Forced to Marry the Earl

The Earls of the North
Book 2

Elizabeth Heights

ARE YOU SIGNED UP FOR DRAGONBLADE'S BLOG?

You'll get the latest news and information on exclusive giveaways, exclusive excerpts, coming releases, sales, free books, cover reveals and more.

Check out our complete list of authors, too!

No spam, no junk. That's a promise!

Sign Up Here

www.dragonbladepublishing.com

Dearest Reader;

Thank you for your support of a small press. At Dragonblade Publishing, we strive to bring you the highest quality Historical Romance from some of the best authors in the business. Without your support, there is no 'us', so we sincerely hope you adore these stories and find some new favorite authors along the way.

Happy Reading!

CEO, Dragonblade Publishing

Additional Dragonblade books by
Author Elizabeth Heights

The Earls of the North Series
Gambling with the Earl (Book 1)
Forced to Marry the Earl (Book 2)

Chapter One

Year of Our Lord 1298. A fortified settlement in the windswept north-west of England.

THE MAIDS HAD lit a fire in the castle bedchamber to ward off the slight evening chill, but despite the flickering flames, Ariana could not keep warm. She drew a woolen blanket around her shoulders and wondered if it was trepidation that made her shiver.

"Just because I've married him, it doesn't mean he owns me," she stated, with more bravery than she felt. Her voice rebounded around the whitewashed walls, almost seeming to mock her plight.

"My dear Ariana," said Merek, the closest thing she had to an ally here in Darkmoor. "I'm afraid you'll find that's exactly what it means."

Ariana folded her arms across her ample bosom and turned her face away so the gray-haired castle physician wouldn't see her distress. She was a proud daughter of Kenmar, long accustomed to masking her emotions. Although she had formerly considered Merek to be a family friend, all contact between them had ceased when he first took employment in Darkmoor. Before today, she had not seen him for several summers; she would not weep before him now.

Merek picked up the glass vial of amber-colored liquid he had brought up to Ariana's bedchamber in anticipation of her state of mind.

"Drink this," he advised her. "It will calm your nerves. You're not the first young bride to be overcome on her wedding night."

Ariana obediently knocked back the tincture, wrinkling her nose at the sour after-taste. Yes, she was a young bride, shivering at the prospect of bedding her new husband, but her anxiety was not for the reasons Merek suspected. At the tender age of twenty years, Ariana was an innocent, but she did not dread the night ahead so much as the challenges that would come after it.

That afternoon, Ariana had married a man she had been raised to see as a sworn enemy. Their betrothal had been short, the ceremony swiftly arranged. Ariana had still not fully recovered from the shock that had chilled her blood when her father instructed her to prepare for marriage to the new Earl of Darkmoor, Otto Sarragnac: the merciless warrior whose name she had only ever heard whispered in fear.

The very same man who had recently ordered the arrest of her kinswoman, Ysmay, who must be held captive somewhere in this very castle.

Ariana's hands shook so violently she struggled to keep hold of the blanket. Impatiently, she tugged it from her shoulders and busied herself with folding it and placing it neatly on the back of a polished wooden chair near the fire. Her eyes lingered on a lion's head which had been expertly carved into the headrest.

"You are Ariana Sarragnac, the Countess of Darkmoor, now," Merek advised her, softly. He sank down onto a long, embroidered footstool at the foot of the canopied bed and rubbed his face wearily. "'Tis not my place to give you instruction. But take heed of my own experience within these walls." He leaned closer and lowered his voice. "It is safer to submit."

Ariana turned her green eyes to his, unwilling to acknowledge her new reality. Only one thought sustained her. "You know the real reason my father agreed to this marriage?" she asked, breathless at her own daring.

"Hush," he cautioned, his furrowed brow creasing further.

"Messages from Kenmar have reached me, yes. But we must not speak of this here." His watery eyes widened in warning, and he raised a gnarled hand to plead for silence.

She swallowed hard, understanding the risks but still clinging to her goal like a small boat in a mighty storm. "I have reasons of my own for agreeing to it. Now that I am here, there is something I must do."

But could she really fool the mighty Earl of Darkmoor?

A movement to her left made them both turn, and Ariana couldn't help shrinking backwards as the imposing figure of her warrior husband loomed in her bedchamber doorway. He was a man bred for battle: tall, broad-shouldered, and narrow-hipped. A man revered by his friends and feared by his enemies. Ariana's people had always spoken of him in hushed tones, as if he was the very devil himself and mentioning his name too loudly might summon him.

Merek rose to his feet and bowed to his master. "Good evening, my lord."

Otto inclined his head. "Good evening to you, Merek. I am come to ask after my bride."

Ariana bristled. *Then why did he not address her directly?*

She met his gaze without flinching. "I have been well looked after, thank you."

But Ariana's breath caught in her throat as the Earl of Darkmoor walked further into the small antechamber that had been set aside for her. Otto's thick black hair had been neatly combed for the ceremony, but his wedding finery hung like a costume on the powerful shoulders of a man clearly more accustomed to armor.

She was suddenly all too conscious of her own appearance. The maid had already undressed her down to her smock and combed out her long dark hair to leave her ready for the night ahead. Without the security of the blanket, she felt naked and exposed. Her hands trembled as she tightened her arms defensively across her chest. What must Otto think of her? Was he disappointed in the plain looks and buxom figure of his bride? Did he hanker after a maid with a waist he could span with his powerful fingers? Her father had always said she would be an unsatisfactory match for any man.

As if thinking his name had conjured him out of thin air, Ariana heard her father's voice speaking sharply in her head. *"Have I raised a jittering fool?"*

This was no time for self-pity.

With her heart beating painfully against her ribs, Ariana took a deep breath and fought to conquer her fears. She couldn't forget what she was here to do. Yes, she was the bride of Otto Sarragnac. Yes, their wedding had forged an alliance between two of the most powerful families in the North.

Yes, as a wife, she now had duties to her husband, including what would happen in this room, tonight.

But more importantly than that, Ariana had obligations to her people. Namely, her mother's sister, Ysmay, who stood wrongfully accused of the death of Lord Ulric, her new husband's father.

Ariana was young and inexperienced, but she had the wisdom of the druids flowing through her veins from her mother's side. She would not be cowed by a bully.

Just feet away from the Earl of Darkmoor, Ariana of Kenmar held her chin up high.

With elaborate casualness, Otto raised his arms above his head, stretched and scratched his head. The actions of a man at home in his body—and accustomed to being around only other men. As the white sleeves of his tunic fell aside, Ariana caught a glimpse of his muscular forearms and the vivid blue line of a tattoo.

Blood pounded in her ears as she imagined those powerful arms closing around her.

He raised a mocking eyebrow. "And have we met the high standards you are accustomed to, Lady Ariana?"

Her cheeks flamed red. Otto knew that she was accustomed to far less. Darkmoor was nestled above a wooded valley, where the sound of birdsong filled the air. The castle itself was four-square and strong. Tapestries hung on the walls and the household sipped from silver chalices in the great hall. It was all a stark contrast to her childhood home. Her father's lands were high and bleak, Castle Kenmar itself was cramped, cold, and devoid of comfort. Although she was the daughter of a nobleman, Ariana had been brought up to know the meaning of hard labor. Everyone worked in Kenmar, and her hands gave as much away. They were rough and reddened, where they should be soft and white.

She clenched them into fists behind her back.

"Only time will tell," she said shortly.

His full lips curved into a crooked smile at that. "You have fire in your belly."

Merek bowed low. "I will leave you my lord, my lady." He inclined his head to each of them, then walked swiftly from the room, his gray cloak billowing behind him. Ariana swallowed the urge to call him back.

She was alone, for the first time, with her husband. The *Feared One*.

His dark gaze looked her up and down, like a lion eyeing his prey.

"You are young," he commented, a note of surprise in his gravelly voice.

Ariana raised her head. "I am past twenty."

"Old enough then."

He took another step towards her, and she inhaled his manly aroma of clean sweat and polished leather.

"I am old enough to be your bride," Ariana answered steadily, knowing she must not make a foe of this man at this time, even if she had no intention of being a submissive wife.

"Your father certainly believes so."

Otto came to stand directly in front of her. Ariana fixed her gaze on the orange glow of the fire, but her heart hammered against her ribs as she imagined his fierce, hunter's eyes looking directly through her thin smock to the pink of her flesh.

She had never been touched by a man.

Bracing herself, she met his gaze without flinching.

She had never been looked at the way Otto was looking at her now, like he could devour her whole.

Back home in Kenmar, she had experienced little in the way of unwanted attention from her father's warriors. Her station as Sir Leon's daughter had not granted her much protection, given that his disregard for his only child was only too apparent to everyone, but her wide hips and clumsiness on the dance floor meant that other young ladies were wined, dined, and held in higher regard than she.

Here in Darkmoor, the reception she'd received had been quite different. It was as if she had stepped out of her old identity to be exposed, for the first time, as a vulnerable and defenseless woman. She flinched as Otto put a hand to her waist. His hand was warm, his grip firm. He tugged her towards him with no hint of a smile.

She swallowed her fear and stared boldly into the face of the man who would take her innocence. Otto's brow was heavy, and a silver scar traced a path from his temple down to his neck. Dark stubble coated his cheeks, and Ariana couldn't help imagining how those sharp bristles would cut into her own tender flesh. His lips were full and sensual. His expression was as closed as a book.

His left hand fastened itself around the other side of her waist. She was his captive now, held tight within the clutches of a warrior who could snap her like a branch. The chamber was silent save the crackling of the logs in the fire. She could almost imagine the darkness outside pressing against the granite walls, complicit in keeping her trapped.

"You must bear me a son," Otto said.

Ariana knew what was expected of her. The mighty Sarrag-nac line must have an heir, one of good breeding from a legitimate marriage.

She didn't falter under his gaze. "You can do with my body

what you will."

Finally, an answering emotion flickered across Otto's rugged face. Was it surprise, or something else?

He didn't step away, but he didn't pull her closer either. Instead, he brought one hand up to her shoulders and brushed his fingers against the curve of her collar bone. His touch was light and surprisingly gentle. Ariana's earlier chill was now swallowed up by a fever which raced up her backbone and settled in her flushed cheeks. Several moments passed before he spoke again.

"You need not fear me, Ariana."

His words came as a surprise. She hadn't expected mercy of any kind within the fortified walls of Darkmoor Castle, especially not from the ruthless earl. But she didn't dare let her guard down. This was not a man she could trust.

"You are entitled to take what is your due," she said, stating a fact, ignoring the heat building in her limbs.

His lips creased into a smile that was not entirely humorous. "I'm glad we understand one another, Lady Ariana. And know this, I *will* take what is mine." His gaze locked with hers and as she looked into his unreadable eyes, Ariana felt her knees start to tremble. "But not tonight," he added.

He dropped her like a hot coal, leaving her limp and breathless with surprise. She covered her modesty with shaking fingers while he strode from the room without a backwards glance.

Just like that, she was dismissed.

The relief surging through her body was tinged with disappointment, and not simply because the deed she dreaded would not be over with this night. In his proximity, the overpowering masculinity of her new husband had nudged at something that slumbered deep within her.

Ariana walked to the narrow window and gripped the wooden ledge. Through the gathering dusk, she could just about make out the daunting outline of Otto Sarragnac stalking across the courtyard. Even as she baulked at his presence, Ariana had been expecting his kiss and his touch, on this night of all nights. Had he gone elsewhere to seek such pleasures?

Was her father right? Had Otto found her appearance so unsatisfactory that he couldn't bring himself to consummate the marriage?

So be it! She'd long witnessed the pretty ladies of Kenmar gaining advantage through their looks. This reprieve was an advantage of sorts; one which she was grateful for.

She sat down on the comfortable bed but stood up again a moment later and started pacing the room restlessly. It was no good. She couldn't settle. She was as likely to sleep here in Darkmoor Castle as she would in a den of thieves. Enemies surrounded her. The very walls throbbed with menace.

But what better time than this to seek out the information she required? No one would anticipate her leaving her chamber on her wedding night.

Acting swiftly, before she could change her mind, Ariana rummaged through her meagre travelling chest until she found a serviceable dress, which she pulled roughly over her head. Next, she reached for her cloak, pinning it in place with fingers that still trembled. She picked up her candle, opened the door and looked carefully from left to right. No one was about at this late hour. The knights and other members of the household would be sleeping in the great hall. Where Lord Otto had gone, Ariana had no idea, but she shook this from her mind.

Earlier that morning, upon her arrival in Darkmoor, she'd been quick to look around and gather her bearings. She knew that Merek's chamber was just beyond the keep. The door would be directly beneath her.

Ariana held her breath as she descended the stone staircase, the cold seeping through her goatskin shoes even as her body grew warm at her own daring. If she was stopped and questioned, her mission would end before it had even begun. Torches still flickered on the high walls of the entrance hall, though Ariana's eyes had already adjusted to the dark. She had the instincts and senses of her mother's people, the druids. She sank into the shadows and made herself invisible, her heart thudding with relief when she heard the drunken snores of the guard who had made too merry at the wedding feast.

Merek's door was locked, but he answered her tentative knock and ushered her inside. The acrid smell of a physician's work immediately made Ariana's eyes water, and she drew her cloak across her face as he bolted the door behind her.

"My lady," he said, his old eyes uneasy. "I did not expect to see you again this night."

"That's why I took the opportunity to come. We have no time to lose." Her curious gaze drank in shelves piled high with glass bottles of all shapes and hues. The flagged floor was bare, and the room sparsely furnished, but Merek pulled out a wooden stool and directed her to sit.

"Ariana," he said softly. "We must tread carefully, both of us. Lord Otto is not a man to play games with. Do you know why they call him the *Feared One*?"

"I'm not here to play games. I'm here to rescue Ysmay, my kinswoman." Ariana spoke more forcefully than she intended, for she knew the physician had already risked a great deal even in opening his door to her.

Merek gripped her arm. "Not tonight," he urged. "Ariana, you are a new bride here. Bide a while. The right time will come. I have been keeping watch over Ysmay. No harm has befallen her as yet."

"And nor should it. She's done nothing wrong," Ariana blurted out.

"Not all see it like that," Merek answered gravely. "Not the knights of Darkmoor, and not your husband."

She shook her head. "I don't care what Otto thinks." But she felt suddenly small inside the formidable fortress.

Merek sighed. "You should, my lady. He's a powerful man. And a dangerous one. How come you to be out of your bed-chamber on your wedding night?" He lifted his candle towards the bolted door as if he believed Otto may be searching for her.

Ariana shrugged her shoulders to hide her embarrassment.

"Otto has gone." She affected not to care. "He must have other pleasures to attend to."

But Merek looked somber in the cheerless room. "Not him," he told her. "Since the battle of Branfeld, where his father lost his life, Lord Otto takes pleasure in nothing. He is much changed."

Ariana recalled the snaking scar and Otto's forbidding expression. "He is a cold man," she declared.

Merek shook his head. "Troubled," he corrected her. "He has seen horrors on the battlefield. And the death of his father, Lord Ulric, lies heavily on him."

Ariana pursed her lips. "How so? Otto must have seen many battles and witnessed many men die." She couldn't help an unladylike snort. "Better men than Ulric, late Earl of Darkmoor."

Merek looked as if he might clamp a hand around her mouth. "Bide your tongue, my lady," he advised. "The court of Kenmar is slack, but here the very walls have ears, and all will be reported back to the earl." He pulled out another stool and sat beside her at the scratched wooden table. Ariana tried not to imagine the gray stone walls listening in to their hushed conversation. "My Lord Otto spoke out against his father about going into battle with Sir Leon at Branfeld," Merek continued. "He weighed the expansion of Darkmoor lands against the risk to his men and found no value in waging war with Kenmar. Not for such poor scrubland that only the druids inhabit. But Lord Ulric would not be swayed. The rest, I am sure you know."

Ariana rearranged her long legs on the low stool. "All I know is that Ysmay was wrongly charged with Ulric's death."

"Lord Ulric was an old man playing a young man's game. He was cut down at the first charge. Otto left the battle and took him to the druid camp to be healed, appealing to their clemency and hoping for help."

"Help which they freely gave," Ariana spat.

"But they couldn't save him," he continued. "Not even Ysmay, the wisest healer our lands have ever known. My teacher," he added. "In his grief, Lord Otto rode away and while he was gone, the knights of Darkmoor took their revenge."

"Upon peaceful people." Ariana's eyes flooded with tears. Her father had done his best to keep her away from the druids. He made no secret of his regret over his match with Ariana's mother and his shame at the muddied lineage of his only child. But despite his efforts, the druids had found her in the fields and forests of Kenmar. They visited frequently, bringing her gifts, showing her kindness, and claiming her as one of their own. She couldn't bear the thought of Otto bringing violence and bloodshed to their camp.

Merek nodded. "But for Otto's return, your aunt would likely have been killed," he said flatly. "I tell you, there is good in Otto Sarragnac. I came to Darkmoor when he was but a young knight, and I have watched him grow. He may yet be your ally."

Ariana couldn't imagine such a thing. "I have no friends in Darkmoor, none but you, Merek. I am relying on your help."

The physician took her hand in a fatherly manner. "And you shall have it, Ariana. Before she died, your mother was very kind to me. I will not let you or your people down."

Ariana raised a questioning eyebrow. "Even if it means turning against the earl?"

Merek shuddered at the thought. "I hope and pray that it will not come to that."

"My father wants me to find the Rose of Kenmar—the jewel my grandmother passed down to Ysmay. The one she wore always around her neck." She swallowed, suddenly nervous of revealing her plan. "But I care naught for rubies. I intend only to free my aunt, the real Rose of Kenmar."

Merek opened his arms. "Neither of those tasks will be easily accomplished. Not here, amongst so many mighty warriors, not least your own husband."

Ariana leaned closer to the respected physician. "Do I look like a simpering bride? No," she answered her own question. "I am a woman, but I am strong, and I am resolute. In this, I am a match for any man," she said, slowly and clearly. "Including the

Earl of Darkmoor."

He met her eyes. "My lady, I am depending on it."

Chapter Two

OTTO'S HEAD WHIRRED with emotion as he left Ariana's bedchamber and stumbled past the sleeping guard. He was so caught up in his own confusion that he didn't even pause to rebuke the man who had put drink before duty. But out in the courtyard, the cool night air helped to calm his thoughts.

What had he done?

If his men discovered that he had walked away from his virgin bride on their wedding night, he would be a laughingstock. If his father were still alive, he'd be furious. Lord Ulric would have expected Otto to claim Ariana of Kenmar as his own—as Darkmoor's own.

Show no weakness, show no mercy. The words reverberated inside his mind like the banging of a drum. They formed the knights' code; a code by which he had been raised. Strength in battle, power, and potency in peacetime. And all for the continued glory of Darkmoor.

Potency, pah! Otto kicked a loose stone that bounced right across the courtyard to the gatehouse. The only thing to be penetrated this night was his own personal armor. He'd looked down at the quaking young woman he had clasped between his two hands, and the courage in her unfaltering gaze had pierced him more sharply than any blade.

She had felt fear, he'd seen enough of it to recognize it, but she had stood tall and willed him to do his worst.

As she walked towards him at the altar, Otto had formed little impression of his bride, save for her height and forbearance. A giant of a man himself, he'd been gratified to note that his new wife was just a head shorter than he. But just now, in her bedchamber, he'd seen a flash of spirit in her eyes. A glint of steel, which intrigued him.

His intrigue was unnecessary. Their marriage was nothing more than the final stage of a drawn-out peace treaty between the neighboring lands of Darkmoor and Kenmar. A treaty which was generations overdue. If only his father had seen fit to negotiate with words rather than muscle and blade… no, he stopped himself thinking down lines which led only to pounding headaches, clenched fists, and a suffocating feeling of impotence. Lord Ulric's death had been violent and unnecessary. But nothing Otto could do now would change that.

In those dark days, it had seemed prudent to agree to Sir Leon's terms—terms which took him very much by surprise— and accept Ariana's hand in marriage. A small sacrifice to save further blood from being spilled; further lives from being needlessly lost. A political alliance, not a love match. But Otto had never expected anything more. Love had no place in his life; no place in the powerful lands of Darkmoor either.

The castle guard stood sharply to attention as Otto passed by the gatehouse.

"Stand easy, Tom," he spoke into the night air. As the new earl, he supposed he should adopt his father's air of indifference towards the guards and servants. But Otto still considered himself a warrior first and foremost. A man among men. The equal of those who willingly followed him rather than the master who ruled over them.

"Aye, milord."

"Is all quiet beyond?"

"It is. Nothing has stirred."

Otto's wooden pattens sounded noisily across the drawbridge in the stillness of the evening. He could breathe more easily once he reached the outer courtyard. Somewhere an owl hooted, and he paused, large hands on narrow hips, to look up at the vast night sky. The darkness was infinite, studded with tiny twinkling stars. A soft breeze brushed his cheek, like a caress which was long overdue. He had not known true affection for many years.

From an early age, Otto had learned that conquering neighboring lands to expand the Darkmoor estate was his life's highest purpose. It was all Lord Ulric lived for and dreamed of. He had seen height, strength, and natural fighting ability in his only son, and ensured that young Otto developed into the mighty warrior he was today. The *Feared One*. The leader of the legendary knights of Darkmoor.

But with every passing year, Otto silently questioned his father's vision more and more. This latest squabble with Kenmar should have been just that. Not a bloodbath that saw the ageing Lord Ulric cut down from his charger to die in his son's arms.

"Otto?" The voice came out of the darkness, making him startle.

"Who goes there?" he challenged, one hand instantly reaching for his sword.

"'Tis only I. Your cousin Guy."

Otto's stance relaxed as his eyes made out the looming figure of the Earl of Rossfarne coming from the stable block, his broad shoulders and curling dark hair illuminated by a flickering torch attached to the granite wall. "What in heaven's name are you doing out here at such an hour?" he demanded. But before the man could answer, he extended his arm and the two clasped each other's forearms in time honored tradition. In addition to being kinsmen, Guy and Otto had been fast friends and allies since childhood, and the battle-scarred knight was one of very few men in whom Otto would declare full and complete trust.

"I could ask the same of you!" Guy declared, clapping him on the shoulder with a heavy hand. "Is this not your wedding night?"

"Pray, do not go there," Otto growled. "We do not all enjoy the same wedded bliss as you and your good wife."

Guy held up a palm in a show of understanding. "I know that

yours is not a love match. But I hope in time you may find some degree of happiness with Ariana of Kenmar."

"I am not so ambitious as to seek happiness," Otto declared, slapping at an insect which buzzed near his unshaven cheek.

"Come now. It is not so much to ask." Guy folded his arms across his muscular chest, his eyes dancing in the torchlight.

Otto couldn't help his heart softening at the sight. Not so long ago, the Earl of Rossfarne had been a broken man, both physically and emotionally. Now, he was not only back at full health, but he also boasted that rare thing, a happy hearth and home. A beautiful wife and a baby on the way.

"Aye, well," he muttered cryptically. Though Guy had found love and contentment, Otto was not so naïve as to believe these things were there for the taking. Not for men such as himself.

"I am glad to have seen you. I will make my way home at first light. That's why I'm out here—checking my horse is fit and well, ready for the long journey east." Guy inclined his head towards a half-open stable door, where a glossy chestnut mare pawed impatiently at the ground.

Otto nodded in understanding. Guy had served King Edward for many years and no matter how many servants he had in the stables, he could not rid himself of the habit of taking full responsibility for the horse that carried him into battle.

"You are not staying for tomorrow's joust?"

Guy's mouth twitched up at the corners. "Do you wish to see me clapping your victory from the stands?"

"My victory is not guaranteed," Otto countered.

"I beg to differ." Guy leaned back against the bailey wall and gazed up at the starry sky, his expression growing dreamy with nostalgia. "I like to remember our jousts when we were boys, and I had some chance of beating you."

"That's not how I remember it." Otto schooled his face into a serious expression, but he could not hold it for long. Both men smiled at one another, lost for a moment in the safe memories of a childhood summer. "I trust your horses and your men have been treated well during your stay?" Otto knew a brief stab of remorse that he had not paid more attention to the wellbeing of his cousin, who had answered his plea for assistance within days of Lord Ulric's death. The arrival of Guy, complete with a small guard of well-trained soldiers, had helped smooth the choppy waters between his father's funeral and today's hastily arranged marriage.

Guy inclined his head. "Well indeed. I fear I have grown too used to the luxuries of Darkmoor. My castle at Rossfarne will seem bleak and empty after these weeks of company. You keep a fine army, cousin. I have learned a lot from training with the knights of Darkmoor."

"You are too kind." Otto clapped him on the shoulder, conscious of how evenly matched they were in height and strength. "But do not pretend you haven't been counting the days until you can return to your lovely wife."

Guy laughed. "That I will not do. I have missed Kitty, and I'm not ashamed to admit it."

"You're a lucky man," Otto stated, with genuine feeling. "Do not let me keep you out of doors on this night, especially with such a long ride ahead of you."

"I'll take my leave." Guy paused for a moment. "But should you ever need my assistance, my friend, please send word right away." His sharp gaze flickered over Otto's face. "I see no need to fret over the fortunes of Darkmoor," he added softly. "England's greatest fortress is safely in the hands of our greatest warrior."

"Get out of here, man, before you have me blushing like a maid," Otto retorted, raising a hand in farewell as Guy picked his way back through the courtyard towards the keep.

A faint wicker from the stables told him that he had been spotted.

Otto felt a smile crack the rugged lines of his face as he smelled the sweet scent of hay and raised his palms to greet another old friend.

"Hello, girl," he whispered, running a hand along the smooth, muscular neck of his favorite black mare.

His horse whickered again, nudging at his tunic and looking for treats.

"Here," he opened the stable door and walked quickly inside, holding out a small apple on the palm of his hand.

She crunched up the apple, then dropped her head, allowing him to place one hand on either side of her face and look deeply into her wise brown eyes.

This was the horse who carried him unflinchingly in battle, who galloped straight as an arrow in jousting tournaments, who had been his companion since youth. She was the fastest horse in Darkmoor, probably the fastest in the North. But more importantly, she trusted him, had faith in him, even amidst the chaos of battle.

If only Otto could summon the same instinctive faith in himself.

Show no weakness, show no mercy.

"I begin to tire of this old dictate," he admitted, in the privacy of the stable.

He was jolted from his thoughts by a discreet cough from beyond the wooden door.

Otto looked up sharply, one hand going again to his sword belt. "Who's there?" he demanded for the second time.

A young stable boy stepped forward. "It is I, Matthew, milord. I heard a noise, so I came to check on your horse."

Had he been eavesdropping? A spy of Otto's enemies? For he had many, he was sure, both inside and outside the castle walls. A flash of anger flared in Otto's chest and his fingers tightened on the hilt of his sword.

"How long have you stood there?"

"No time at all, milord."

Otto breathed deeply, unable to quell his unease. His father's brother, Althalos, was a powerful man with many loyal followers. He had come to Darkmoor upon Lord Ulric's death and remained here still. Was Althalos plotting against him?

"I'm sorry, milord," the boy continued, a tremble in his voice betraying his unease. He was barely more than a child.

Otto felt a wave of nausea wash over him. He had been named earl, heir to Lord Ulric, with Althalos putting up no objection. Would he allow such fear and suspicion to plague him forever? If so, then self-doubt would be his undoing, and faster than an enemy's sword.

And his father's tyrannical reputation with the servants would soon extend to him as well.

"Have no fear, Matthew," Otto said, unclenching his hand. "Your keen ears do you credit."

"Thank you," Matthew breathed, his relief evident in the slope of his slender shoulders.

The stable boy disappeared into the shadows and Otto felt the lateness of the hour catch up with him. He'd been up since dawn, training with the knights, and the enforced ritual of his wedding to Ariana had been a further ordeal. The afternoon of drinking and feasting in celebration of a loveless marriage had not passed easily for him.

He could go to the village and seek comfort in the arms of willing women; forget his cares in the warmth of their tender flesh. He knew of many a door that would open to him. But since the battle of Branfeld, when Lord Ulric had lost his life—and later, when Otto had watched his own men take their revenge upon peaceful people—he had lost all appetite for such earthly pleasures.

Blood. Vengeance. Retribution. When would it end?

How many more unnecessary deaths must he witness?

So where could he take his ease? As a boy, Otto had spent many a night sleeping under the stars, enjoying the vast emptiness of the outside world after the close restrictions of stone walls and duty, but the Earl of Darkmoor could do no such thing.

With a reluctant sigh, he swiveled around and returned to the keep. To his own cold bedchamber, where the fire had been left unlit in the expectation of his absence. This was his wedding night, after all.

Otto felt the familiar weight of obligation settle on his shoulders. Tonight, he had shirked from his duty; tomorrow would have to be different.

⚜

"VICTORY SHALL BE yours." Sir Althalos clapped Otto on his armor-clad shoulder. "Be sure to make it so," he added before turning away, his gray eyes cold and distant as they raked over the jousting arena in the shadow of Darkmoor Castle.

Otto bowed his head in deference to his uncle, even as his jaw tightened at this unwelcome reminder of his father's unquenchable thirst for success. The desire to win, at any cost, ran thickly through the veins of the Sarragnac men. But despite his instinctive recoil, he knew that Althalos was correct. Defeat today was not an option.

If yesterday's wedding had been a brief and hurried affair, this was a time for glory and feasting in Darkmoor. Red and gold crests fluttered gaily above hundreds of townsfolk who had crowded into the wooden stands, laughing and jeering before the jousting tournament had even begun. A smell of dust, ale and hot bodies hung in the air.

The yearly Joust of Darkmoor didn't just draw an eager crowd of onlookers, it also attracted the finest knights in the North to try their luck against the undefeated champion, Otto Sarragnac. All around him, horses pawed at the hardened ground and servants ran back and forth as their masters prepared to prove themselves in the infamous arena, where men sought glory but all too often encountered injury and defeat. The fact that entrants would now be pitting themselves against the newly ordained Earl of Darkmoor added an extra frisson to this year's event.

Robin handed Otto his highly polished helm. "Good luck, milord," muttered the young page.

Otto gave a small nod of thanks, though he had no need of luck. Speed, strength, and skill were the required components for success in the jousting arena. He had an abundance of all three, and everyone here knew it. With his reputation whispered far and wide, Otto's victory was all but sealed before his horse even set foot in the ring.

His eyes scanned the crowd, resting finally on the gracious figure of Ariana as she made her way to her seat of honor next to Althalos in the royal enclosure. He had not had the opportunity to speak to her this morn and was surprised by a brief stab of remorse. Had she known any kind words of welcome since waking in what must feel like a strange and unfamiliar place?

He shook the concern from his mind. Ariana would have to grow used to their ways. Neither warmth nor welcome were bywords in Darkmoor. Still, Otto's brow darkened as he saw his uncle rake her over with his critical gaze. His bride was clad in a cloak of deep blue which clung to her generous curves. As she pulled back her hood to reveal her shining mane of glossy black hair, the crowd let out an appreciative murmur, but Althalos grimaced with disapproval. Clearly the new countess was attracting more attention than his father's brother deemed appropriate.

Like his brother before him, Althalos only had time for war and warriors. Women were of little value to him, necessary only for childbearing and the relief of certain urges. Otto hoped that Ariana would find herself equal to the disdain radiating from her new kinsman. But as she straightened her back and folded her hands, her green eyes resting steadily on the empty arena, he once again glimpsed the steely resilience which had so intrigued him the night before.

Soft curves, glinting eyes, and a backbone of steel. Ariana of Kenmar was proving to be a more enticing bride than he had imagined.

Shaking off the brief distraction of an unanticipated tremble of desire, Otto gathered up his reins and sprang lightly into the saddle. His charger snorted and shifted beneath him, plate armor gleaming in the morning sunshine. Otto tightened his grip around the lance and urged the horse forward into the arena, into a wave of deafening cheers from the expectant crowd and the certain victory that was his to claim.

But Otto's mind was not on his opponents, or the physical challenges he had yet to face. His head was full of Ariana, of her shimmering cloud of hair and her untouched skin which had shown through her cotton smock last night.

Ariana, whose own father had so carelessly handed her over to a sworn enemy. Who had arrived in Darkmoor alone and undefended. Who displayed equal might and bravery to any contender now circling the jousting arena.

He knew a jolt of electricity as his eyes met hers across the ring. Suddenly, the roaring of the crowd dimmed in his ears, and he grew oblivious to the side-stepping of his horse. All he could see was Ariana, with her steady gaze and unflinching demeanor.

His horse reared, and Otto came to his senses just in time. The starting flag went up and his charger surged forward, like the well-trained fighting machine she was. Otto balanced himself in the stirrups and thrust his lance into his opponent's armor, splintering the wood and unhorsing Sir Ralph of Crawshaw with one powerful blow.

He removed his helm and held it high for his victory lap around the ring. The crowd went wild with approval, the familiar chant already echoing around the castle walls.

Otto, Otto, Otto.

But one glance towards the royal enclosure told Otto he had yet to impress the one person who suddenly mattered. Ariana's face was as calm and watchful as his uncle's.

She'll make a daughter of Darkmoor yet, thought Otto, as he trotted out of the arena and back to the knights' tents.

He accepted a small cup of ale and congratulations from the waiting physician.

"Thankfully I have no need of your skills or potions, Merek,"

Otto said.

Merek inclined his head. "Not so your opponent. I'm afraid Sir Ralph has broken two ribs."

Otto shrugged, not allowing any concern to show. "Every knight knows what he risks when he rides against me."

Merek bowed low. "Indeed, my lord."

Otto turned to Robin. "Who do I face next?"

"It is Lord Gawain's youngest son. His name is Benedict."

Otto spat out a mouthful of ale. "Isn't he just a boy?"

Merek agreed. "He is nearing sixteen summers."

Otto looked around the bustling field in search of Gawain's yellow crest. He soon spotted the flag proudly hoisted above a small crowd nearby. Benedict was a head shorter than his attendant page. As Otto watched, the boy removed his helm and dropped to one knee for his father's blessing.

Benedict had brown curls, which lifted in the wind.

He was too young for this, just as Lord Ulric had been too old.

Otto leaned an arm across his horse's steaming flank and breathed deeply as the pain of loss and guilt crashed over him.

"Are you quite well, my lord?" Merek's voice came as if from a great distance away.

A vision of his father's face swam into view and Otto straightened up.

Get a hold of yourself, boy.

Althalos was watching. Nay, most of the North was watching. He knew he must fight. He must win. He must remain undefeated. For the glory of Darkmoor.

"It's time, milord," Robin said, nervously.

Without a word to his companions, Otto mounted his horse and re-entered the arena where the noise from the crowd had swelled to a constant undulating wave. Half a smile cracked his uncle's frozen expression as he witnessed the victories of Darkmoor's finest warriors. All of whom had been trained by Otto.

His horse wheeled around, and Otto reined her in.

"Easy girl," he murmured.

She tossed her mane and snorted, ready to charge. Otto raised his lance.

Show no weakness. Show no mercy.

The man before him was a trained warrior, a challenger like any other. He must be overpowered.

Benedict, the boy who just two years ago had run races in the castle fields, flipped down his visor.

The flag went up. Otto urged his horse forward and focused on his target, but Benedict's charger was fast and came upon them at surprising speed. Otto's thrusting blow was sound, but not powerful enough for the clean, decisive victory he sought. Benedict was injured, bent low over his horse's neck, but he was not unseated. They must ride again.

Perspiration beaded beneath Otto's heavy helm and ran into his eyes as he cursed his own stupidity. He yanked at the reins, furious with the horse that had let him down. He could hear his uncle's mocking voice in his head.

"So, not the fastest horse in Darkmoor today."

Benedict steadied his lance. They were ready.

Otto rammed his spurs into the horse's sides, making her rear with alarm, then bolt forward with a surge of energy, like lightning striking a tree. Otto readied himself for the blow, closing his ears to the roar of the crowd, seeing only his opponent and the point at which he must strike.

Benedict slumped to one side; his feet still tangled in the stirrups. His horse bolted and the boy was all but unseated, but at the last moment he regained his balance. The crowd gasped, and Otto cursed savagely under his breath, reining in his horse beside the royal enclosure.

"Let him retire," came the call from the stands. A woman, most probably a mother herself, wrung her hands in alarm.

Otto flipped up his visor to see a blood-soaked Benedict struggling to remain in the saddle.

"Send for the stretcher bearers," he ordered. His voice carried easily through the arena.

Althalos stood slowly, shaking his head. His natural air of authority made all around him fall silent. "The competitor is still mounted," he declared. "The joust must continue."

Otto's chest tightened in anger. He was the earl. How dare Althalos question his judgement? But at the back of his mind, he knew the rules of the joust were clear. His uncle was correct.

For the second time, his head whirred with confusion. Under his father's rule, Otto knew there would be no doubt. He would ride out once more against Benedict, even if the boy was killed in the process.

The crowd was growing restless. Some shouted out their agreement with Sir Althalos, others their disapproval. Otto's heart pounded beneath his chain mail. This was his chance to assert his rule.

"The competitor is but a boy. One who may yet rise to become a knight of Darkmoor," he stated firmly, raising his voice to be heard above the clamor from the stands. "But not if his back is broken here today."

This time the chorus of approval was deafeningly loud. Otto beckoned for the stretcher bearers to enter the arena and cantered out, dismounting as soon as they were safely out of sight. He removed his helm and wiped the sweat from his brow.

The horse's flanks were flecked with blood from his spurs. Her mouth foamed and her eyes bulged with fear.

Behind him, Otto heard weeping as Benedict's mother ran towards her fallen son.

Otto looked over to the ancient trees of Darkmoor Forest. They waved slightly in the breeze, peaceful and calm.

He laid a hand on his quivering horse.

"I'm sorry," he mouthed, silently.

Chapter Three

THE CROWD WERE restless after the injured boy was stretchered out of the arena, but they soon settled when the next riders came into the ring. Ariana, however, felt her attention wandering to her new husband. He had cut a masterful figure astride his powerful horse, but more surprising than this had been his show of compassion.

It was not what she had been expecting from the Earl of Darkmoor.

"Your husband will be victorious today," Sir Althalos commented drily, seeming to read her thoughts. His mead-stained lips curled up in a grimace as if the idea did not wholly please him.

"I have no doubt of it," Ariana answered steadily.

"What think you of our yearly joust?" he continued. "The might of Darkmoor makes a worthy display, does it not?"

"Indeed, sir." Ariana kept her reply short, not allowing Otto's leering kinsman to rile her. She recognized him as the kind of man to make a sport of unsettling the ladies of the castle.

"And all in your honor," Althalos concluded. He leaned back in his wooden chair, his arms folded across a sumptuous crimson cape which billowed in the breeze. His dark hair hung greasily around a pointed chin and his beady eyes, which missed nothing, were fixed on Ariana. She could feel his probing gaze sear into her mind. Looking for what? Impertinence? Fear? The latter probably. She could well imagine Sir Althalos enjoying her fear.

She lifted her chin higher, conscious that Otto had entered

the ring for his final joust. The winner would hold high the silver shield and, finally, this ordeal would be over. She could stretch her legs and retire from the curious gaze of the public. Even better, she could put distance between herself and Sir Althalos.

Although she would not be cowed. Not by an aging man with yellow teeth and foul breath.

"I am more blessed than any bride," she chirped sweetly, folding her hands in her lap.

Althalos raised an eyebrow in surprise. "You are happy in your match?"

"How could I not be?" Ariana gazed deliberately at the musclebound knight on the prancing horse, readying himself for a final charge. "I am wedded to the greatest warrior in the North."

She chose her words carefully and saw that her arrow had met its mark. Althalos narrowed his cruel eyes but could say nothing, for the competitors were once again galloping towards one another, lances poised and ready. The crowd held its breath; Ariana among them. She cared little for the wellbeing of her husband, but divined that the day would pass more smoothly if the Earl of Darkmoor claimed victory in the jousting arena. Dust rose in a cloud around the two horses, so for a moment it was difficult to see the sequence of events, but the unmistakable sound of splintering wood reached her ears, followed by the thud of a fallen horseman.

The townsfolk of Darkmoor erupted into cheers; the swell of celebration hitting her like a strong wave. Ariana steadied herself against the handrail, blinking dust out of her eyes. Otto had won. Her vision cleared in time for her to see the triumphant lap of honor on his snorting charger. Otto swung his helm high above his head, the sun glinting on the metal, and his adoring crowd roared with delight. She couldn't help a small smile at her husband's obvious elation. A smile which turned to genuine pleasure when he dismounted and extended a hand to his fallen competitor.

The other man, whoever he may be, accepted Otto's arm and

struggled to his feet. Arm in arm, the contenders acknowledged the crowd and Ariana watched with growing confusion.

How come the man known as *the Feared One* was showing such humanity?

She felt Althalos appear at her side before he spoke. Her flesh prickled with distaste as his warm breath hit her neck.

"Have you no token, my lady, for your husband?"

His voice was mocking, and Ariana felt her cheeks redden. Of course, it was expected that a new bride would present the earl with a gift at this moment. But she had nothing prepared. Here in Darkmoor, she had no one to advise her, and had only learned of the joust after breaking her fast.

All at once the eyes of the crowd fell upon her, like a leaden weight dropping onto her shoulders. Althalos had attracted their attention with a gallant wave and Otto was already approaching the royal enclosure, his helm tucked beneath a muscular arm.

She swallowed drily as he walked closer, each step of his leather boots kicking up a small cloud of dust. Otto was breathing heavily, his cheeks flushed with exertion and the heat of the day. He would not be pleased to be brought here for nothing.

Which Althalos well knew.

Ariana fished in her pockets and drew out an embroidered handkerchief, a gift from her ladies in Kenmar. Chiara, the castle cook and a dear friend, had also presented her with a basket of her favorite pastries, but Ariana hadn't been able to face them in the tumult of her hasty departure. This handkerchief was all she had of her past life, but now it must be surrendered. As Otto came to stand before her, she dipped into a small curtsy, her head held low.

"You need not curtsy before me," he said gruffly. But he returned her courtly favor with a low bow, which prompted a ripple of applause to reverberate around the stands.

Ariana's hands trembled as she leaned forward to fasten her handkerchief to Otto's chainmail, where it fluttered gaily. Biting down on her lip in concentration, she gave thanks for his height which meant she could reach out to him with ease. Her body felt unsteady with nerves, as if she might tumble out of the enclosure with little warning.

Quest accomplished, she tried to lean away from the heat and masculinity of her warrior husband, but Otto had already closed his fist around her wrist. She looked down in alarm.

"I thank you, Ariana," he said, in a voice rich with surprise.

"It is nothing, my lord."

"It is a mark of your esteem, is it not?"

Did he mock her? Ariana's gaze flew upwards, but Otto's face bore no trace of disingenuity. His eyes met hers, wide and honest.

"You rode well today," she said. "Especially against the young boy, Benedict." Her heart pounded at her daring, but it was true. Otto's leniency in the ring had impressed her.

He raised an eyebrow quizzically. "Not all would agree with you." Did she imagine it, or had his head inclined slightly towards Sir Althalos?

Ariana pressed her lips together. This feeling of connection between them was unexpected. She spoke up before she could think better of it. "Not all are so noble minded."

She had gone too far. Fear twisted a knife into her stomach. Too late, she remembered Merck's words of caution and she fought an urge to pull backwards as Otto's shuttered off face creased with a sudden show of emotion. Was he enraged?

No. When she at last dared to glimpse upwards, she saw that the *Feared One* was amused.

"I am pleased to learn of such compassion in my bride."

His words flummoxed her. Ariana lowered her face and fastened her gaze on the dusty ground. When she looked up again, it was to find Otto's fierce brown eyes hovering inches from her own. Her breath caught in her throat as she inhaled his masculine aroma of heat and leather. And when his lips grazed against her cheek, she felt a shiver travel the length of her body.

His strong fingers finally released their grip on her wrist. "I bid you farewell, my lady," he said.

"Farewell, my lord." Heat rushed into her cheeks before she could look away, but Otto gave no sign of noticing her embarrassment. As he walked back to his horse, she slowly became aware of the clamoring crowd and the disdainful presence of Sir Althalos behind her.

"The earl puts on a show for his public." Althalos spat out the words as if he had a nasty taste in his mouth.

Ariana straightened her back, determined not to be diminished by his bile.

"The people of Darkmoor are most loyal," she stated. Althalos looked at her sharply and opened his mouth as if to speak, but Ariana cut him short with a dismissive nod of her head. "I bid you farewell, Sir Althalos," she said, in a knowing parody of Otto.

And Althalos could do nothing but bow low as the new Countess of Darkmoor swept past him, away from the royal enclosure.

Ariana kept her head held high and her breathing steady until she reached the safety of her room, then she unfastened her cloak and clutched the back of a chair, sucking in lungfuls of air as a cool breeze wafted around her body.

The morning had unsettled her. Spiteful attention from a man such as Althalos was nothing new, but she was unused to being on public display, and totally unprepared for the rush of feeling she'd experienced when Otto's lips met her cheek.

She put a hand to her face, as if a trace from his lips might still linger there. A tremor passed through her; one she didn't fully understand. Otto Sarragnac was a sworn enemy of her people; a warrior she'd been raised to hate and fear. But in the short time she'd known him, he'd shown both compassion and kindness.

More than her own father had exhibited in many a year.

She had expected coldness and cruelty from the Earl of Darkmoor. It would have made her intended betrayal easier for her conscience to bear. But now this!

Ariana tugged absently at her loose sleeves as she paced the length of the room, recalling the moment their eyes had met across the jousting arena. She had experienced such a jolt of energy; it was like falling from a tree. Such a surge of awareness, of anticipation. Of life.

She made herself come to a standstill; her hands crossed over her heart so she could feel its frenzied rhythm.

This would never do.

Maybe Otto Sarragnac had put her under some kind of spell, for she was forgetting who she was and why she had willingly come here.

Not to play the part of an adoring wife in the stands, but to right a grievous wrong.

A wrong committed by the man she now called her husband.

A serving boy knocked on her half-open door and came into the chamber with his eyes cast studiously down.

"A letter has come for you, milady."

"Thank you."

She took the proffered roll of parchment and waited until the boy had bowed and left before opening it out. Her heart sank as she recognized her father's inelegant scrawl.

Sir Leon wasted no words enquiring after his daughter's happiness but got straight to reminding her of her duties to Kenmar. *Ariana, he wrote, must recover the famous Rose of Kenmar; a beautiful ruby which once had belonged to Ariana's grandmother.*

Upon her death, it had not passed, as he'd hoped, to Ariana and thus to the coffers of Castle Kenmar, but instead to her Aunt Ysmay, the druid priestess. She had worn it always on a chain around her slender neck, its fiery colors matching the brightness in her eyes. Since her capture, the jewel had been claimed by Darkmoor, falling even further from Sir Leon's clutches.

Ariana's hands shook as she folded the parchment and placed it at the bottom of her travelling chest. If any of the maids should see it, her father's plans would be revealed. And she, mayhap, would be considered complicit.

Then what? Her pulse quickened at the thought of how the

Earl of Darkmoor might punish a disobedient bride. But a shudder rippled through her as she imagined the cold eyes of Sir Althalos lighting up in pleasure at her plight.

With a surge of impatience, she slammed shut the wooden chest and paced over to the narrow window. Her father wanted too much, and too soon. She had been a bride in Darkmoor for little more than a day. Did he expect her to already have gained access to the vaults? She was sure the prized ruby would be locked away somewhere in the castle. None could see it and not realize its rarity.

But it was a rarity that mattered little to Ariana. Recently among the druids, the Rose of Kenmar had come to mean not just the precious jewel, but also the beautiful woman who wore it. Ysmay, the greatest healer Kenmar had ever known.

Ariana had every intention of rescuing Ysmay from her wrongful imprisonment in Darkmoor. As for the jewel, she would deal with that later. Her father would be furious, but what did it matter? She was a daughter of Darkmoor now. He had signed her away with his own hand.

But Sir Leon would not rest until he had her reply. She must send one soon, else her days would be plagued with his missives.

Deep in thought, she didn't hear the approaching footsteps and jumped in shock when the earl's looming figure appeared in her doorway. Otto was so tall and broad he took most of the light; his shadow fell across the wooden floor onto the neat linens on her bed.

He inclined his head. "My lady."

She dipped into an answering curtsy. "My lord."

Impatience flashed across his eyes. "I have been Earl of Darkmoor for less than a month but already I grow bored with the bowing and scraping. Stand tall, Ariana, when I enter the room. You are my wife, not a servant."

Though his words were generous, his commanding tone was harsh, and Ariana's limbs trembled with anxiety. Not least because of the quest she had been contemplating just moments earlier. Nonetheless she gathered her composure and acquiesced with a graceful nod. A lock of her long hair fell across her cheek, but she resisted the urge to push it away. Instead, she linked her fingers together tightly, lest the earl see their tremors.

Otto put a hand to his brow. His chainmail had been removed and he was clad in a dark tunic embroidered with fine gold thread. It fell away from his shoulders to reveal his bronzed skin and the merest hint of a carved, muscular chest. Ariana's nerves intensified into a small ball in the pit of her stomach. She pinched her nails into the backs of her hands until the pain steadied her thoughts.

"I have come with an offer," he stated. His voice was rich and deep, like a cool river on a hot day.

She took a breath. "I should be pleased to hear it."

He raised an eyebrow and all at once she was flooded with trepidation. Had the earl come to claim his bride, in the way she had expected last night? It was nothing more than his due. She had no right to resist him. But all at once, the trembling in her limbs intensified. She reached out to steady herself against the back of a wooden chair as Otto stepped forward in alarm.

"Are you unwell, Ariana?" He reached out a strong hand towards her and she couldn't help an instinctive flinch away. Realization flashed across his rugged face, closely followed by annoyance. He cleared his throat and looked away, towards the narrow window. "I meant only to invite you on a tour of the castle."

A potent mixture of relief and embarrassment made her weak. Heat suffused her spine and sprung into her cheeks. She smoothed her sleeves and swallowed. "I should like that."

He nodded sharply. "I have some time before luncheon."

"I have no engagements." It was a statement of fact, but bitterly made. Ariana hated to be idle. Back home in Kenmar, she was kept busy with work around the humble castle. And when work was done, she would ride out into the hills with her charcoal and a roll of parchment, always keen to snatch a moment to sketch—sometimes basing her line drawings on the bounteous nature all around, sometimes letting her imagination run wild. She had never been one to while away her days with chatter and embroidery, the way she suspected the Countess of Darkmoor may be expected to.

Although she had not yet been introduced to any ladies to chatter to. The great hall of Darkmoor Castle had been filled mainly with men during yesterday's wedding feast. Back then, she had been relieved to have no scathing eyes raking over her gown and finding it wanting.

Otto inclined his head. "Shall we?"

He did not hold out his arm for Ariana to take, but she had not been brought up to expect chivalry. Pausing only to fasten her cloak and pull up her hood, Ariana preceded him out of her bedchamber and out onto the sunlit gallery.

"Where shall we go?" She couldn't help a flicker of excitement at Otto's attention, but she told herself this was because he was unwittingly playing into her hands. If she could discover where the dungeons were located, mayhap she could locate Ysmay this very day.

"This way." Otto strode past her, taking the lead down the spiral stone staircase and out of the grand entrance doors to the inner courtyard. Ariana had to hurry to keep pace with him, wary of tripping on her long skirts.

The late morning sun had grown strong; Ariana's fur-trimmed cloak was unnecessary. She felt heat building at the back of her neck as she followed her husband around a corner towards a lawn of sparse grass. She looked around at this unfamiliar part of the castle, where weeds grew up through cracks in the rough stone. All around them, servants paused in their work and bowed low as they passed. Ariana knew they would be judging her, gossiping about her uncommon height and unfashionable wardrobe.

Smoke billowed out of the bakehouse, which was at least twice the size of the one in Kenmar. Shouting and banging from within indicated a frenzy of work in progress. Ariana flinched away, reluctant to be a nuisance, but Otto veered from the gray-stone building and turned sharply to the right, bringing them to a sudden halt by a circular tower which had loomed up out of nowhere.

She put out a hand to the sun-warmed stone. A strong breeze cooled her cheeks and brought birdsong floating up from the woods below them.

"What is this?"

He glanced down at her with all-knowing eyes which made her stomach twist. "Come and see." He fished in his tunic for a long iron key and swung open the door. "After you, Ariana."

She picked up her skirts and walked past him, conscious of the need to brush against his broad chest. Had he stood so close on purpose?

The air inside the tower smelled dank after the freshness of the day and she had to blink until her eyes adjusted to the gloom. The stone steps were narrow and steep. She concentrated on where she was putting her feet, trying to stay away from the gray walls which ran with damp.

She had expected wealth and riches from the famed fortress of Darkmoor, not poor accommodation such as this.

All at once, apprehension sized her. She paused and felt the commanding bulk of Otto press against her back. "Why have you brought me here?"

"You will see." His voice was gravelly and deep, giving nothing away.

Had he already discovered her treachery? Had he brought her here to imprison her—or dispose of her?

A thrill of fear made her blood run colder than the tower she was forced to ascend. But with the bulk of the earl behind her, she had no choice but to continue. At least she was walking towards a bright chink of sunlight; one which grew bigger and more welcoming with every twist of the stairs.

Finally, she emerged into a spacious, circular chamber. It was flooded with sunlight from several large windows which had been cut into the stone. After the gloom of the stairwell, the brightness was a blessing. Relief made her knees weaken and her chest heave inside the restrictive bodice of her gown. She put out a hand to a tapestried wall while she caught her breath.

Barely affected by the steep climb, Otto walked to the center of the chamber and put his hands on his slim hips.

"What do you think?"

She pushed back her hood and lifted her dark hair away from her neck while she cast her eyes around. Two upholstered chairs were positioned near an unlit fireplace and at the other side stood a large wooden table. Other than that, the room was empty.

"What is this place?"

"It is my tower." He smiled slightly. "Come and look."

He waved her over to one of the windows and after a moment's hesitation, she came to join him. Side by side, they gazed out at an unparalleled scene. Ariana couldn't help a gasp of surprise. Up here, they were far above the treetops. All of Darkmoor spread out before them in a patchwork of rolling fields. Here and there, small dots indicated cattle or men working the land. If she shaded her eyes, she fancied she could see a shimmering line on the horizon which must be the sea.

"It is beautiful," she exclaimed, honestly.

"It is useful," he corrected her. "From this tower, I can see to the very edge of our dominion. None can enter into Darkmoor lands from the east without my knowledge."

His words made her knees start to tremble once again. Why was he telling her this? Had he somehow divined her intentions?

She made her voice light. "Surely you have castle guards for such a chore?"

He pursed his full lips, and she once again noticed his chiseled cheekbones, so sharp they might cut her. "Of course. We have many guards here. But I prefer to keep an eye on things myself."

"You have no one to entrust with this task?" she questioned.

He shook his head.

Her pulse quickened and to buy herself time, she strolled casually over to another window. But she no longer had any interest in the view. "That must be very lonely for you," she commented.

His hunter's eyes followed her every move. She was trapped here, she realized. No one knew where she was. No one would hear her if she screamed. Though that mattered little, for even if her plight was known, no one in Darkmoor would dare stand against the earl. Far above them, the sun shifted behind a cloud and the tower room was plunged into shadows. Otto became one with the darkness. A masculine force of muscle and brawn. A warrior, trained to trust only himself.

"I have been raised to expect little else," he stated.

Ariana's growing anxieties were tempered by a small jolt of recognition. *Nor me*, she wanted to say. But the words dried on her tongue.

She swallowed and dampened her lips. "What about me?" she forced out. If a confrontation was coming, then she would prefer to get it over with. "Can the Earl of Darkmoor not trust his wife?"

All at once, she regretted her bravado. Otto stalked over to her, like a lion approaching its prey. "What about you?" he murmured, bringing his warm, bronzed hand to her flushed cheek. "Can I trust Ariana of Kenmar?" His gaze tightened; eyes boring into hers. "Let's talk about that, shall we?"

Chapter Four

A S HER GREEN eyes met his, the flick of passion in Otto's gut began to take hold. He longed to run his fingers through her cloud of hair, to press those sweet lips with his own.

She was his bride, after all.

But why had she such anxiety stamped across her face? He had brought her here so they could talk and get to know one another without constant interruption from his knights or other members of the household. Otto had barely known a moment's peace since becoming earl.

Did she expect him to maul her like a dog?

"Can I trust Ariana of Kenmar?" he muttered, tracing a soft line across her pink cheek. The question was partly rhetorical, for she was but an innocent maid and he earl of the mighty lands of Darkmoor.

Should Ariana trust him? That was a question more worthy of consideration.

But for the moment, he silenced the nagging voice of doubt and allowed himself to breathe in his wife's subtle fragrance of rose water. She was a beautiful flower, as yet untouched, unspoiled. The only thing in this castle to remain untarnished.

She shifted slightly at his touch, like a frightened horse not sure whether to acquiesce. He placed his hands gently on her shoulders and inhaled deeply as he came to a decision.

"I hope that, in time, we may come to trust one another," he said throatily, honestly.

He felt her thrill of surprise. For a long moment, neither spoke. Otto had dampened down his carnal desire, but he still wanted to touch and explore. His hands ran down Ariana's arms and found her trembling fingers.

"A wife must obey her husband," she said, finally.

"Aye," he agreed, entwining his fingers with hers and raising their joined hands to place them over Ariana's heart. "But I want you to trust me in here."

Her eyes widened in confusion. "Trust you?"

He smiled at her reaction. "It is a novel idea, I know." He bit his lip in frustration, searching for the words to explain. "When a horse trusts its rider, they are as one. When an army follows a trusted leader into battle, they are as one." He nodded, pleased with the analogy.

"But you are Otto Sarragnac," she whispered. "You're the…"

"The *Feared One*?" he finished for her, raising an eyebrow at her embarrassed stammer. "I know what they say of me in enemy lands. I know the reputation of the warriors of Darkmoor. It is one I helped my father to maintain." He broke off at the swell of grief in his chest.

"And you want me to trust you?" Her eyes were wide open like a child's.

"Let us consider it an experiment."

"An experiment?"

"Ariana, our relationship will grow much easier if you refrain from repeating everything I say."

Immediately she cast her eyes down. "Forgive me, my lord."

He shot out a hand and raised her chin, so they were once more gazing into one another's eyes. "When you are ready, we will know one another as husband and wife." He was charmed by the rush of color to her cheeks. "But only when you are ready."

Ariana opened her mouth and closed it again. He gently skimmed his finger over the fullness of her lips.

"But I should like to kiss you now, if I may?"

His question unnerved her. He saw it in the way she held

herself. It wasn't fear, not exactly. More a kind of confused surprise.

"You may," she whispered, so quietly he had to lean closer to catch her words.

His lips were already inches from hers. What a blessing to have a wife who stood so tall. He smoothed his hand into the small of her back and nudged her towards him, before planting the smallest of butterfly kisses at the corner of her mouth. Her lips parted in wonder. Emboldened, he did it once again. She exhaled and the sweetness of her breath mingled with his own. Otto held her more firmly and moved to the other side, keeping all his actions small and deliberate. He must not scare her off with a display of passion, however much he could feel it gathering within him.

She leaned closer to him, and he knew a swell of victory more meaningful than any he'd felt in the jousting ring. Instinctively, one of his hands rose up to stroke her thick tresses of hair. He cupped his hand around the back of her head and gently pressed his lips against hers. A small moan escaped her, and he was momentarily undone. Pushing caution to the wind, he parted her lips with his tongue, and she responded with an eagerness he had not anticipated, tilting her face to one side and running her hands over his shoulders. They fit together, like two parts molded explicitly for one another. Electricity fizzed up his spine and he knew he must stop, else he'd betray the pledge made mere moments earlier.

Slowly he withdrew his lips, though he continued holding her face in his hands and caressing the fullness of her cheeks with his roughened fingers.

"Thank you," he said, surprised by the throatiness of his voice.

Ariana broke their gaze to look over his shoulder. "It is I who should thank you, for your kindness." Her voice trembled, though Otto fancied it was not from fear.

"Kindness you did not expect?"

Her eyes slid back to his. "I have not been raised to expect kindness."

"'Tis the fate of those who are first-born."

She opened her mouth to reply then seemed to change her mind. "We must all accept the lot we are born with."

"Indeed."

Her words stirred the turmoil inside him once again. He heard his father's voice extolling the Knights' Code. *Show no weakness; show no mercy.* Rules he had broken more than once on this day.

All at once, he grew tired. It was not yet noon and hours of tasks lay ahead of him. What foolish impulse had led him to bring Ariana up here? He took a step backwards.

"I have little time." His voice was short, and he saw her heed his change of mood.

"Pray, do not let me detain you further."

There was no coyness in her manner. No hint of vanity or guile. He couldn't help but be charmed.

"Tell me, what would you like to see?"

Her eyes widened. They were a beautiful color, he realized. Green and blue, like the sea.

"In the castle?"

He nodded and watched as indecision raced across her face. "The morning room has been set aside for you. 'Tis a pleasant enough room. Shall I take you there?"

She cleared her throat. "One of the maids can show me, I suppose?"

"Of course."

"I should like to see somewhere the maids do not tread."

He frowned at her request. "But the maids have the run of the castle."

"Of course." She nodded hastily. "I only meant, as your time is so short…" Her voice trailed off.

"You want to see something that only I could show you?"

Her gaze flickered around the tower room as if she was thinking fast. "The might of Darkmoor is known far and wide."

He shifted his stance. "What of it?"

"I have often wondered," she paused and took a breath. "I have often wondered, my lord, how the prisoners are treated here."

Her question took him entirely by surprise. "The prisoners?"

She nodded. "Our priest taught me that the justness of any ruler is shown by his treatment of those at his mercy." He frowned in puzzlement and all at once he felt her pull away. "Forgive me. I have spoken out of turn."

"We do not take many prisoners," he responded. It was true. Most opponents were slaughtered on the battlefield. "You make an unusual request, Ariana."

She swallowed. "It was but a foolish notion. Please, think no more about it."

"I have nothing to hide," he countered. "No reason not to show you the dungeons. But they are no place for a lady."

He saw the debate rage behind her eyes. "My father raised me to be a ruler first, a lady second."

Surprise made him pause. There was that glint of steel once again. The unflinching manner he so admired. "Very well," he decided. "Let us go and see the dungeons. Though I warn you," he continued, holding up a finger to quell her expression of gratitude, "I have not ventured there myself since the last battle. I know not, exactly, what we may encounter."

Was that fear he saw race across her face?

But if it was, she pushed it firmly away. Ariana nodded her agreement. "I understand," she said levelly.

"Then follow me."

He led her back down the winding stairs, conscious of the narrow stone treads and the steepness of the descent. But Ariana did not clutch her skirts and grasp for his assistance the way he had expected. Nay, she walked with a surety and composure he had rarely seen.

What a curious creature he had wedded.

The sweetness of the outside air was always a relief after the confines of the stairwell. From the corner of his eye, he saw a pair of castle guards stand sharply to attention. Good. They should not stand easy. Yesterday's feast had brought merriment to Darkmoor after the bleakness of mourning, but he must ensure standards of vigilance remained high.

"This way," he said.

They walked side by side, unspeaking, to the western edge of the outer courtyard, chickens scattering in their path. Their squawking and pecking unsettled him somehow, and the curious gaze of women from the washhouse increased his irritation. But he had offered to show the castle to Ariana. In the future, he would take care to be more specific.

An acrid, unwashed smell reached them, and he paused to offer her his handkerchief. "You may wish to cover your nose," he advised.

"I have one of my own." Her hand went to her side and then faltered. "Oh, I had forgotten…"

He gave a small bow, lips curling upwards at the memory. "You were kind enough to present it to me." Her eyes lifted to his and once again he knew a strange jolt of recognition. "Take this," he urged.

She held the handkerchief daintily to her nose as they reached the imposing granite overhang of the Darkmoor dungeons. The guard was ready for them.

"My lord, my lady." He bowed to each of them in turn.

"How many prisoners have we?" Otto asked.

Surprise flickered across the guard's face, but he answered readily enough. "No more than six, my lord."

"Are they all men?"

He turned in surprise at Ariana's question. "Of course," he answered, before the guard could conjure a response.

Her cheeks colored pink. "What of the women prisoners?"

He frowned, genuinely perplexed. "Why should we have women prisoners?" The tolling of the noon-time bell alerted him to the passage of time and the urgency of the tasks still awaiting him. "Well, seeing as we are here, shall we continue?"

Ariana nodded her assent although he sensed her interest had waned. No doubt because of the smell, he thought, holding his breath as they passed beneath the overhang and into the dank confines of the dungeon. The ground beneath their feet was wet with moisture from the rocks. Torches affixed to the granite walls gave off little light, but his eyes adjusted quickly. He held out a hand to steady Ariana and was pleased when she took it.

"I hope you shall see that we treat our prisoners well," he stated, leading her towards the cells. "As well as can be expected," he amended. The wretch in the first cell was sitting on a wooden stool facing away from them. He turned when they approached, his eyes widening in surprise. "You see?" Otto gestured impatiently. "You are provided with food and water, are you not?" he demanded of the man.

The prisoner nodded.

Otto looked over at Ariana, but she was rooted to the spot, her eyes scanning the rocky corridor leading further into the dungeons.

"Do you wish to see more?" She shook her head, and he cursed his foolishness when tears brimmed at the corners of her eyes. "Then let us go."

He took her elbow and led her forcibly out into the freshness of the outer courtyard. Ariana gagged with his handkerchief pressed against her mouth.

"A terrible place," she gasped. "No light, no air."

"They are prisoners," he observed, "not guests."

"I see they are not held in chains, nor starved, nor flogged," she permitted, straightening her back. She shook out his handkerchief, then folded it neatly. "What are their crimes?" The question was flung out carelessly, but he sensed her interest in the answer.

Otto folded his arms, reluctant to talk more on this subject. "Theft, mostly."

"What of more serious crimes?" Her gaze met his.

He raised his eyebrows. "Such as?"

She opened her mouth, then hesitated. "Mayhap causing injury or death?"

Otto ran a hand through his hair, displeased with his wife's morbid interest. "Those guilty of killing are treated in the usual way." He turned back the Keep, determined to put an end to this peculiar line of questioning.

Ariana ran a few paces to catch up with him. "What is the usual way?"

He stopped abruptly and turned to face her. "What kind of questions are these, Ariana? Do you think me an earl or a saint?" He didn't wait for her answer. "Any man who kills another man outside of battle is put to death. The same in Darkmoor as Kenmar or anywhere else in this land, of that I'm certain. Those prisoners don't even see these dungeons. They are held else-where, at Traitor's Gate." He paused and added grimly, "But not for long."

His words were harsh, but he did not expect the rush of despair which creased Ariana's lovely face with fleeting sorrow.

Her next question was so quiet he could hardly hear the words.

"Women as well?"

"A killer is a killer," he declared.

A moment later, she had pulled up her hood and lowered her head.

"Thank you, my lord," she said, her voice muffled by the hood. "I will take my leave."

Otto started in surprise. He was the earl. He should be the one to take leave of Ariana. But his bride had already turned and fled, her long legs striding over the rough grass like a colt.

Otto folded his arms across his chest and watched her go. What had he said to upset her so? And why had she been so insistent on seeing the dungeons?

His brow darkened. Sir Leon had always been as crafty as a

fox. Was Ariana her father's daughter, after all?

Whatever Ariana was planning, he was determined to find out. His teeth clenched at the idea she might be deceiving him. But no sooner had this resolve hardened within his gut, than he remembered their kiss in the tower. She had felt right in his arms. Soft, warm and above all sincere. For a moment, he had known peace.

Otto picked up a piece of flint and flung it over the castle wall with an exclamation of impatience. Married life was proving to be far more unpredictable than he ever could have imagined.

Chapter Five

A RIANA PUSHED SHUT the wooden door of her chamber and flung her cloak onto the bed. She was flushed with heat and an inner conflict that showed no sign of abating.

That kiss.

His lips on hers, feathery light. The broadness of his shoulders. The sinewy strength of his arms that held her so gently.

The coldness in his eyes when, just minutes later, he condemned anyone believed to be guilty of crimes against Darkmoor.

Ariana clamped a hand over her mouth, fearful that the turmoil churning her stomach may come pouring out of her in a wail that would be sure to bring her maid running. She couldn't bear to be seen like this.

She was too hot. How could she think straight in this dreadful heat which covered her like an itchy blanket?

With shaking fingers, Ariana gathered up her long tresses of hair and tied them in a plait over her shoulder, relieved to feel some cool air against the back of her neck. She walked over to the nightstand and poured herself a small cup of ale from the earthenware pitcher, sipping it slowly.

That was better. Gradually, her heartrate slowed along with her racing thoughts, leaving her to confront an uncomfortable truth which her wildest dreams could never have foreseen.

She found her husband attractive.

Ariana squeezed her eyes shut in an effort to repel the notion, but it could not be denied. Otto's image flickered before her. Tall, strong, irrefutably male. A potent concoction of untamed power and unanticipated kindness.

He had infected her, like a fever. See how she trembled like a foolish maiden? Ariana straightened her shoulders. This would never do. She was Ariana of Kenmar, made of sterner stuff than the silly ladies who simpered and giggled in her father's hall. But in less than a day she had fallen prey to that very same affliction.

Which was ridiculous indeed. Her husband, forced upon her by circumstance, was Otto Sarragnac, *the Feared One*. And hadn't he proved himself worthy of his reputation when he spoke so unfeelingly about the prisoners held at Traitor's Gate?

Ariana shook her head to dispel any remaining confusion. Rescuing Ysmay had to be her number one priority. She couldn't allow her resolve to weaken with memories of how it had felt to stand encircled in Otto's arms. To feel his warm breath against her cheeks. The rasp of sharp stubble before the softness of his kiss.

Memories which gathered force within her, threatening to undermine everything.

She crossed her room and rummaged deep within her travelling case, breathing a sigh of relief when her fingers closed over the letter from her father.

She would write her reply, this very minute. What better way to channel her roving thoughts?

Ariana sat at her writing desk, bidding her hands to be steady else the ink would splatter everywhere. Though Sir Leon had never cared about the neatness of his daughter's hand, Ariana prided herself on the flowing lines of her letters. Somehow, the act of marking empty parchment with lines that would last longer than she, had always calmed her. It was the same with her sketching; a pastime that never failed to bring her peace. She lowered her head and concentrated on her task, writing with studied concentration of her intentions to free the Rose of Kenmar at her first opportunity.

Sir Leon, of course, would assume she meant the ruby; the precious jewel which his avaricious mind could not forget. But no matter. The task had quietened her thoughts and clarified her resolve. For all his brooding masculinity and sudden smiles, the Earl of Darkmoor could not compete with the love and affection Ariana felt for her aunt.

She would free Ysmay.

Ariana waited for the ink to dry, then folded and sealed her letter, acting hastily now for fear of being interrupted. Sure enough, no sooner had the wax settled than she heard a knock on her chamber door and the maid, Allys, entered.

"I am to help you dress for dinner, milady." The maid bobbed a curtsy and waited expectantly.

Ariana couldn't help a sigh of regret. She had always hated the charade of dressing for dinner. The restrictive gowns. The hairpins that dug into her scalp. The knowledge that no matter how much time the maids spent pinning up her hair or straightening her skirts, she would never hold a candle to those dew-eyed young ladies whose hair fell into natural ringlets and who somehow knew how to hold their fans just so, batting their eyelids and quirking their pink lips into perfect smiles. Mayhap if her mother had lived for longer, or she'd had an older sister to guide her, she'd have found it all less daunting.

"I was hoping to have a tray brought up to my room," Ariana tried. "I am weary from the events of the day." Her halting words failed to sound credible to her own ears.

Allys shifted her weight from one foot to the other. She was a short, slender girl with straight brown hair and a level gaze. Was she pleased to find herself elevated to the position of lady's maid, Ariana wondered, or did she prefer the bustle and camaraderie of the kitchen?

"The earl has requested a place be laid for you in the great hall," Allys said tonelessly.

Despite herself, Ariana felt her heart lift at this. Otto was thinking of her, wanting her company. How could she refuse him?

How could she refuse anyway? She had neither power nor agency in the halls of Darkmoor.

"Very well," she sighed, dragging her feet over to the vanity table where Allys waited, hairbrush in hand.

Sometime later, attired in her best emerald-green gown with her hair carefully piled onto her head and a necklace of gleaming pearls fastened around her neck, Ariana was declared ready. Her corset pinched and she dared not make any sudden movements, lest her hair come tumbling down, but she correctly divined that the Countess of Darkmoor could not publicly dine without such pomp and ceremony.

"Please can you see that my letter is delivered to Sir Leon?" she asked Allys.

"Very good, milady." The maid bobbed another curtsy and then left the chamber, pulling the door closed behind her noiselessly.

Left alone, Ariana felt a clutch of fear. She must descend to the great hall alone. At least in cold Castle Kenmar, feasting and ritual had been uncommon occurrences. There, she had been largely left to her own devices, eating from a trencher of bread and cheese which Chiara the castle cook had willingly brought up to her chamber when hunger dictated. But when the niceties were observed, perchance when Sir Leon entertained company, Ariana had always known that she would be amongst other women. A couple of them kind, most of them not. But all of them well able to attract the attention of her father's men, drawing their eyes blessedly away from Ariana.

She had never before faced the prospect of being a lone lady in a hall full of warriors.

Ariana fingered the pearls that dipped into the hollows of her throat. She was Countess of Darkmoor now and must greet whatever obstacles came her way. She would hold her head high and remember that rescuing Ysmay was the only thing that mattered.

Still, her courage failed her at the entrance to the great hall and she ducked behind the high stone archway to better compose herself. The rumble of conversation was distinctly masculine, with guffaws of laughter and much scraping of chairs. Ariana risked peeking around the archway to scan the room for a familiar face. She knew that Merek took his meals in his chamber. Her only friend here could be Otto.

At first, she could see nothing but a blaze of light, for the hall was illuminated with flaming torches as well as a multitude of candles which flickered from the mighty pillars. The vast room was full of people, of *men*. All of them clad in the red and gold colors of Darkmoor. How could she recognize Otto amongst so many seasoned fighters?

She knew a thrill of relief when she spied him sitting high on the dais beside another man whom she hadn't seen before. Once identified, his height and bearing made the Earl of Darkmoor unmistakable. Although the shuttered expression on his rugged face bore little resemblance to the courteous husband who had invited her on a tour of the castle. Ariana felt a thrill of foreboding travel up her spine. She had risked too much when she asked him to show her the dungeons. Pushed her advantage too far. Amidst the clamor of the knights and soldiers, her vulnerability was all too evident. She must stay on her guard around the *Feared One* and his men.

"Are you quite well, my lady?"

She jumped at the voice, smooth as oil slick, which came from behind her. Ariana recognized it at once and her heart sank as she turned to acknowledge Sir Althalos.

"Just getting my bearings," she lied. "Good evening, Sir Althalos."

A knowing look passed across his small dark eyes. He knew she had cowered here, intimidated and maybe even afraid. Ariana cursed herself for her foolishness, and for giving this weaselly man some advantage over her.

He proffered an arm, which she had no choice but to take.

"Allow me to escort you to your seat."

"You are most kind." She inclined her head and rested the tips of her fingers against his crimson sleeves.

All conversation ceased in the great hall as they made their stately procession to the dais. Ariana felt hundreds of eyes turn upon her, felt her nostrils assaulted by the stench of sweat mixed with cooked meats. Well-honed fighting men sat on wooden benches pulled up to trestle tables all around the hall. Their bodies were loose, their limbs carelessly outstretched, meaning she must pick her way carefully around muscular legs and heavy boots. She deliberately held herself tall, refusing to repeat her earlier show of weakness, however much her heart pounded and perspiration gathered beneath the folds of her gown.

They clambered up to the dais and Althalos pulled out her chair with an overdone display of chivalry. "My lady." He bowed low.

"Thank you, Sir Althalos."

With as much grace as she could muster, Ariana lowered herself into her chair and only then raised her eyes to her husband. "Good evening, my lord."

Otto seemed momentarily surprised to see her there. The earl had been deep in conversation with the man at his side, merely picking at the platter of tempting morsels before him. "Ariana." He nodded with just the merest flicker of a smile. "Let me pour you some wine."

She thanked him, though she wanted neither food nor wine. Her stomach churned with a mixture of apprehension and exhaustion. Had it really been just one day since her wedding ceremony?

"Allow me to introduce my distant cousin and good friend, Angus de Neville." Otto nodded to the man beside him; a tall, golden-haired giant of a man, clad in rich furs with eyes as blue as a summer sky. "Angus, this is my bride, Ariana, Countess of Darkmoor."

The title tripped from his tongue clumsily, as if Otto shared

Ariana's incredulity that the worthy moniker should apply to her.

The golden-haired nobleman raised his goblet and smiled broadly. "Delighted to meet you, Countess. I apologize that I was not here for your wedding. Alas, I was detained in Wolvesley."

Otto snorted before Ariana could think of a suitable reply. "Detained how, Angus?" he enquired mildly. "Perchance were the pleasures too manifold for you to take your leave?"

Ariana felt a blush stain her cheeks at her husband's rudeness, but his friend laughed it off easily. "It is true, Countess, that in comparison to my cousin here, my life is one of idle enjoyment." He took a long sip of wine. "I would not have it any other way."

"Angus is the younger brother of the Earl of Wolvesley," Otto commented drily. "He enjoys all of the riches and none of the responsibility."

"And will you stay with us long?" Ariana asked politely, her voice sounding weak amidst so much clamor.

"Have no fear, my lady." Angus bowed his head gallantly toward her. "I will be out of your way come the morrow. I must make haste to Hexham. Besides, I have no intention of overstaying my welcome with the wild warriors of Darkmoor." He winked at her before raising his eyes to Otto and guffawing with mirth.

Ariana was mortified that her polite enquiry had been misinterpreted. "There is no need for you to leave us so soon."

"Ah, but there is," Otto injected. "Angus is unused to rough living. Our halls are not great enough, is that not right, my friend?"

"On the contrary, your halls do very well. Outside of Wolvesley, there is nowhere else I would rather be."

Otto gave a burst of laughter which took Ariana by surprise. For a moment, the *Feared One* morphed into a genial young man with a solid sense of humor.

"You lie, Angus, but I thank you for the compliment. What about the beautiful Lady Emelia Foxton, your betrothed? Surely, she will be missing you?"

Angus straightened his face and nodded with a show of sobriety. "I am sure she is distraught at my absence."

"Should you not do the lady a favor, and marry her already?"

"The favor is the lady's to take, whenever she wishes. I await her word." Angus paused to drink deeply from his goblet. "Although I have always believed that marriage is not a state to be hurried into." He paused, as if remembering both his manners and the hurried nature of Otto's recent nuptials. "But of course, if one's betrothed is as lovely as the Lady Ariana, why wait?"

Ariana's cheeks stung with heat at the falsehood. She had little experience of society, but tales of the redoubtable Lady Emelia Foxton, beloved companion of Princess Mary, had reached even her father's chilly outpost. Lady Emelia was one of the wealthiest heiresses in England and a beauty in the bargain. By her side, Ariana was as lovely as a farmer's daughter just in from working the fields.

Angus de Neville was toying with her.

If she had felt out of place before, now Ariana was awash with self-awareness. Thankfully, having paid their dues to the lady present, the men now paid her little heed, resuming the close conversation they'd been enjoying before her entrance. Ariana toyed with the food on her trencher, half wishing to re-join the banter, keenly aware that the eyes of Darkmoor were upon her. Surely if the men-at-arms saw her interacting with their lord and master, their interest in her would wane? They would look away, anxious not to be caught prying.

But Otto and Angus were as thick as thieves, and humble modesty prevented her from speaking up. She had no wish to converse with Althalos, and dared not so much as glance sideways towards him for fear he may try to engage her. As the seconds ticked by, her silence became inescapable. She was like a young child allowed to dine with the adults for the first time. A cold flower of anxiety unfurled in her stomach as she watched Otto's long fingers grip the stem of his goblet.

Was Otto displeased with her?

Worse, had he discovered her missive to Sir Leon?

Surely not, she reasoned, dampening down her panic. Why then would he have greeted her and poured her wine? Even requested her presence in the great hall?

A flurry of footsteps announced the arrival of a fourth man who was to join them on the dais. He was tall and gray-haired, with a kind but noble face. He bowed low, first to Otto, then Ariana, and finally to Angus de Neville. His nod to Sir Althalos was distinctly more abrupt.

Otto raised his hand towards the man. "Ariana, this is Gaius, one of my longest-serving knights."

"I am pleased to meet you," she said, smiling. Perhaps Gaius would inspire some conversation in which she could participate. She would feel so much more comfortable if she could talk and laugh with another.

"You, too, my lady." His blue eyes were crinkled with sincerity, but no sooner had he settled himself than Otto turned to bring him into conversation with Angus.

Ariana's spirits sank.

Althalos, who was seated at her left, leaned closer. "You are not eating, my lady. Allow me to assist you."

Ariana steeled herself not to flinch away from the sourness of his breath. "I have little appetite," she replied, honestly.

It was the wrong thing to say. Althalos quirked an eyebrow. "Perhaps the Darkmoor kitchens are not as well equipped as those you are accustomed to?"

His words met their mark, but she cleared her throat and spoke to him levelly. "I believe you know that is not true, Sir Althalos."

Her brutal honesty made Althalos choke on a mouthful of food, and her lips twitched into a smile, but she regretted her impulsive words almost immediately. Her husband's uncle was an unpleasant man; it would not do to make an enemy out of him.

"On the contrary," she continued, "it is the case that I am

unaccustomed to such rich and wonderful foodstuffs." She waved her hand over the laden tabletop which groaned with roasted meats.

"Perhaps you would prefer a bowl of broth?" Althalos suggested drily.

"Indeed, I would."

She had not counted on the hovering page who scampered off to the kitchen to repeat her request; one that surely would not endear her to either the servants or the household.

How could she ask for mere broth when she was seated in such company?

Her spirits plummeted further when their handsome guest, Angus de Neville, gave her a quick glance over the rim of his goblet. What must he think of her?

What must Otto think of her?

Ariana folded her hands in her lap and looked down, avoiding further conversation. When a bowl of steaming broth was placed before her, she surprised herself by sniffing hungrily, tempted by the simple fare.

She met Otto's eye as she picked up her spoon and he treated her to another slight smile. Small comfort, but there nonetheless.

The vegetable broth was quite tasty. Ariana found herself relaxing in her high-backed chair. Gradually the chatter in the great hall resumed to its earlier levels. She was a novelty no longer. Within days, hopefully her presence on the dais would warrant no comment.

A fearsomely tall, broad-shouldered man made his way up the steps of the dais to speak to Otto, his thunderous footsteps making the ground beneath them shake. She watched from the corner of her eye as the men conversed; one warrior to another. The new man's thighs, encased in breeches, were as wide as tree trunks. No wonder the might of Darkmoor was feared far and wide, with men such as this to fight for it.

No wonder the druids had crumbled so quickly.

With shaking fingers, Ariana placed her spoon carefully in her bowl, but she could do little to stem the tide of memory. She heard Merek's voice as if he was speaking directly into her ear.

"But for Otto's return, your aunt would likely have been killed."

Was this giant of a man one of those responsible for plundering the druid camp and taking Ysmay prisoner? What hope would those peaceful people have had against such a brute?

She tried to swallow down her last mouthful of broth but found herself choking. One cough, then another. Her hand went to her throat as her chair scraped back and Ariana struggled to catch her breath. In seconds, Otto came to her aid.

"What is it?" he enquired; heavy brows knitted together. "Here, drink this."

Ariana clutched at the goblet and desperately gulped down the wine, which washed down the stubborn broth. Her sides heaved as her breathing returned to normal.

"Thank you," she managed.

"Take a moment," he advised.

The eyes of Darkmoor were upon her once again. Ariana grew even hotter with the realization she had acquitted herself badly. She wanted to leave now, before anything else could go wrong, but Otto was already righting her chair and guiding her into it.

"Better?" he asked.

"Thank you, my lord." She dared not look at Sir Althalos, nor Angus, nor the assembled soldiers below her. When would this ordeal end?

Otto returned to his own place, but she felt the force of his gaze still upon her, while Angus and Gaius looked studiously away.

"There are no other women here," Otto announced, as if newly surprised by their absence. "I apologize for it, Ariana. It is only right that you should have female company."

She inclined her head. "Please, do not trouble on my account."

Otto waved his hand expansively. "It is no trouble, and it is no less than your due. We have been the preserve of men since my mother's death and I'm sure our manners are the worse for it." He paused for a moment as Angus spluttered his agreement. "My father did not encourage distractions, but there are noble ladies, wives and daughters of our knights, who we could invite to the castle," he floundered, clearly unsure what women might do when left alone together.

Ariana smiled her thanks, carefully masking her fears. "That would be most pleasant."

"Good." Otto's face was transformed by his smile. "Robin." He clicked his fingers towards his page. "See that Lady Elspeth and Mistress Lucietta receive an invitation to dine with us tomorrow."

Lady Elspeth and Mistress Lucietta, Ariana recited their names in her head. Names which told her nothing about the women she would meet. Would they become kind, supportive confidantes, like Chiara back home in Kenmar? Or would they snipe and snigger behind her back, like so many others in Sir Leon's castle?

She shook herself out of her reverie to find Althalos's cold eyes set upon her, a small smile playing over his lips. What lapse of etiquette had she displayed now?

Ariana pressed a napkin to her lips, determined to remain an object of ridicule no longer. She raised her chin and sought out Otto's gaze. "Forgive me, husband, but I find myself out of sorts. I will retire early." She pushed back her chair and stood from the table, before any of the men assembled could react.

Otto was the first to his feet. "I shall accompany you," he said, making Ariana's heart leap.

But Althalos was also out of his chair and lifting a restraining hand to his nephew. "I will not hear of it, my lord. I shall escort Lady Ariana. Pray, be seated now and finish your meal."

Ariana pressed her lips together, silencing any plea for Otto's support. Althalos could hardly insist on accompanying her all the way back to her chamber. What harm could another minute in the man's odious company do her?

She inclined her head to Otto, Angus and Gaius, the elderly knight, allowing Althalos to take her arm and lead her down the wooden steps of the dais. With her eyes fixed on the arched doorway and freedom, Ariana cared less about the keen appraisal of the men as they paraded through the great hall. Soon she could close her chamber door and pull her hair free of its ridiculous trappings.

She turned to face Althalos as soon as they passed into the stone-flagged entrance hall. Standing beneath the mighty Darkmoor coat of arms, she pulled herself up to her full height.

"I bid you good evening, Sir Althalos."

She expected him to bow and take his leave, but instead he held tightly to her arm, keeping her prisoner by his side.

"I am surprised you agreed with such good grace," he announced, cold eyes raking her over. Making her feel foolish and worthless, as was no doubt his intent.

She could wrench her arm free and walk away. He could hardly chase after her. But after the scene on the dais, Ariana had no wish to create another.

She swallowed; aware she was walking into his trap. "Agreed to what?"

Althalos smiled. "Why, to the earl installing his whore here in Darkmoor Castle, right under your very nose."

Chapter Six

THE MORNING SUNLIGHT filtered through the mullioned windows of the castle solar, casting bright patterns onto the walnut desk and dark shadows onto the tapestried walls. Otto sat in the large, ornately carved chair that had once belonged to his father. His long fingers drummed an impatient tattoo on the desk as he tried to work out his next move.

He had spent a restless night, tossing and turning in his bedchamber with the whispered words of his young page echoing clearly through his mind.

"Sir Althalos has told the countess that you are installing your whore here in the castle."

Such a rage gripped him that he had risen from the dais and strode from the great hall, with no thought to the scores of men watching the family drama play out. In that moment, Otto wanted only to find his uncle and grip him by his scrawny neck until the man apologized. But by the time he reached the inner courtyard, there was no sign of either Althalos or his bride.

It had come as no surprise to him that Althalos sought to undermine his relationship with Ariana. His uncle was a coldhearted, cruel man who enjoyed making others squirm. Otto was sure that Althalos's intentions were purely to bring the new Countess of Darkmoor down a peg or two, but the question remained, how should he be punished?

If he should be punished.

Otto had spent enough time with his new bride to understand

that she was no simpering maid in need of a protector. She could fight her own daily battles, as he had already been pleased to witness, but in questioning Otto's fidelity and undermining his authority, Althalos had gone too far.

"Damn him," Otto swore quietly.

If it were anyone else, he would see him chased from the castle grounds. But for his many sins, Althalos was the closest family Otto had left. More importantly, he was a man of great wealth and substantial following. It would not do to alienate him, especially when Lord Ulric was not yet cold in the ground. Otto knew that amongst his own people, many held Sir Althalos in high esteem. Would they march behind him if they were forced to choose?

He did not wish to find out.

Bone weary, he leaned forward in his chair and ran his fingers through his tousled hair. He had been married for less than two days, and already the institution had proven more than troublesome. Mayhap he should forget the whole sorry affair. Push the incident from his mind and leave Ariana to entertain her doubts and suspicions as she saw fit.

But no sooner had this thought crystalized in his mind than he pushed it away. *No.* His bride did not deserve that. He pictured her steady green gaze and her dark cloud of hair. The softness of her lips. The steely determination he had glimpsed on more than one occasion. The unexpected connection which drew him to her like a magnet. After the honest conversation they had in the tower, he could not leave her to imagine him bedding his whore under the same roof as she.

His lip curled in disgust. Only a man with the moral deficit of Althalos would have planted such an idea in her head.

He should approach Ariana then, not Althalos. Tell her the truth.

He paused at that. *Could Ariana handle the truth?*

"Damn them all," he swore again, pushing himself up from the chair with a surge of impatience and pacing the length of the room. He paused beneath a life-sized frieze of his father, Ulric, Earl of Darkmoor, which had been painted onto the white-washed wall when Otto was a boy and Ulric still stood tall and strong with a full head of dark hair.

Bold tempera had brought life and energy to the portrait. His father's imperious gaze seemed to look straight out of the painting to land, scornfully, on Otto.

"Show no weakness, show no mercy," Otto imagined him saying.

Lord Ulric would have wasted no time in pondering the well-being of his wife, nor anyone else for that matter. He believed in action, not words and certainly not sentiment.

But was that the sort of man Otto wanted to be?

Was that the sort of husband he wanted to be?

Seized by a new idea, he walked back to the desk and began to hunt through its multitude of drawers. It was many years since he'd last glimpsed the object he sought, but he had an idea Lord Ulric would have secreted it somewhere here. After all, it was not costly enough to be locked away in the vaults. Its value was purely sentimental, and therefore measured little to his father.

Finally, he glimpsed a flash of bronze metal, and his grasping fingers retrieved a medium-sized broach set with glittering amethyst stones. His mother's. Otto closed his fist around it, clamping down on a swell of emotion. He had never known his mother and had learned little about her from Ulric.

"What's past is past," his father had told him. "Your future lies on the battlefield boy, not in grasping after ghosts."

He brought the broach closer to his face, squinting at its condition. The metal had grown dull, but a quick polish would restore its shine. He would make it a gift to Ariana, in return for the token she had bestowed upon him after the joust. The idea felt good and right, and his lips turned up at the corners.

A brisk knock sounded at the solar door, jolting him out of his reverie. He opened his mouth to invite entry, but the door was already opening.

Althalos walked into the solar with a confident gait and his head held imperiously high, as if he was the Earl of Darkmoor and Otto some lowly servant.

"The men have been asking where you are," he stated.

Otto folded his arms across his embellished tunic. "Good morning, Althalos." He put his head to one side, considering his uncle.

"Shall I tell them you will be out soon?" the old man asked irritably.

Otto walked over to the window with deliberate slowness. It was a lovely morning, with sunlight dappling through the distant trees. "Out where?" he enquired, his voice mild.

"To morning training." Althalos took a few steps towards him. "It would not do for you to miss it."

Otto slipped the broach into his pocket and grasped the back of his ornate desk chair. "Would not do for whom? I am the Earl of Darkmoor. Can I not do as I please?" His rhetorical question was calmly delivered, and he sat down to busy himself with a roll of parchment before Althalos could answer. Otto kept his eyes affixed to his desk, though he would have dearly liked to glance up and see the effect his question had on a man unused to being challenged.

Althalos cleared his throat. "Nephew, I speak only out of concern for Darkmoor and the estate passed down to you by my own brother. Your skills have always been in combat, not government. You must know this?" Althalos paused for an acknowledgement, which the younger man was not inclined to give. Instead, Otto templed his fingers beneath his chin and waited with a display of patience for his uncle to continue. "The knights follow you because you are a formidable warrior. But if they cease to see you as such. Well…" Althalos finished his sentence with an eloquent shrug of his shoulders.

Otto leaned back in his chair, trying for now to control his rising temper. "I hardly think the men will leave Darkmoor in droves if I miss one training session."

"It is your opportunity to demonstrate your right to be earl."

"A right I have demonstrated many times." Otto's voice rose in warning. "And I shall continue to do so. But not today. I'll ask you to leave me now, Althalos."

It was the first time he had expressed hostility towards his uncle and even as the words left his mouth, he half regretted them. Althalos may be a brute, but he was a brute with wisdom and experience to share. Not to mention a loyal following of well-armed, battle-honed fighting men. Were it not for his deliberate goading of Ariana, Otto would have bitten his tongue until Althalos saw fit to leave Darkmoor for his own, lesser estate.

But Althalos did not so much as flinch at Otto's words. He considered his nephew with his head on one side, before swiftly swiveling on his heel.

"Very well," he spoke over his shoulder, leaving the solar door open behind him.

Otto brought his fist crashing down onto the desk, frustration surging through his veins.

"Damn him to hell," he swore again.

His blood was up and the silvery scar across his face began to throb. He had received the scar on one of his first outings in battle—when he was mayhap little older than young Benedict. For several days, it had refused to heal, causing their ageing apothecary to wring his hands and Ulric to search far and wide for a more talented physician. By the time Merek arrived in Dark-moor, Otto's fever had been raging and hopes for his recovery had begun to fade. But Merek had closed the wound, staunched the bleeding, and restored him to health. These days, his scar only troubled him during times of high emotion.

Otto flung the parchment aside and rocked backwards in his chair. He knew he would find no further peace in the solar, no solace in work. Were it not for his implacable stance against Althalos, he would have stridden outside and plunged himself deep into a knights' training session. Right now, there was nothing he would like more than to throw an axe against a far-off target or draw his sword against a worthy opponent.

Another image flashed across his mind. The lovely Elspeth Woodruffe, with her willowy limbs and ready smile. At one time, she would have happily offered him a form of solace.

Otto ground his teeth. Thinking on the matter, she was perchance not the best choice of companion for his young wife. But the woman was quick-witted and articulate, exactly the type to put Ariana at ease. *That* had been his sole consideration in the moment when he'd mentioned her name. He certainly had no designs on her now. God's Bones, he was a better man than to go whoring after a one-time mistress while his wedding vows still echoed around the chapel.

His eyes flickered again to the window. A lovely morning, he confirmed. Why spend it stewing inside?

Energized, he leapt to his feet. He would take his horse and gallop down to the river, where the fresh air and rippling waters would chase away the black cloud that had gathered around him. Calling to his page, Otto walked from the room with long strides, already imagining the release he would feel when the horse gathered speed beneath him.

So caught up was he in this vision, that he failed to see the tall young woman standing hesitantly on the threshold of the solar. It was only when she scuttled backwards in alarm, his arm having made contact with the softness of her chest, that he realized who she was.

"Ariana," he said, coming to an abrupt halt. "Forgive me, I did not see you there."

"It was my mistake, my lord." Her cheeks flushed pink as she straightened the deep blue skirts of her simple gown. Her hair was loose upon her pale shoulders. He liked the way it billowed around her. Unfashionable, maybe, but Otto had always preferred the natural look.

"Come now. You have every right to be outside my door. Is there something you desire?"

Her face was pained with indecision. "I was looking around the keep."

He put his hands on his hips and considered her. "You have still not had the chance to explore?"

"Not properly." She hesitated. "But to tell you the truth, I long to be outside on a day like this."

"That's exactly where I was going." He clicked his fingers, gripped with new resolve. "Why don't you accompany me?"

At once he saw that she wanted to agree, but nerves or propriety held her back. "Accompany you, my lord?"

"Accompany me," he confirmed, then couldn't resist teasing. "Do you worry that might be improper?" He nudged her with his shoulder and laughed down at her.

She bit down on her lip, her cheeks crimson. "I only…"

"Forgive me," he repeated soberly. "I have had a trying morning, Ariana, and I long to be free of the tension building around my shoulders. It increasingly feels as though you are the sole person within these castle walls who wants nothing from me. Am I right?"

Her beautiful green eyes widened. "I don't know, my lord."

"Otto," he corrected.

"Otto," she mumbled.

He sighed. "A horseback ride down to the river. That is all I am offering, Ariana. A change of scene. A breath of fresh air." He leaned closer. "The chance to spend an hour or two away from Sir Althalos."

She couldn't fully repress her smile. "That I would like, very much."

"Come then." Acting on impulse he reached down and took hold of her hand. "Let us waste no further time."

ARIANA WAS A natural horsewoman with a good seat and a courageous connection with her horse. They had trotted sedately through the outer courtyard, but once they were out in the fields,

Otto felt confident enough in his companion to urge his horse into a gallop. A quick glance over his shoulder assured him that Ariana was secure in the saddle, enjoying the speed and exhilaration as much as he was. Desire, deep and unanticipated, stabbed through him. His bride was an intriguing prospect, the more time he spent with her, the more curious he became.

He pulled up at the far side of the meadow, where the grass grew long and the ground began to slope down to the river. Just seconds later, Ariana arrived at his side. Her eyes were bright and her cheeks flushed from fresh air and exercise.

"Are you well?" he asked, happy to note her enthusiasm. "Enjoying the ride?"

"Very much," she answered. And he could tell that she had bitten back the words 'my lord.'

Good. At last, they were getting somewhere.

Ariana gathered her reins in one hand and used the other to scoop her long hair away from her face. Her gown had gone askew during their ride, falling tantalizingly low over her generous breasts. Otto's instinct, as a gentleman, was to look away. But this was his wedded wife, he reasoned, and he enjoyed the view as she better secured her hair.

"Would you like to lead the way?" he asked.

She twisted in the saddle to look at him and he knew another rush of desire. "But I do not know the way."

"Simply follow the path," he assured her. "Anyway, the horses know where they are going."

He had an ulterior motive asking Ariana to go ahead. From behind, he could gaze at her soft curves and the bewitching fall of her hair without fear of being caught.

All too soon, they reached the river, a wide ribbon of water which gushed over jutting stones and widened into a welcoming pool where colorful birds flittered in search of food. For a while, all they could hear was the rushing of the water and the rhythmic singing of an ousel perched nearby.

"It's beautiful," Ariana breathed.

"As are you." When her cheeks colored again, he simply shrugged. "I only speak the truth."

"You embarrass me," she said, but her lips curled upwards into a smile, and he knew he had pleased her.

"Let's stop here a while," he suggested. When she nodded her assent, Otto flung a leg over his horse and dismounted, then held Ariana's hand while she slipped from the saddle.

"What about the horses?" she asked.

"They will be fine." He looped both sets of reins over a branch, before unclipping a blanket from the back of his saddle and spreading it over the soft grass. "Come and sit beside me. Only for a moment," he added, noting her hesitation. "We deserve a rest after our rough ride, do we not?" He stretched out, enjoying the view of both the river and his young wife.

"As you wish." She picked her way over the uneven ground towards him and carefully lowered herself down onto the blanket, arranging her skirts so they fell respectfully over her legs. "I have not ridden with such speed and freedom for too long."

He plucked a long blade of grass and twisted it through his fingers in an effort to distract himself from her alluring closeness. "Why is that?"

She gave him a small smile. "My father wished to ensure no harm should befall me…"

"Quite right," he interrupted.

"In the days leading up to our marriage," she added, a slight shrug of her shoulders indicating her indifference.

He followed her gaze to a series of ripples on the surface of the river, indicating fish swimming deep below. It seemed as though they were the only two people for miles around. "Were you surprised to discover your father's plans?" he asked hesitantly.

"To marry you?" She turned to face him; her eyebrows raised in disarming honesty. "Of course."

He allowed the grass to fall through his fingers, breathing in the smell of spring. "You were not pleased?" he guessed, speaking quietly, unsure why he was pressing on with this line of questioning.

Her chest rose and fell with her breathing. She had grown anxious and suddenly he wanted nothing more than to reassure her, but she spoke up before he could find the words.

"At first, I was shocked, afraid even." She glanced up and once again he was impressed by the courage shining in her green eyes. "You have a considerable reputation throughout the North."

Otto pressed his lips together as a cloud passed over the sun overhead, casting them into shadow. "I know what they call me." He had never flinched from his reputation, but the idea that brave Ariana had feared him made him strangely uncomfortable.

She shifted on the blanket and lowered her head so he could not see her expression.

A kingfisher darted by in a sudden flash of glistening blue. It dived into the river and emerged victorious; a small fish clamped inside its beak. The horses watched with their ears pricked forward, then lost interest and began to crop at the grass.

Otto felt as if a vise was closing around him. A vise formed from the reputation built for him by Lord Ulric. A reputation that helped ensure prosperity for Darkmoor, but at what cost? Was he a man or a mere fighting machine?

"Everything I do is for the good of Darkmoor," he said, unsure why he felt the need to speak so forcefully.

But Ariana surprised him by laying one of her cool hands over his. "I know," she said.

The fact of her reaching out to him took his breath away. When was the last time anyone had shown him such spontaneous affection?

"You do?"

"I have seen another side to you," she said simply.

He thought to make some quip about keeping such insights to herself, but the words dried on his tongue when a sudden breeze brought a waft of clean, citrussy scent from Ariana's hair.

He closed his eyes and inhaled, twisting his hand so their fingers entwined. When she didn't pull away, he leaned in closer, so their sides were touching. A frisson passed through her. Fear, or mayhap just awareness. But he cautioned himself to move slowly.

"You bring that other side out in me," he told her, surprising himself with his truthfulness.

She tilted her face upwards, her beautiful eyes just inches from his, and for a long moment they gazed at one another. Then, as if moving of one accord, they closed the gap between them and kissed.

As much as he longed to claim her mouth with his own, Otto made sure he stayed soft and gentle. But he couldn't resist twining a hand through her hair and pulling her head closer to him. She gave a low moan which seemed to uncork something inside him, and he encircled his arms around her, delighting in the softness of her curves. She positioned her hands on either side of his face, responding to his kiss with renewed urgency and releasing a current of desire which bolted straight to his core.

"Ariana," he whispered, pulling away before he lost control and ravished her by the river.

Her cheeks flushed pink. "Don't stop," she said, so quietly he wasn't sure he had heard her correctly. But when she moved against him and tentatively placed her palms against the hardness of his chest, her meaning was clear.

"Lay back," he told her, his voice coming out in a rasp, as he gently lowered her to the blanket. Her green eyes locked onto his, following his every move. He kissed her cheeks, dropping butterfly kisses onto the side of her mouth, and then moved down to her neck. He deliberately kept his hands away from her body, but when she traced her fingers in a line from his chest to his navel, he was undone.

With a groan of pleasure, he cupped a generous breast with the palm of one hand while the other fastened around her waist. His kisses grew hotter and more urgent, his tongue darting out along her collar bone. Ariana twisted with anticipation, arching against his hand until he couldn't help but reach beneath her gown to find the hard nub of her nipple.

Her response to his touch was electrifying. His desire for her strained at his breeches, but he was determined to give her pleasure first. With trembling fingers, he unfastened her gown until her breasts sprang free. Ariana bit down on her lip and he instantly covered her mouth with kisses, warding off any embarrassment.

"Your body is beautiful," he murmured, stroking her firm breasts with delight.

She pulled him closer towards him. "I never thought..."

Her sentence trailed off as he gently fastened his mouth against one rose-colored bud. She groaned, twisting her fingers in his hair and driving him wild with longing.

He couldn't help it. He had to explore more of her. Without shifting his position, and still paying homage with his tongue to the wonder of her breasts, he lifted her skirts and traced a gentle path up the velvety softness of her inner thighs.

She tensed and he immediately stilled, determined not to move faster than she was ready for.

"Otto," she breathed.

He raised himself onto his elbow and looked down upon her. Her face, which had been flushed with pleasure, was now creased with alarm and he cursed himself for letting his desire get the better of him.

Ariana was struggling into a sitting position, and he wanted to tell her he was sorry, but she was already grasping at her open gown.

"What is it?" he asked, surprised by the sudden shift.

"Voices," she said, her eyes wide with alarm. "Can't you hear them?"

His attention had been firmly attuned to Ariana, but now he could discern the chatter of distant conversation from further along the river. His first reaction was to stride out and tell them to take another path. These were Darkmoor lands, and he was the earl. If he wanted to banish everyone from this patch of land so that he could bed a woman on the banks of the river without being disturbed, it was no more than his right. But one look at Ariana's anxious face told him that her sense of shame was too great. Their moment had passed. The best they could hope for now was an appearance of propriety.

"Here." He gently pushed her fumbling fingers aside and fastened her gown with practiced dexterity. "No one will know," he told her firmly. "And if they do, then so what?"

She caught his eye, smiled, blushed, and looked away.

"We are husband and wife, are we not?" he continued lightly. "And I for one was very much enjoying getting to know my wife better."

She bit down on her lip. "As was I."

He caught her hand in his and brought her fingers to his lips. "Then let us reconvene at the first opportunity." He leaner closer and whispered, "Tonight, mayhap?"

Her blushing smile warmed his heart. "Tonight."

Chapter Seven

ARIANA FOLLOWED OTTO into the castle feeling as if she were walking on air. Her husband had shown her more than kindness that morning. He'd introduced her to a level of pleasure she'd never believed possible. Although her gown was now demurely fastened, her skin still tingled from his kisses, and she imagined her decolletage must still bear the visible imprint of his ministrations. Surely, everyone they met could divine what they had been doing?

And he so darkly handsome, so fearsomely tall and broad, so unequivocally male. It filled her with satisfaction to recall that she had made a man so powerful hunger for her touch, too. She had made him groan. The memory made her insides quiver like a jelly. If only they hadn't been interrupted at such a vital moment. Blood rushed to her cheeks as she imagined what might have happened if they had only enjoyed a few more minutes of uninterrupted time. The act she had once feared now called to her with incessant longing.

Once inside the stone-flagged entrance hall, Otto turned to face her. His fierce hunter's eyes captured her face, and she pushed down the idea that he could read her thoughts, relishing what he had glimpsed in her mind's eye.

"I have something to show you," he said, taking her hand. She looked up at him, feeling dainty and feminine at the side of his height and strength.

Would he take her to his bedchamber? Finish the act they had begun? Despite herself, that was what Ariana hoped. She felt as if a delicious meal had been placed before her, then removed before she could take a bite.

However, Otto did not lead her towards the staircase, but beyond it. They walked together down a narrow corridor lit with torches and emerged at the back of the castle, an area she had yet to explore.

"In here," he said, releasing her hand to push open a large wooden door.

"Oh." She could not help her exclamation of surprise. For where most rooms inside Darkmoor Castle were overshadowed and imposing, this one was flooded with light thanks to a row of windows set into the south-facing wall. The air was fragrant with lavender from the fresh rushes on the floor, a small fire flickered in the grate, and comfortable looking chairs invited them to sit. Everything about the room projected an air of cheer and welcome. "What is this place?"

"The morning room." Otto seemed to be enjoying her reaction. "In truth, it has not been used in many years. But I had the maids prepare it for you. I thought you might like it."

"I do," she nodded, with one hand at her throat as she looked out at the expanse of gardens. "I like it very much."

"It was my mother's room," Otto flung out carelessly as he walked over to the windows. "My father shut it up after she died. There was little call for it, I suppose."

Ariana stilled at this mention of his mother. It was the first time Otto had mentioned her. "Did you never know her?" she asked, greatly daring.

"Never." Otto turned to her with a smile and a shrug. "My father told me I couldn't miss what I had never known."

She held her breath at this unanticipated reveal of such personal information. "And did you?"

"Miss her?" He raised his eyebrows. "Mayhap a little, but my father was correct. How can you miss what you have never had? Sit down, Ariana. I have something for you."

Though his tone was light, she felt the reprimand in his words. The Earl of Darkmoor did not like to discuss any perceived weaknesses. She would tread more carefully in the future.

"But you have already given me so much," she said, crossing over to an upholstered chair by the closest window. "I mean…" her sentence trailed off and she felt heat rise to her cheeks as she recalled their morning's activity.

Otto smiled down at her. "There's so much more I intend to give you," he whispered, his breath warm on her skin. "But first this." He fished in his pocket and pulled out something small. "Open your hand."

She did as he asked, opening her palm to receive his offering. "What is it?"

"It is a token, in return for the one you presented to me."

She brought it closer to her eye, smiling in genuine pleasure as she saw the delicately wrought broach studded with pretty stones. "It is a gift of greater worth than the one I gave to you." She spoke without thinking, surprised by the generosity of the gesture.

Otto closed her fingers around the broach. "It once belonged to my mother."

Her heart beat quickly at this. "Thank you," she whispered. Otto had given her a gift, a *personal* gift. Husband to wife, *lover to lover*. It was far more than she had ever expected from him. Or from their transactional marriage.

"Will you wear it?"

"Of course." He had asked the question lightly, but she could see her answer mattered to him. "Will you…?"

With his dark eyes burning into hers, Otto gently took the broach from her and fastened it to her bodice. The warmth of his hands transported her back to the riverbank where his expert touch had delivered such exquisite pleasure.

"It looks well on you," he said, dropping his arms to his sides.

"I shall wear it always." A strong emotion swelled within her bosom and after a moment she realized what it was: happiness. Unfamiliar and unanticipated.

He nodded once, and he looked as if he might say something further on the subject, but then he pressed his lips tightly together. Outside, a cloud drifted over the sun and the morning room was cast into temporary dullness.

"There is another matter we should discuss." Otto's voice had become firm.

"Oh?"

"I know what Sir Althalos said to you last night."

His abrupt words brought her free-floating emotions crashing down. Her hands fluttered into her lap where she folded them together, searching her mind for a suitable answer.

She pondered for too long. Otto sprang from his position by her chair and paced back to the far windows, his arms crossed over his muscular chest.

"It was a lie," he stated, addressing the gardens.

A lie. His bold declaration made her flesh grow cold.

Why would he claim that Althalos was lying?

Ariana followed his gaze to the thin swoop of light falling over the well-tended lawns. She shifted uncomfortably in the chair, aware that with every beat that passed, Otto's stance grew stiffer.

"I have known men such as Sir Althalos all my life," she said eventually, forcing her words through lips that had become dry. "I know that they seek out ways to undermine the confidence of others. I have learnt to pay them little heed."

Relief washed over Otto's face. "The women I named will not come," he stated. "When you are better settled in Darkmoor, we shall hold a banquet so you can meet our noble families. After that, you may select your own lady friends to stay with us."

He smiled; no doubt assured his solution was one that would appeal to her. Ariana hastily buried the fears and insecurities his words had planted in her gut. *A banquet.* Where she must be on show for the whole of Darkmoor to see and judge and find wanting. She looked down, lest Otto somehow divine her true feelings. She must not appear ungrateful.

"You are too kind," she managed.

One of his large, warm hands fell onto her shoulder, squeezing gently. "It is no more than you deserve."

But his words of affection could not reach her, for she knew he had told her an untruth. And this untruth now sprouted roots, growing into a barrier which blocked the path to a heart which had been so newly opened. Ariana could only nod silently, her lips curling into another smile which did not reach her eyes.

Her heart beat shallowly as disappointment wrapped itself around her. She could not, in good spirits, accompany Otto to his bedchamber now. *Please don't ask me*, she prayed silently.

Thankfully there came a knock at the chamber door.

"Come," said Otto.

Gaius, the knight she had met last night, walked diffidently into the morning room and bowed low to both Otto and Ariana. He carried himself with his usual air of composure, but Ariana saw that his gray hair was ruffled and dried mud clung to the edges of his dark cloak.

"My lord, I'm afraid to report a disturbance has broken out in the lower field."

Otto raised his thick eyebrows. "What kind of disturbance?"

Gaius hesitated, one hand at his chest. "There was some unrest among the squires."

The change in Otto's demeanor was instantaneous. Ariana was reminded of her first impression of her husband when he came to her bedchamber on their wedding night. Before her wary eyes, he transformed from a gentleman into a warrior.

His hands clenched into fists, making his muscles ripple beneath his loose-fitting tunic. "I shall not tolerate disobedience," he growled.

Gaius inclined his head and allowed a moment to pass. "I understand that Merek, the castle physician, had to be summoned."

A pulse jumped in Otto's jaw and Ariana instinctively flinched backwards into her chair, making herself as small as she could.

But her movement attracted attention. Otto's eyes flickered towards her, and he gave a curt bow. "I must attend to this situation."

"Of course." She made to get up, but Otto was already striding out of the room with the aging knight scurrying in his wake.

Ariana waited until the door had banged shut behind them before releasing the breath she had been holding. But her relief at the reprieve was short-lived. Fast on its coattails came a whirlwind of emotions which left her insides churning. So much had happened in one short day. She clutched her hands to her stomach, trying to calm her racing thoughts.

Otto had lied to her, without reason, and just when she had believed them to be on the cusp of something wonderful and new. He had proven himself to be considerate, kind even. They had conversed easily. She'd felt herself warming towards him. Liking him. Believing, readily, that there was more than one side to the *Feared One*.

And then he had kissed her. And partially disrobed her. And awakened her desires so her body still ached for his touch. As a crowning moment, he had presented her with this beautiful broach. Her fingers sought it out, proving with their touch that it had been no dream. They had been stumbling together towards real feeling. Real *affection*.

Why? Why had he lied?

Unable to sit still, Ariana pushed herself up from the chair and followed her husband's pacing path to the windows and back again.

Last night, on the stone-flagged floor of the entrance hall, Althalos's words had affected her hardly at all. She knew him to be a poisonous snake who sought only to cause her pain. But back in her bedchamber, with her curiosity burning like an itch that demanded to be scratched, she had casually enquired of her maid if she knew anything of a Lady Elspeth or a Mistress Lucietta.

Allys had answered her readily enough. Mistress Lucietta was an accomplished horsewoman. The daughter of a knight. Lady Elspeth, she said, was a beautiful lady with golden ringlets and the singing voice of an angel, who had once been a favorite of Lord Otto.

As she uttered those final words, Allys had flushed and grown so nervous that the pins she was extracting from her mistress's hair had scattered to the floor.

"I'm sorry milady," she stammered. "'Tis not my place to tell such tales."

Ariana had waved away her apologies as unwelcome knowledge settled in her stomach with the weight of a stone.

Althalos had been telling the truth. Otto had bedded this Lady Elspeth.

But when the maid had left and Ariana was alone with peace and time to reflect, she'd scolded herself for her naivety. So Otto had a past. What of it? She had never expected the Earl of Darkmoor to be an untouched virgin. Laying in her clean, white sheets, she even smiled at the thought. He was a young, virile man. Of course he had taken lovers. The important thing was that since her arrival in the castle, he had treated her with unfailing kindness. *And honesty.* Ariana gazed out of the tall window with unseeing eyes. Usually, a couple of deep breaths helped to calm her, but not today. Perhaps not ever again. Otto's passionate kisses had awakened more than just her desires, leaving her mired in a sticky marsh of unfamiliar emotions. Possessiveness, jealousy, a craving for his touch.

He had undermined her hard-won self-control. *And then he had lied to her.*

The truth, she could have handled. Even if a flare of jealousy brought warmth to her blood and a series of unwelcome images to her mind. *A beautiful lady with golden ringlets and the singing voice of an angel.* How could she hope to compare?

But Otto's needless evasion was so much worse.

With a sigh of frustration, Ariana gripped the sleeves of her gown and forced herself to focus on the present moment. If she concentrated hard, she could discern a far-off clamor of horses' hooves and shouted instructions. Somewhere beyond the morning room, a door closed, and rapid footsteps sounded on a stone floor. She breathed in the scent of lavender, fixed her gaze upon the gardens, and considered that Otto had made special instructions for this lovely room to be furnished especially for her.

It was no good, her mind refused to be calmed.

What else was the earl keeping from her? she wondered, as a strong breeze lifted the branches of the distant trees. Was this Lady Elspeth still his lover? Was that why he lied?

Although how could she anticipate honesty, given the secret she was hiding herself?

At once, her anger subsided leaving a chill of apprehension in its wake.

What start to married life was this? Lies and deceit, even as they grew closer in mind and body. Otto did not trust Ariana with the truth about his lover. She could never hope to share her intentions to rescue Ysmay from Traitor's Gate.

Her beloved aunt.

The woman he held responsible for his father's death.

At once the full weight of their situation fell upon Ariana's shoulders. It was a burden that threatened to bury her. Her lips parted in fear as she recalled how quickly Otto's temper had flared when he learned of unrest amongst the squires.

"I shall not tolerate disobedience."

How then would he react were he ever to find out about her true intentions to rescue Ysmay?

The answer crystalized in her mind. *He must never find out.*

She gripped her beautiful broach unconsciously as the realization flooded into her veins. With every moment she spent with Otto, she put herself in greater danger. The Earl of Darkmoor had got under her skin. With his smiles, his unanticipated understanding. *His kisses.* She was forgetting herself and the real reason she had come to Darkmoor.

She was falling in love with him, that was the unwelcome truth of it. But she must never forget that the man her heart increasingly craved was the *Feared One*.

And she was the traitor in his castle.

Chapter Eight

"I GIVE YOU my word, my lord, all was peaceful before Sir Althalos intervened." Gaius swallowed the last mouthful of ale and carefully positioned his empty tanker on an upturned haybale.

The two men had retreated to the lofty haybarn to talk in private, Otto first making sure the stableboys would keep a distant look out. He didn't fully trust anyone with this situation, and that included his father's old friend. But he needed to hear both sides of the story, and the experienced knight had once been something of a mentor to him.

"Tell me what happened." Otto sat back on a small wooden chair and folded his arms. The air was sweet with the smell of hay and a shaft of sunlight fell across his face. If he closed his eyes, he could remember simpler times, happier times. But the band of tension across his chest was too tight to be dispelled by nostalgia.

"We were training, as usual," Gaius spoke quietly. "Nothing was amiss." He shrugged. "Not that I could see anyway. My eyes though, are not as young as they used to be."

"Your eyes are perfectly fine," Otto said sharply. "It is your account of the morning that I want."

Gaius inclined his graying head. He was a tall man, not yet shrunk with age, though his shoulders were not as broad as they had been in Otto's youth. He could still wield a sword with venom, and Otto would not hesitate to ride out to battle alongside him.

"The young squires were jousting," he continued. "Yesterday's tournament was fresh in their minds. While two of them rode against each other, the rest stood near the tent to watch."

"And?"

Gaius shrugged. "They must have grown rowdy. Said things they did not mean." He avoided Otto's gaze.

"Such as?" he prompted.

"When Sir Althalos arrived, he claimed that two of them were starting a rebellion against you." Gaius delivered the news calmly. "He had his men strike them down and ordered them to leave the castle immediately. Said they were lucky not to be strung up as traitors."

Otto's fingers drummed against his thighs. "I oversaw their training personally," he mused. "Until today."

"They were loyal to Darkmoor," Gaius spoke up. "At least, that is what we all thought."

"Could Sir Althalos have been mistaken?" Otto asked the question which was at the forefront of his mind.

Gaius's hesitation spoke volumes. "In truth, I was not standing close enough to hear what was said."

"Was anyone?"

"None but the other young squires."

Otto scuffed his boot against the wooden floor in frustration and dust motes flew around them. "Then it is their word against Sir Althalos's. And none would dare speak against him."

Gaius pursed his lips in agreement. "It is a sorry situation, my lord."

The rhythmic sound of his horses chomping hay in the nearby stables helped to channel Otto's thoughts.

"If there was a rebellion brewing, Sir Althalos did well to dispel it," he said, watching Gaius closely for a reaction.

Gaius's stillness proved he knew he was being observed. "Indeed, my lord."

"But you do not believe it?"

The old knight looked at first surprised, then resigned. "All I know is that the men are unfailingly loyal to you."

"All of them?" Otto demanded.

Gaius inclined his head.

"Come now, Gaius. You and I have marched alongside each other more times than I can count. No army is unfailingly loyal." Otto fought an impulse to spring up from his chair.

The open window let in a stream of sunlight which fell on Gaius like a halo. He leaned towards Otto and spoke in a whisper.

"You are a great leader, and your army is well-fed." He paused and fixed his eyes on the dusty floor. "There is but one thing that causes unrest amongst them."

"And that is?"

Gaius took a deep breath. "The presence of Sir Althalos. His men take the best food, the comfiest beds, the choicest women. We all of us wonder, when will they be gone?"

Despite the seriousness of the situation, Otto felt a low rumble of laughter in his chest. "It is as easy as that? I ask Sir Althalos to leave, and harmony shall return to Darkmoor?"

Gaius looked hurt. "You asked for the situation as I see it."

Otto raised his hand in apology. "Forgive me, my old friend. Since my father died, it seems there are twists and turns at every step of the road."

"Lord Ulric was proud of the warrior you have become." Gaius spoke with feeling.

Otto raised his eyebrows. "He made me the warrior I have become."

"Darkmoor is safe in your hands," Gaius continued. "I know this, and your men know this."

Otto straightened his arm and clasped Gaius's forearm. "Thank you for your honesty. And your loyalty."

Gaius got to his feet and Otto followed suit. "You will have my loyalty until the day I die." The knight made a smart bow and then turned to leave.

Otto watched his stately progress across the outer courtyard, then went in search of his young page.

"Robin," he called when he spotted him sharpening swords in an adjacent barn. "Go and find Sir Althalos. Tell him to meet me in my solar."

OTTO DID NOT plan what he would say to his uncle, confident that the necessary words would come to him. His intention, however, was clear.

First his impudence to Ariana. Now this.

Althalos would be gone from Darkmoor before nightfall.

Otto sat back in his ornately carved desk chair and let his head fall backwards. In truth, he was relieved to have been forced into action. His uncle had overplayed his hand, and now Otto had every reason to demand his departure.

As the day had progressed, the sunlight had moved over to a different side of the castle and now the solar was overshadowed and dull. The maids had already been in to light the candles and a fire crackled in the grate. Otto was impatient for the deed to be over with. Then he would be free to find his bride and finish what they had started down by the river.

Ariana, what a revelation she had been. In her embrace, he had been able to put aside his cares, losing himself in her sweet warmth.

The steady clip of approaching footsteps made Otto sit upright in his chair. This time Althalos knocked and waited for Otto's response before walking into the room. His sharp face was expressionless, but he had changed into a smart dark tunic, laced with gold thread and overlaid with a plush, finely trimmed cloak. A statement of wealth, no doubt.

A statement which would soon make him uncomfortably warm, Otto reflected, deliberately motioning for Althalos to take a seat by the fire.

"You asked to see me, nephew?" Althalos inspected his clean, well-polished nails. His hands were small and pale. Those of a commander, not a warrior.

Otto saw little reason to prevaricate. "I take no pleasure in this. But I must ask you to leave Darkmoor, tonight."

No surprise showed in the older man's face. "May I enquire why?"

Otto took a steadying breath. It would not do to display his gathering temper. "It is simply time, Uncle. You first came here to honor your brother. And I was grateful for your assistance during those difficult weeks."

Althalos opened his palms but said nothing.

Otto was forced to continue. "But I shall do well on my own now, thank you."

He had said his piece. He was the Earl of Darkmoor. Althalos would have no choice but to acquiesce.

"I see." His uncle plucked an invisible thread from the deep folds of his cloak. "So it is time for me and my men to return to my own estate."

"That's it." Otto felt the beginnings of relief.

"Leaving you here, alone, with the army of Darkmoor."

"An army which I have led for many a year." Otto gripped the desk, breathing in the scent of woodsmoke from the fire and reminding himself to stay calm. "You know, Althalos, that my father handed that responsibility over to me long before he died."

Althalos nodded slowly. "Ulric told me everything." He lingered over the last word, but Otto would not give him the satisfaction of asking after his meaning.

"You are welcome to use the carriage," he said instead.

"You are most kind." Althalos did a poor job of hiding his smile. "But I shall not need it, not today."

Damned impudence.

"Have I not made myself clear?" Otto's voice came out with a growl.

"Perfectly, but you are not yet furnished with all the facts." Althalos sighed. "Facts regarding loyalty."

Otto recalled his conversation with Gaius. "I am the Earl of Darkmoor, and I command the loyalty of my people,"

Althalos inclined his head. "You are the Earl of Darkmoor, yes. And you command the loyalty of *most* of your people. But dissent is growing, Otto. And you have been distracted." Althalos waved his hand in a contemptuous manner.

Otto felt his scar begin to itch. He clenched his fingers together and bade himself to show no signs of agitation. "At which point was I distracted, uncle? Was it when I won the joust? Or when we defeated the troops of Sir Leon in Kenmar?"

Something flickered behind Althalos's eyes. "The outcome of the battle of Branfeld was not clear."

"It was clear enough to me," Otto replied shortly "My father died for it." He wanted to bang his first down onto the desk, but contented himself with a hard, unwavering glare at the man he was beginning to think of as his enemy.

"Lord Ulric died before his time." Althalos held Otto's gaze. "His people were not ready for it." His voice grew softer. "His son was not ready for it."

A log flared and cracked in the fire. "I was born and raised to be earl," Otto said, slowly and deliberately.

"And you will be a great one." Althalos leaned forward, the heat from the flames seemingly not affecting him. "I will make sure of it."

Otto ground his teeth together, resisting the urge to reach for the sword which hung at his hip. "Your assistance is no longer required in Darkmoor."

"Only this morning I caught your own men plotting against you." Sir Althalos raised his voice, his composure finally ruffled. "What would your father say?"

The question brought Otto up short. He knew what his father would say. *Show no weakness; show no mercy.*

If Althalos had caught the men plotting, as he claimed, then he had reacted the way Ulric would have wanted. Even a potential traitor must be banished from Darkmoor. Else their poison would spread like wildlife.

Unwittingly, Otto's gaze flickered upwards to the frieze of Lord Ulric. *What would his father have him do now?*

Althalos shifted on the chair, seeming to come to a decision. "I understand you wish to be left alone, to rule Darkmoor as you see fit." His voice had become accommodating, benevolent even. "You are newly married, Otto. And I remember what it is to be a young man. I have no wish to stay beyond my welcome. But long ago I made a promise to my brother. And it is one I intend to keep."

The itch of his scar had settled into a burning ache. Otto rubbed at it absently, knowing he had to ask even though he didn't want to. "What was this promise?"

"That if he died young, I would stay in Darkmoor until you had full command of your new position."

Otto pushed himself forward over the polished desk. "What will convince you, uncle? Should I have my men swear an oath of allegiance?"

He had meant it as a dig, but Althalos seemed to consider his proposal. "That is most likely not necessary," he eventually concluded.

Otto raised an eyebrow and stayed quiet, anger slowly giving way to weary irritation.

"Let us stay, just a few weeks more," Althalos continued. "Allow me to satisfy myself that those two foolish squires did you no lasting harm, that no further rumors of rebellion are circulating. That way I will rest easy in my bed, knowing that you can rest easy in yours."

Otto placed the palms of his hands together. This was not what he had wanted, but somehow Althalos had backed him into a corner.

"A few more weeks?" he clarified.

"Beltane is almost upon us. By midsummer's eve, I shall be gone." Althalos smiled. "And that, nephew, is a promise."

When Sir Althalos had finally taken his leave, Otto poured

himself a generous goblet of wine and downed it in one long gulp. As the last of the day's light slipped from the sky, Otto sat and gazed at the portrait of his father, noting how the tempera colors seemed to glow even more luminous in the shadows.

His father's rule had brought glory and prosperity to Darkmoor, that fact was indisputable. Thanks to Lord Ulric, their people had coin in their pockets and roofs over their heads. Their lands were fertile and well-farmed, their harvests bountiful. They lived in difficult times, but despite their proximity to the wild borderlands of Scotland, no raiding parties had successfully breached their defenses since Ulric was made earl. His policy of warfare worked, both as a deterrent to would-be attackers, and a means of accruing riches.

But this was just one part of the story. Otto twisted the silver goblet and squeezed his eyes shut to rid himself of the unwanted images playing on a reel inside his mind. Violence, shouting, the clash of steel on steel, injured men staggering towards their enemies, panting horses rearing in fear. He had seen it all a thousand times.

Must he endure it a thousand times more?

What about any sons he may have? Even grandsons?

Would Otto himself sacrifice his life in vain pursuit of land and coin? There was already wealth enough in the castle coffers to pay the wages upon which his people depended.

These were questions he had asked himself many times, and he doubted he would find the answer tonight. The conflict tearing through his soul had begun long before the ill-fated battle of Branfeld. His father's counsel sat on one shoulder, like a wise owl, parroting the words of advice Otto had grown up hearing.

Suffer no fools.

Rule through fear.

Show no weakness; show no mercy.

Dictates that Sir Althalos would have him adhere to still.

But on his other shoulder sat a more peaceable mage. One who suggested a different path forward, a path paved with the flags of peace.

Peace.

The idea tugged at him, harder and harder to ignore.

Days earlier, on his way about the castle, Otto had passed by Traitor's Gate and heard a faint singing coming from its forbidding walls. The haunting melody seemed to speak of forgiveness and healing, unlocking some bittersweet melancholy deep inside him. He had halted his horse and listened, as if under a spell.

Memories had assaulted him from the terrible moments immediately after the battle of Branfeld. Moments when, gripped by despair, he had ordered the capture and imprisonment of the druid healer who had kneeled by Ulric's side as he passed. Caught up in his grief, he had considered her complicit in his death, as culpable as the man who swung the sword into his father's ribs.

Sitting quietly, astride his horse, he had begun to question those convictions. The druids were a peaceful people. Was he guilty of meeting their compassion with battle-honed aggression?

Should I release the druid and redress this wrong? Inside the solar, his father's portrait seemed to gimmer in a silent rebuke, telling him what he already knew. His men expected vengeance. Althalos would countenance nothing less. If Otto wished to tread a different path, he would find no support within Darkmoor.

And where else mattered?

He had two powerful allies in Guy, Earl of Rossfarne and Angus de Neville. These were boyhood friendships, lasting ever since they had trained together at the Lindum Academy. In more recent years, Otto had travelled solely at his father's command. His life had been one of obedience to Lord Ulric; even quashing his youthful ambitions to serve under the King.

Instead, he had remained here, leading his father's army. Gaining a reputation as the *Feared One*.

How could he make further allies and forge a path towards peace when his instincts were to trust no one?

Otto set the goblet spinning on the polished surface of the desk, hardly caring when the sticky residue spilled out.

There was one area in his life in which he enjoyed absolute clarity: Ariana.

He would leave these ruminations for another day and seek out the manifold pleasures of his bride's company. Desire flickered through him at the memory of how her curvaceous body had responded to his touch. Ariana of Kenmar was proving to be a woman full of surprises.

He was beginning to feel fortunate to be her husband.

"Tonight," he had suggested, down at the river. And she had readily agreed.

Seized with new energy, he walked hurriedly from the solar and strode through the corridors of the castle, acknowledging the servants and knights who paused in their tasks to stand aside for him. He bounded up the staircase with the enthusiasm of a boy, feeling the tensions of the afternoon fall from his shoulders as he reached her chamber door.

But before he could raise his hand to knock, the door swung open and Merek came out. The older man was startled by his presence and made a hurried bow.

"Forgive me, my lord, I did not see you there."

"Forsooth, Merek, can those potions of yours not help you see through walls?" Otto spoke with irony and saw with satisfaction the glimmer of an answering smile on the physician's face.

"Not quite." Merek was holding a large bag which he twisted anxiously in his capable hands.

Otto was gripped by sudden alarm. "You have been summoned to see Ariana? Is she well?"

Merek nodded and held up a hand to allay his concerns. "She is quite well, I assure you. Merely tired and a little," he hesitated, "overwrought."

"Overwrought?" Otto raised an eyebrow.

Merek nodded slowly, closing the door fully behind him and stepping to the side. "It is only to be expected, my lord. A young woman. A new bride." He inclined his head delicately. "Lady

Ariana requested a sleeping draught."

His words felled all Otto's aspirations and he put a hand to the cool castle wall to steady himself. "So the lady wishes to sleep?"

Merek was wise to avoid the question. "Once she is well-rested, she will be better able to fulfil her duties to Darkmoor."

"I certainly hope so," Otto declared bluntly.

Merek made another bow. "If you will excuse me, my lord, I have another patient to attend to."

"Yes, of course." Otto cleared his path. "I thank you for your ministrations."

Merek hurried away, his cloak swinging beside him, leaving Otto to gaze at the closed door like a lovesick squire.

He had been spurned by his bride.

The sting of rejection quickened his temper and Otto half raised his hand to knock and demand entry. But sense prevailed. He had been the one to tell Ariana to take all the time she needed. And that had been just yesterday.

His shoulders drooped and he rested his forehead on the unyielding oak of the door, weariness claiming his limbs. Were he not primed to always stay on high alert, he would have been inclined to call Merek back to administer a second sleeping draught.

He must stay true to his promise. They would move at a pace dictated by Ariana. Only when she was ready, would he bed his bride.

But she was ready, his mind raged. Down at the riverbank, she had wanted him just as much as he wanted her. *Hadn't she?*

Distant footsteps jolted him from his reverie. The Earl of Darkmoor must not be caught sulking out here. Quickly, he covered the distance to his own bedchamber where he flung the door closed in frustration.

He had obviously misread Ariana's signals. Inadvertently, had he pushed her too far that morning? Maybe even frightened her? *Overwrought*, Merek had said.

Otto had never pushed his advantage with a woman, and he didn't intend to start with his innocent bride. He would keep his distance from Ariana. That was the only way.

And so the die was cast. He would stay away and let her come to him.

Otto pursed his lips as he surveyed his empty room. He may be sleeping alone for some time yet.

Chapter Nine

T ALL AND CONFIDENT, the young knight strode through the trees, sparing hardly a glance towards the poor figure huddled to the side of the woodland path.

Safely hidden by the heavy folds of a woolen cloak, Ariana breathed a sigh of relief as he passed.

She had chosen this narrow path, believing it to be hardly used. Her heart had nearly jumped out of her throat when she heard the firm footsteps and clanking of spurs behind her.

Thank goodness for her disguise.

The knight continued on his way, arms swinging by his sides as he whistled tunelessly. The woodland birds piped their own songs over his head, creating a cacophony of joyful sound entirely at odds with the apprehension twisting inside Ariana's chest.

Could a rough cloak fashioned from the poorest wool, really provide the protection she needed?

It would have to. It was the best she could do. And it had worked, so far. Yesterday, Ariana's frustrations had reached boiling point. As Countess of Darkmoor, eyes followed her everywhere. She could not walk as far as the inner courtyard without maids bowing their heads and guards standing to attention. She would never find Ysmay under such scrutiny.

But luck was on her side. Once a week, villagers and farmworkers living beyond the castle walls were permitted to hawk their wares within the lower courtyard. On this day, the services of the castle physician were available to all. When Ariana spied an elderly peasant with an aching back come to seek a remedy from Merek, the plan had popped into her head. While the physician attended to his patient, Ariana swapped the peasant's cloak with an old one of her own.

It had taken some practice to adopt her own natural stance to the shuffling gait of a peasant. Ariana had stood in front of the looking glass in her bedchamber, deliberately rounding her shoulders and hunching her back, quite enjoying the overt rejection of grace and femininity. At last, she felt confident enough in her deception to try it in public, donning her disguise once outside the keep.

Her skin crawled with trepidation as she shuffled past the first set of guards. How on earth would she explain her actions if she were caught?

But the guards had afforded her no attention. Neither had the men working at the gatehouse. In one afternoon, Ariana had successfully worked her way around the whole outer perimeter of Darkmoor Castle, with no one pausing to question her.

As a poor, elderly peasant, she was all but invisible.

What liberty!

And even better, as the shadows began to lengthen, she had caught sight of what could be the entrance to Traitor's Gate. Today she would find out for sure.

But first, her eyes could not help but follow the path of the young knight. He must be on his way to train with the infamous army of Darkmoor.

With Otto.

She hadn't seen Otto for two whole days. Not since the scene in the morning room. On the first day, she had jumped at every footstep, half expecting his looming figure to appear around every corner. Her heart longed for his presence, while her mind told her to stay away. By the time the bell had rung for the evening meal, her head was throbbing with indecision. She instructed the maid to say she was ill and had a tray brought up to her room.

Surely, she'd reasoned, Otto would come to see her the next

day.

But he hadn't. And now even Ariana's traitorous heart had hardened against him. Despite her best efforts, she couldn't help but imagine Otto seeking his pleasure elsewhere. With you a young woman who boasted golden ringlets and the singing voice of an angel. Alone in her bedchamber, Ariana had fingered her dark, unruly locks and scorned her presumption that a man such as Otto would ever choose a woman such as her.

She had provided but momentary distraction, that was all. Otto was accustomed to seducing women. She had merely become one in a long line. Now he had moved onto the next.

But what if some other reason had kept him away?

What if he was injured? Or had been summoned from the castle?

She bit down on her lip as her pulse jumped at the possibility. A pipe dream, no doubt, but it would take mere moments for her to find out for sure. Then she could resume her quest to find Ysmay with a quiet mind.

Keeping closely to the cover afforded by the overhanging branches, she slipped through the trees after the young knight, his scarlet tabard easy to spot amongst the greens and browns. Soon the tranquil sounds of the forest were replaced by the clash of swords, shouted instructions, and occasional barking laughter. The knight broke into a jog and emerged out onto the lower field. Ariana ducked behind a gorse bush and peered out cautiously.

What a sight greeted her. It was as if a great hunting party had descended, complete with fluttering flags and majestic silken tents. Fine horses pawed at the ground and a rippling mass of fighting men moved as one, commanded by an unswerving voice of authority which carried across the grassy field and brought goosebumps to Ariana's flesh.

Otto sat astride a gleaming black horse, facing his knights, his own plate armor glinting in the morning sunshine. He was some distance away from her, but it was impossible not to feel the magnetism radiating from him. Ariana suddenly understood that out here, amongst his men, Otto was his true self. *A warrior.* A fighter. One which would strike terror into the heart of an enemy. Before her eyes, he reached behind his back and brought forth a sparkling dagger. With barely a moment's hesitation he flung it out so it flew in a graceful arch through the air, landing forcefully inside the head of a dummy soldier strung up on the far side of the training ring.

Was this the same man who had touched her so gently?

Breathing hard, she sank down against the rough trunk of an ancient tree and placed her head against her knees. Never had she imagined that seeing Otto again would have this effect on her.

Like a fever, she remembered. And she was infected, whether she liked it or not.

She had been right to stay away from him. He would be her undoing. Hers and Ysmay's.

Unless she fought the sickness.

Without another glance towards the training ring, Ariana pulled her hood more securely over her head and set off again into the dense cover of the forest. She walked quickly along a faint rabbit path, keen not to waste any more time. The hidden building she'd glimpsed yesterday was some distance from the main castle, and she must return to her quarters before luncheon else risk awkward questions. Otto may not notice her absence, but the maids would. And the careless talk of maids could cost her dearly.

The woods had fallen quiet now, as if all the birds and hidden creatures were holding their breath, waiting for something. Dark clouds scuttled overhead, and the very air felt heavy with anticipation. Ariana scalded herself for her fancy. What she felt was no more than a premonition of rain. But still, her heart beat hard beneath the rough woolen cloak and she couldn't help but swing her gaze from left and right as she picked her way amongst the twisted tree roots, expecting all the while a strong arm to reach out and grab her.

Less than a week within the walls of Darkmoor Castle, and you have become a foolish chit of a girl, she told herself sternly. What would her father say if he could hear her wild fancies?

Her cheeks colored at the very idea. Sir Leon would laugh, cold and humorless, his dark eyes sliding over the disappointing figure of his only child, as they had so many times before.

"You know the trouble with your mother's people?" he would ruminate. *"They have no discipline."*

Ariana pursed her lips. Part of her wished her father could indeed see her now, to bear witness to the extraordinary feats of discipline she displayed in her determination to free her aunt from the clutches of Darkmoor.

Though Sir Leon would prefer she turned her attention to finding his ruby. *Ysmay's ruby.*

A stone in which she had no interest at all.

She had reached the end of the woods. If memory served her correctly, she must turn away from the outer wall of the castle and head down to where the river carved a deep path to the sea. The towering gray castle walls seemed to mock her as she slipped on a loose patch of sand, but she pressed on, peering desperately into the gloom of the valley for the flash of carved stone she had spied yesterday.

There it was. The arched perimeter of a squat tower, hiding amongst the gnarled branches. She slowed her pace and took a welcome lungful of air, wishing she could push back her hood and let the strong breeze cool the back of her neck.

This must be Traitor's Gate. There was no other reason to build a tower so far from the castle. And she recognized the elaborate sweep of architectural design, even though here it was far subdued.

Could she simply walk in and find Ysmay?

Her keen eyes fixed on a wooden door set into the stone above the river and a cold stab of disappointment pierced her belly when she saw the crimson flash of a uniformed guard.

Not so simple a rescue then. But she would not be easily

dissuaded, not when she was so very close.

Her eyes travelled up the short expanse of stone to the top of the tower, then back down again. Not so much as a window interrupted the smooth stones. Her hands shook with anxiety. Ysmay had always been a creature of sun and sky. How would she bear incarceration in perpetual darkness?

She wouldn't, Ariana concluded. She would be driven to despair. But Merek had assured her that no harm had come to her aunt.

She scanned the back of the tower, as far as she could see. At first, she discerned nothing save the fast gushing of the river. But then another shape jumped out of the gloom. She took a few steps closer, uncaring of being seen. What was that?

Ariana shaded her eyes against the weak sunlight. A smile creased the corner of her mouth when she finally made out the arch of a covered bridge, jutting over the fast-flowing greenish water. The bridge led to another tower, taller this time, at the other side. Both were half-hidden amidst the abundant trees.

Was this where Ysmay was being held? But there was no way over the river save by the squat tower and the guarded bridge. And even a poor, unremarkable peasant would not be granted entry to Traitor's Gate. Ariana chewed on her lip, ruminating hard. She already knew that the river would not be safe to cross. One false step and she would be swept away.

Once more, she scanned the tall tower which reared up to the tops of the trees. Her gaze fixed on the battlements, which were no longer so uniformly gray. Someone was up there. A tall, willowy figure robed in the white sheet of a penitent.

Ariana's heart leaped. It was Ysmay. There was no mistaking her waterfall of silvery blonde hair, nor her gracious bearing. She was thin, very thin. Ariana's spirits sank when she saw how the white robes fell from narrow, almost skeletal shoulders. But the druid healer stood with her head held high, face upturned to the weak sunlight.

She was alive.

She wanted to call out and wave to attract her attention but regained her senses just in time. It would be of no service to her aunt if Ariana's subterfuge was discovered now.

At once, their situation became more dreadful. For although Ariana had found her aunt, the hangman's noose was all but tied around her slender neck. Ysmay lived still, for today at least, but tomorrow was not guaranteed. There was but one way for prisoners to leave Traitor's Gate.

Ariana bit down on her lip and tasted blood, then turned regretfully and started picking her way back through the trees. With every minute that passed there was a greater risk of her being discovered.

Her mind raced as she clambered up the slope, one hand clutching the gaping folds of the cloak. She must find a way to act, and quickly. If only she had a friend to turn to. Her mind leaped from one outlandish scenario to another. Could she summon soldiers from Kenmar?

No, she concluded as she dampened her dry lips with her tongue, wishing she had thought to bring a flask of ale. That idea was worth little consideration. Sir Leon would never spare men for such a task. And none were likely to be equal to it. Ariana shook her head at the ridiculous prospect of one of her father's disheveled soldiers daring to stand against the might of Otto.

Her boot slipped on a tree root and Ariana flung out her hands, only saving herself just in time. Her palms stung and her back ached, and that was when the answer to all her problems became clear.

Merek.

She would beg assistance from her mother's old friend. The physician had already given his promise that he would help all he could to rescue Ysmay from her sentence. And all she needed from him was a sleeping draught. One perchance even stronger than that he had brought to her chamber so recently. Merek was a brilliant herbalist. He could mix a potion so potent that the guard would be felled before he had the chance to raise the alarm.

She paused as a mixture of relief and adrenaline coursed through her veins. She had a plan now. All that remained was the execution of it. And the need to persuade Merek to act against the man he served.

Otto.

The name reverberated through her mind as she passed through a wide meadow, the grass parting before her like a wave. Was he her friend or her foe? In the short time she had known him, he had been both. When she first came to Darkmoor, Ariana had expected nothing but harsh treatment at the hands of the notorious earl, but the reality had been far different.

Otto Sarragnac had proven himself a man of depth and mystery. Did anyone really know him?

Ariana was finally approaching the gatehouse, but she slowed to a standstill as an idea of outlandish proportions occurred to her.

She could simply tell Otto the truth. Plead for clemency for her aunt.

Would he listen? When she thought of the man who had kissed her by the river, the answer seemed to be yes.

But when she thought of Otto Sarragnac the *Feared One*, the merciless warrior she had glimpsed in training, the answer was a resounding no.

Still, it might be worth a try. Ariana fished beneath the folds of the cloak to find the beautiful broach pinned to her kirtle. It had belonged to his mother, but he had willingly gifted it to her. She must mean *something* to him?

She remembered how it had felt to be encircled in his strong arms. To feel the warmth of his lips. To hear the gravelly rasp of his laughter. All of this she had put aside because of some foolish jealousy, based on nothing more than the insinuations of Sir Althalos.

Ariana had to exert all her self-control not to gather up her skirts and run through the outer courtyard. Her path forward was suddenly clear. She would find Otto and throw herself on his mercy. He was a gentleman. He would not put her aunt to death, not when she explained who she was.

The searching gaze of the guard brought her to her senses. Just in time, Ariana lowered her head and bent her back, assuming the tremulous gait of an old woman. The guard grunted and stepped aside, allowing her to pass, but a clatter of horse's hooves made her look up once more.

The gleaming black charger coming towards her was instantly recognizable as belonging to Otto, but the man on his back was almost a stranger. His hair was freshly combed and his beard neatly trimmed. Beneath a sumptuous scarlet cloak, he was dressed in finery the likes of which Ariana had not seen before. Not even on his wedding day had the Earl of Darkmoor been so well-presented.

Ariana couldn't help her lips parting in surprise.

Where was he going?

Who was he going to see?

His horse snorted, dust flying around his hooves as Otto spurred him into a canter. In a flash, horse and rider had passed her. She pressed back against the gray castle wall, cringing into the safety of the cloak. But it was too late. Even as she pulled the folds over her face, she felt Otto's eyes burning into her.

She glanced up, pulled by a force beyond her control, and their eyes met across the sun-dappled courtyard.

"Ariana?" he mouthed, his face twisted in confusion. But then he clattered over the drawbridge and was gone.

HAD IT REALLY been Ariana?

By the time he had craned around in the saddle for a better look, his fleet-footed charger had already carried him beyond the confines of the castle walls. From a distance, the hunch-backed, shuffling figure clad in poor woolens bore little resemblance to the proud poise of his bride, but there had been no mistaking those wide green eyes, nor the tilt of her chin.

Why was the new Countess of Darkmoor sneaking around the castle disguised as a peasant?

Such was Otto's confusion, he sat deeper in the saddle and pulled back on the reins, bringing his horse to a snorting halt.

Surely, he must be mistaken.

But no, the more he thought on the matter, the greater became his conviction that he had, purely by chance, happened upon Ariana in the midst of some devious plot. Why else the disguise?

He shook his head in bafflement as his horse executed a prancing side-step, eager to be off once again. Otto twisted his head towards the castle, wanting to chase back over the drawbridge, find Ariana and demand an explanation. But the hunched figure was long gone. And he knew that if he were to track Ariana down to the morning room, she would have cast off the shabby cloak and would no doubt deny all knowledge of it.

Would he have to accuse her of falsehood?

The question danced around his head, demanding an answer. Any answer bar the obvious one which was too terrible to countenance.

Was Ariana being untrue to him?

The very idea put him in a greater rage than he'd experienced since the nightmare of Branfeld. *How dare she?* Especially when he had shown her such courtesy and consideration as to delay his own dues in the bedchamber. Did she repay him by taking her pleasures elsewhere?

Black rage descended and he jammed his spurs into his horse's side, making him rear in alarm.

"Steady there, steady." Otto extended a hand and rhythmically stroked his charger's muscular neck, bringing him back under control.

The horse's fright had restored his senses. It was foolish to suspect Ariana of cheating. Who in Darkmoor would dare to bed the earl's new bride? Otto's lips curled up at the sides. No man would be so bold. And Ariana herself had not appeared carefree and cunning beneath her dull disguise. On the contrary, she had been pale and anxious. In the days since she had come here, she had grown gaunt.

She was unhappy. The knowledge slammed into him like a blow from the hilt of a sword. But it did little to alter the fact of her subterfuge.

The weak spring sunshine was now high overhead. Otto swore under his breath. It was past noon and he had promised Gaius he would be with him before then. For a moment, he dallied with indecision. Should he return to the castle and confront Ariana? Or continue to the house of Gaius, to take luncheon with the knight and his wife? The choice would have been easy, had Gaius not hinted of some new information he wished to impart.

Given recent events with the squires, Otto could ill afford to ignore any counsel freely given. With a dark grimace, he turned his horse's head towards the sea and urged him forward.

Today would proceed as planned. But tomorrow he would get to the truth of Ariana's actions. He was the Earl of Darkmoor, and he would not be taken for a fool.

Chapter Ten

ARIANA'S NERVES WOULD be the death of her.

That's what she told herself as she lifted the hem of her beautiful gown and ascended the smooth steps to Traitor's Gate with as much grace as she could muster.

Yesterday, she had tripped and stumbled through the undergrowth, a poor creature in disguise. Today, she was the Countess of Darkmoor, come to deliver Beltane mead to the guard. She had donned a shining emerald-green gown for the occasion, though her hair was left loose to tumble over her pale shoulders as she had risen long before the maid was due to attend her. With luck, she would be back between the sheets before Allys came to draw open her blinds.

Her hand shook as she walked closer to the squat tower. The first rays of morning sun cast a dappled hue onto the gray stone, though the sun did not yet have any strength to it. Ariana would have been chilled, were it not for the fire of anxiety burning in her belly. All she had to do was convince the guard to drink the mead. One small and simple task. The potion Merek had slipped her was potent enough to act instantaneously. When the guard woke up, he would remember nothing of her visit. Ariana would have been and gone, Ysmay would be free.

Once this latter point was discovered, the poor guard would be in trouble, no doubt. But there was nothing she could do about that.

Her hands trembled so violently that the precious liquid

contained within the goblet all but spilled over the edge. She bit down on her lip in fierce concentration, holding the goblet as far from her body as she dared in case the heady fumes made her woozy. She was nearly there. Above her, she could see the black boots of the resting guard, crossed at the ankle.

He slumbered on duty. Obviously not one of Otto's finest.

She had never done anything like this before.

She took a deep steadying breath. With another step, she would be fully in the guard's line of sight. There would be no going back.

She had to be convincing.

For the hundredth time, her mind raced back to the ladies in Sir Leon's feasting hall, recalling how they would simper and sway, eyelashes fluttering, bosoms pressed forward.

"Halt, who goes there?"

The guard's voice was louder and harsher than she had expected. No more prevaricating. It was time to act.

Ariana pushed back her shoulders and drew her lips up into a smile. "It is only I, Countess of Darkmoor." She allowed the guard's surprised gaze to travel the length of her body before resuming her ascent of the wide stone steps.

"Countess." He dropped into a hurried bow. "I was not expecting…" he trailed off, embarrassed no doubt by his unfastened uniform and disheveled appearance. His sword belt was propped against the arched doorway of the tower and his helm was nowhere to be seen, allowing her to speak to him as a person, not an anonymous guard in gleaming silver.

"You were not expecting me?" she suggested, making her voice purr like a cat.

"I was not," he confirmed. "Forgive my sorry state."

It was nothing short of a crime, she realized, for a guard of Darkmoor to be caught unarmed and undefended. Perchance her quest would be easier than she had feared?

She forced herself to stand still and look him in the eye. She was still a couple of steps below him, and therefore able to tilt her head coquettishly upwards. "You were not expecting anyone, were you?"

The guard stammered, unable to deny that he had been neglecting his duties. Ariana knew a sudden rush of power, correctly divining his fears that she may report his laxity back to Otto. She drew herself up to her full height, conscious of the strain of her bosom against the delicate fabric of the gown and the natural slant of the guard's eyeline.

"I was not, milady," he said in a rush.

He was no older than she, Ariana realized. Bored and lonely most likely. Relegated to a job that no one else wanted to do.

Her smile became more genuine, lighting up her eyes. "Have no fear," she said, lifting her skirts and traversing the final steps so they stood just feet apart. "I will say naught of this." She dipped her head towards his abandoned sword belt, making it clear that nothing had escaped her notice.

"I thank you." He swallowed and straightened his shoulders. "How can I help you, milady?"

"Oh no." She tossed back her hair with a small giggle. "I have not come all the way here in search of your assistance. I have come with an offering." He raised a puzzled eyebrow and she pressed on, ignoring a fresh assault of anxiety. "Where I come from, it is customary for the lady of the house to offer refreshments to all who serve her on the feast of Beltane."

It was a bare-faced lie. Sir Leon would no more offer hospitality on Beltane than on any other feast day. He was a parsimonious lord and master, who kept a dour and cheerless household. But this lowly guard of Darkmoor was not to know that.

Ariana smiled again, conscious that her mask had slipped. She must appear carefree, nonchalant, a follower of the Beltane rites. She stepped forward and pressed the goblet into the guard's hands, exerting pressure when she felt his initial resistance.

"Drink," she urged. "You have stood on duty all through the night. It is only right you should have refreshment."

"The earl does not like us to take intoxicating liquor when we are on duty," he tried, a faint blush staining his pale cheeks.

Ariana shifted her stance so her skirts swayed around her ankles. "The earl is not here," she whispered, greatly daring.

Had she gone too far?

Just when the hammering of her heart had grown loud enough to rival the overhead morning chorus, the guard finally allowed himself to smile.

"We always kept Beltane back home," he nodded behind him, towards the village beyond the castle walls, before pressing the goblet to his lips and drinking deeply.

Ariana's relief was but momentary, for he drained the goblet and handed it back to her, apparently unaffected by the potent sleeping draught Merek had so reluctantly provided for her. But no sooner had her mind leaped to this alarming possibility, than the young man swayed on his feet, frowned in puzzlement, and slumped to the ground.

Cautiously, she extended her foot and prodded him on the shoulder. The guard didn't stir. He lay as still and lifeless as a rock. Alarmed now, Ariana pushed her hair away from her face and ducked down beside him. She held her palm close to his nostrils, weak with relief when she felt the warmth of his breath.

He lived still. Thank goodness.

But her time was limited. She had been entirely focused on drugging the guard but now the task ahead of her loomed large and insurmountable. With fumbling fingers, she fished in his stiff pockets for the large iron keys which banged heavily against her hips. Luck was on her side and the first key she tried fitted the lock of the squat tower. She heaved her shoulder against the unrelenting wood and stumbled through the door.

Darkness surrounded her. It was as if she had stepped into another world from the sunlit cheer of early morning. Here, the thick walls swallowed all sounds. Neither the torrential gushing of the river nor the chirp of woodland birds could permeate the ancient stone. All was silent and the gloom was absolute. Ariana's shoulders shook with a mixture of cold and fear, but there was naught she could do but press on.

She recalled the bridge was set into the back wall of this first tower. That was where she must head. She took a deep breath of stale air and put one foot in front of the other, aware of the chill travelling up through the soles of her feet. After several paces, her eyes adjusted to the darkness, and she could make out the dim outline of walls. A scurrying shape past her feet made her heart leap into her mouth.

Only a rat, she calmed herself.

There must be dozens in here. It was best not to think about it.

Greatly daring, she reached out a hand and traced a line along the damp walls, finding her way from one side of the tower to another. When the featureless back wall loomed into sudden view, she didn't allow her spirits to plummet, but bravely ran her palms all around until she encountered a catch in the stone. The door swung open, taking her by surprise, and as light flooded into the chamber, her knees fairly buckled with relief. She stumbled out onto the wooden bridge without a thought for safety, desperate to get out of the unrelenting darkness of the tower. Outside, the air was sweet and the light akin to a gift from the heavens. Ariana clung onto the wooden handrail and steadied her breathing. Through the wooden slats beneath her feet, she could see the fast-running river far below. She must watch her step. Just one rotten plank would spell disaster.

Easy now, she told herself. One step at a time.

The bridge held firm beneath her tentative footsteps and she arrived at the doorway to the second tower without incident. Here, she was sure she would find Ysmay. On her second attempt, she found the correct key for the doorway, and only then did a new thought occur to her.

What if Ysmay was not the only prisoner in Traitor's Gate?

Worse, what if she was not the only one to be wrongfully imprisoned in Traitor's Gate?

Ariana clung to the stone wall as thoughts chased around her mind. She had come here for one purpose only, to rescue her aunt. Not to mount an insurrection against Darkmoor. Such an action could have terrible consequences. No matter what she found, she would have to steel herself against pity for anyone else's plight.

If she only had a torch to light her way.

Ariana had deliberately stood with her foot blocking the door, so a thin strip of daylight filtered into the gloom of the second tower. But here the darkness was not so absolute, for occasional thin windows allowed in a bleak glimmer of the outside world. Ariana blinked until her eyes adjusted and she could make out a steep stone staircase winding up through the center of the tower, then she moved her foot and the door closed with a dull bang.

Her heart thudded with anticipation. This was the moment she had been waiting for. She lifted her skirts and began to ascend, paying no heed to the rivers of damp running down the walls, nor the chilling echo her footsteps sent reverberating around her. The cold was harder to ignore for it seemed to have crept into her very bones. Though mayhap it was trepidation that made her shiver so. On and on she climbed, in a spiral that became ever tighter, until at last she reached a small galleried opening. She swallowed hard and forced herself to peer between the bars of the cell, fearful of what she might find. But her eyes saw only a poor heap of dirty straw and the remnants of an old candle.

The cell was empty.

Ariana was about to press on when a new sound reached her ears, and she froze in surprise. What was that? Hardly daring to breathe, she listened hard, warmth stealing through her when she realized what was happening.

Someone humming a melody.

It was a voice she recognized. Ariana's spirits soared. It was Ysmay.

The humming dispelled both the gloom and her anxieties.

Ariana ran lightly up the next spiral of the staircase, relieved that as the sound grew louder, the light in the tower grew brighter. Was the force of Ysmay's inherent goodness dispelling the gloom of this dreadful place?

She stumbled out into a large circular room, set with regular square windows. In the center of the room sat a tall, thin woman with long cascading white hair. The woman held herself regally, despite her poor surroundings. She had her eyes closed and her hands folded in her lap. At one side of the room was a pallet of straw covered with a thin blanket. A larger shaft of light came from an opening to the battlements. Ariana crossed her arms over her chest, overjoyed to have found her aunt but reluctant to startle her. The conditions were not as dire as she had feared, but there was no question Ysmay would be cold and hungry. And frightened, knowing the execution that awaited her.

"Ariana?" Her voice was steady. "I knew you would come."

Ariana flung herself forward and kneeled at her aunt's feet. "I am so pleased to have found you."

"My dear child." Ysmay gripped her hand with surprising strength. "You have taken a great personal risk to do so." Her startling blue eyes seemed to look straight into Ariana's soul.

"It is of no consequence." Ariana shook her head so vigorously her hair flew out behind her. "All that matters is that you should go free."

Ysmay smiled. Her face had grown ravaged with age and weariness, but her beautiful smile was unchanged. "That, I fear, would have grave consequences. And for you more than most."

Her aunt's hand was chilled despite her steady grip. Ariana sandwiched it inside her own, trying to inject some of her own warmth and vigor into the woman who had helped to raise her. "Do you know about my marriage to Otto? Otto Sarragnac?" she amended.

Ysmay inclined her head. "I know it was planned. I know it came to pass. What I don't know yet is how much happiness it will bring to you."

Ariana was exhausted after her climb up the tower and all the adrenaline of her rescue seemed to be seeping away. "I cannot be happy with the Earl of Darkmoor, not while he keeps you prisoner up here."

Ysmay's gaze was steady and unblinking. "The earl gave special instruction that I should be treated well. And as you can see, I have been."

"You're a prisoner," Ariana protested. Her eyes raked over the cheerless room, the cold bare floor, and the empty grate. "You should be with the people who love you."

"I admit, I did not anticipate ending my days here." Ysmay held up a regal hand to silence her niece and Ariana bit back her denial. "But I have had much time to think. And this twist of fate may have been necessary. Intended even. If the North is to know peace, Kenmar must ally with Darkmoor. Your marriage to Otto Sarragnac may be the start of this."

Ariana slumped onto the dusty floor, uncaring of her elegant gown. "My marriage to Otto did not have to come at the cost of your freedom." Her voice shook. "Or your life."

Ysmay gave her a knowing look. "For what reason did your father agree to the alliance?"

Ariana paused as the realization struck her. "So that I might reclaim your jewel for Kenmar."

Her aunt nodded. "Exactly so."

"But your life is too high a price for peace between Kenmar and Darkmoor." Ariana shook her head vehemently. "I could not live with myself."

"Ariana, you are young and have your whole life ahead of you. I am old. My days are ending."

"You are not ill?" she asked in alarm.

"Not ill." Ysmay shook her head. "There is strength in my limbs still."

"Good." Ariana pushed herself to her feet, seized with new conviction. "For I am not leaving you here."

"Ariana…"

"No," Ariana spoke over her with all the authority of the Countess of Darkmoor. "Either you allow me to help you down those cursed stairs and out into the light, where you can live freely once again, or we both of us stay here to be found by the guards." She bit down on her lip. "And punished accordingly."

"Ariana, you can't do this."

She smoothed down the folds of her gown. "It is already done," she said airily. "I have committed my own crimes against Darkmoor this day. Crimes which won't easily be forgiven, should they be discovered."

Ysmay shook her head slowly, her eyes shining with love as well as trepidation. "Your future happiness hangs in the balance. I feel it. I know it."

"Once you are free, I will be able to commit myself to Otto," Ariana promised wildly. "I will make my marriage work. I will keep a lasting peace between Kenmar and Darkmoor. All of this and more, I pledge to you, aunt. But while you remain a prisoner, awaiting execution, I simply cannot."

Ysmay pulled herself to her feet, just the faintest tremor in her body betraying her age and weakness. "I see we are at an impasse," she said softly.

"I will not be swayed." Ariana focused her gaze on the leafy treetops visible through the square windows. Gray clouds scudded across the sky, and she thought of the guard laying slumped across the doorway to the squat tower. Merek had said he would sleep until noon. But how long did they have until he was found?

"Very well," Ysmay sighed. "You have your mother's stubborn determination. It is a strength," she smiled, nodding gently. "It will see you well in the future, I am sure."

Hope unfurled in Ariana's chest. "You will come with me, now?"

"I will." Ysmay extended her arm. "And I thank you, my dearest niece, for your love and concern."

They made halting progress down the spiral staircase. Many

times, Ysmay slipped on the damp stone and Ariana had to hold her steady, flinching at the birdlike frailty of the woman who had once appeared indomitable. Despite her physical weakness, the healer brought an air of calm to their journey, and the chambers seemed less dark and forbidding in her presence. They paused at the wooden bridge, Ysmay taking great rattling breaths to recover her strength, and Ariana wondered anew at the flaws in her plan. She had given no thought to what would happen next, imagining her aunt as a healthy druid priestess who longed for freedom and would stride off into the woods with scarcely a backwards glance. The Ysmay of her mind's eye was younger and stronger than the Ysmay of today. Had she made matters worse by insisting on setting her free?

"Do not worry, child," Ysmay whispered, seeming to read her thoughts. "I will follow the river into the lands of my people. It will not be long before they greet me. All will be well."

"I can go with you," Ariana said recklessly, hating the thought of abandoning her.

But Ysmay only smiled. "You promised me your commitment to your husband. And I intend to hold you to that."

Together, they clattered over the wooden bridge. Ariana braced herself for the horrors of the squat tower, but again the gloom was diminished by Ysmay's steady, unflinching presence. Much sooner than she'd expected, they were out in the brightness of early morning.

Ysmay bent with surprising grace to the prone figure of the guard. "He will awaken soon," she pronounced. "Do I detect Merek's work?"

Ariana nodded dumbly, fearful of exactly how soon this might happen. She bent also and replaced the keys in the guard's pocket.

"Merek will be a good friend to you," Ysmay said gravely. "Keep him close."

"I will." Ariana swallowed down a lump in her throat, as she helped her aunt down the tower steps, newly aware that this was goodbye. She flinched at the sound of the cockerel crowing. So much time had passed. She could only hope that Allys had been tardy in her duties this morning.

"I will leave you now, Ariana." Ysmay stood by a copse of holly, haloed by sunlight. "Remember what you have promised me."

"I remember." Ariana pushed down her emotions. "Take good care." Her mind whirred with a hundred things she could have brought to ease her aunt's onward journey. A warm cloak. A flagon of mead. Even a walking stick would have been helpful. Her eyes rested on the guard, and she saw a small flash of steel. His dagger. Ysmay could take that at least, to protect herself. "Wait," she called, already climbing the tower steps to retrieve it.

But when she turned back, Ysmay had gone. From her higher vantage point, Ariana scanned all the woodland paths she could see, but her aunt had disappeared without a trace.

Ariana was left in her green gown, with a slumbering guard at her feet and the growing warmth of the sun stealing over her. The events of the morning already felt surreal; from her terrifying journey through the darkness to Ysmay's reluctance to leave the confines of her cell. It had all been like a dream.

A dream that would quickly turn into a nightmare were the guard to awaken and find her there.

Ariana picked up her skirts and began to run.

She arrived back in her bedchamber to discover that she had arrived before Allys—but with the maid sure to arrive at any minute, there was no time to undress and feign sleep. The stirrings of the mighty keep were impossible to ignore, and she could only send up thanks that no serving maid had spied her unladylike scurry up the stone stairs. Once safely in her room, with the door pressed shut behind her, she splashed cold water on her burning cheeks and dragged a comb through her tousled hair. The young woman peering back at her through the looking glass had a face awash with guilt. Ariana grimaced and tried to settle her features into a more regular pattern.

Allys knocked on the door and entered, blanching at the sight of her mistress already dressed for the day.

"My lady." She hid her confusion behind a curtsy.

"Good morning, Allys." Ariana aimed for bravado but pitched her voice a little too high. She cleared her throat and tried again. "It is a lovely morning." The serving maid shot a puzzled glance towards the closed shutters and Ariana cursed her own stupidity. "I can hear the birdsong," she added quickly.

Allys folded her hands. "You are dressed already, my lady?"

"No." Ariana shook her head. "I woke early and decided to look through the gowns I brought with me from Kenmar, that is all. I have no wish to spend the day like this." She cast another glance into the looking glass, hardly recognizing the tall, elegantly dressed lady reflected back at her. In just a few hours, the false confidence she always attempted to exude had been replaced with something solid and real. After all, she had half-seduced a young guard already that morning.

"But that gown would be perfect for the Beltane feast." Allys stepped forward with a faint smile.

Ariana grasped the lifeline. "The Beltane feast. That's exactly what I was thinking."

"Unless my lady would like to try this one." Allys crossed the room and opened the tall door of the dresser. "The earl himself sent it up for you yesterday." She brought out a sumptuous gown of deepest red and held it against her own slender frame.

Ariana couldn't help a gasp. "It's beautiful." The gown was low cut across the chest with a full skirt.

Allys nodded her agreement. "The earl's boy told me that he would especially like to have you attend the feast in person."

Ariana moved closer so she could reach out and touch the expensive fabric, imagining how such a rich color would look against her skin. She then thought of Otto picking out the gown and sending his boy to request her presence. Her heartrate increased as she remembered the last time their eyes had met across the courtyard. He had been riding away, dressed for some suspicious assignation, while she had been disguised as a poor peasant. Had he recognized her after all? Was this gift of a gown some kind of message?

Her hand fell away, and she blinked in confusion. At her temples, she felt the first throbbing of a headache.

"It would look well on you, I think." Allys paused, her cheeks coloring a little. "But only if it pleases you, my lady."

Ariana turned away so the poor maid didn't have to witness any more of her uncertainty. She walked over to the window and lifted a corner of the shutters, enjoying the rush of sunlight into the chamber. Outside, the courtyard was already busy with the usual milieu of scurrying servants and eager horses.

She couldn't hide up here forever. She would have to face Otto some time.

And she had promised Ysmay that she would commit to her marriage.

Ariana took a deep, restorative breath and turned to face her maid. "Do you know, Allys, I think it would please me very well. Come early tonight and bring the brightest jewels to dress my hair. It is Beltane, after all, and I wish to please my husband."

Chapter Eleven

B ELTANE HAD ARRIVED and the great hall of Darkmoor Castle was all but unrecognizable. Fresh flowers had been brought in from the gardens to brighten every corner and a team of builders had erected a circular stage at the far end, upon which a troupe of musicians now played. Their music was jolly and engaging, under different circumstances Otto was sure his foot would be tapping along with the rhythm. He may even have considered joining the enthusiastic dancers in the center of the floor. But as it was, it took all of his self-control to remain seated with what he hoped was a benign expression on his face.

For as long as anyone could remember, the Earl of Darkmoor had provided feasting and entertainment during the Beltane Festival. In years gone by, two great fires would have been burning outside, with men taking turns to drive the cattle through them in a bid to ensure fertility. In these more enlightened times, Otto kept the merry-making indoors. He ordered the kitchens to put on a lavish banquet and saw the hall illuminated with flaming torches and over a hundred flickering candles. He was more than willing to play his part. He would applaud the musicians and see that the wine kept flowing, until every last servant of the castle was thoroughly sated.

What he was not willing to do was watch his beautiful bride being preyed upon by salacious knights who should know better.

Otto closed his fist around the stem of a silver goblet. If Andreas de Montain allowed his hand to wander any further towards Ariana's waist, Otto would spring down from the top table and slice off his fingers, one by one. His palm unconsciously curled around the hilt of his sword, even as his mind rejected the fantasy. Andreas was a fine swordsman himself. Otto acknowledged that he would need his fingers for the future defense of Darkmoor. The real problem here, was Ariana.

She looked beautiful tonight.

Too beautiful.

He watched her, sitting and laughing with his men, wearing the ruby red gown he had himself picked out for her, and he ached with longing. *Why?* Why did he feel that way? He was the Earl of Darkmoor, damn it. He should be pleased with his beautiful wife.

He should be planning to escort her from the hall to the nearest private spot where he could do with her what he wanted.

Not sitting here like some sex-starved youngling, wondering when she would throw a smile in his direction.

Immediately, his question was answered. Ariana had tipped back her lovely head of hair to laugh uproariously at some joke and across the melee of the feast, her green eyes looked into his.

He held her gaze, fighting down an impulse to smile. She looked so lovely. So happy, in that moment. And happiness was not something readily associated with Darkmoor. He found his defenses wavering. He would return her smile. Get up and join them even. Already he was shifting in his chair. But Ariana's expression changed, became frozen and watchful. Otto realized that he had met her open gaze with a furrowed brow, and it was too late now to summon the necessary smile.

Ariana ducked her head once more, returning her attention to Andreas de Montain and her other gaggle of new admirers. Was it his imagination, or did she twist her shoulders to give Andreas a better view of her wondrous cleavage?

Otto took a mouthful of sweet wine, grimacing at the taste. He was in no mood for sweetness.

In truth, his ill temper had been roused long before his table of knights shuffled up to make room for the new Countess of Darkmoor, urging her to sit beside them just for a short while before taking her appointed seat at Otto's side. Anger had pounded through his veins even before Ariana made her grand entrance in her beautiful red gown. For nearly a whole day now, he had wrestled with the information passed to him by the loyal Gaius. Information which made no sense at all, but which had come all too soon after spying Ariana's ridiculous disguise in the poor cloak of a peasant.

He couldn't help conflating the undeniable fact of Ariana's subterfuge with the news that spies from Kenmar had been captured within the grounds of the castle. These things must be linked. Only a fool would think otherwise.

Otto took another mouthful of wine and then spat it out, uncaring of his manners. Over his shoulder, he waved for his page to bring him some other form of refreshment. Then he resumed his observation of Ariana of Kenmar.

She was radiant tonight.

Surely her eyes had never shone so brightly, nor had her flesh ever looked so creamy and enticing, like a fresh peach. The gown clung to her remarkable curves, dipping low over her generous breasts, and as he watched her talking to a young knight, Otto knew a throbbing in his core which threatened to steal his attention away from the tiresome arguments circling his mind.

Could Ariana have deceived him?

His eyes narrowed in contemplation. The confident young woman seated below him exhibited none of the innocent reticence he had glimpsed during their early interactions. Had that all been a con? His hands gripped the wooden table. It would be the worse for her if he found her to be deceitful.

But his reason was already claiming control over his flailing temper. He had held Ariana in his arms and kissed her. There was neither cunning nor artifice in her manner. Besides, she had not spoken warmly of her childhood, nor of Sir Leon. Surely, she would not risk her own neck to conspire for a cold-hearted father?

Robin, his page, carefully positioned a flagon of ale by his side. Otto nodded his silent thanks and poured some into a fresh goblet. Across the hall, the musicians struck up a lively jig and the floor shook as a dozen new dancers got up to enjoy themselves. Among them, Andreas and Ariana.

Otto tightened his focus. The merriment around him faded as he saw Andreas's courtly bow promptly followed by Ariana's answering nod. Otto had been raised a warrior. His very existence depended upon his being able to read people. He knew in his heart that Ariana was no spy for Sir Leon. But what was she doing now, on the dance floor, with one of his most charming knights?

They made a striking couple. Even in his growing rage, Otto had to admit as much. There was something different about Ariana tonight. She had always commanded his attention; some particular inner spark within her connected with his soul in a way he did not yet understand. But on this Beltane night, Ariana was lit up from within, glowing even, with a delicate flame that caught the awareness of every damn man in the room.

He had sent her the gown as a subtle message to his wife that she need not creep around Darkmoor clad in poor rags. But the joke was on him. For Ariana bore the ruby red robes with all the regal bearing of a queen. A queen who dazzled.

He should have flooded the place with women.

He should have insisted that Ariana stay by his side, up here on the dais.

But he had never believed she would venture into the celebratory throng without him.

He drained his ale and smacked his lips together. Enough was enough. Andreas had snaked an arm around Ariana's waist and was holding her much too close. It didn't matter that such movements were part of the dance. Otto's fragile tolerance was at an end.

He pushed back his chair with a resounding scrape and stood up tall. He would do what he should have done at the very start of this fiasco. Stake a claim to his wife.

If Andreas dared make the faintest sound of protest, Otto would have him thrown into the dungeons for the night.

Seeming to sense his soaring emotions, the minstrels began to play faster as he descended the wooden steps. The music whirled around him, accompanied by a frenzied stamping of feet which was all too reminiscent of the heightened seconds immediately before a battle charge. Otto put a hand to his forehead, momentarily befuddled. He must have drunk more ale than he'd realized.

A pretty serving wench sashayed past him, giving him a wide smile and a generous view of her swaying hips. The sight of her only increased Otto's longing for Ariana. Where was she? Now that he was amongst his men on the makeshift dancefloor, everything was a confusion of flailing limbs and heated bodies. He stood a head taller than most and the crowd parted before him like a wave, just in time for him to see Andreas's hand drift down from Ariana's waist to hover over a place it had no business visiting.

He tightened his fists, a roar of rage erupting in his throat, but before he could stride forward and strike the man for his insolence, Ariana herself took charge. In one swift and sudden movement, she stepped out of his grasping embrace and delivered a sharp slap across Andreas's face.

Otto felt his eyebrows shoot up in surprise as Ariana then bobbed her head and politely took her formal leave of the startled knight. Around them, the music and dancing went on. No one else had noticed.

Otto looked from the frozen figure of Andreas to his departing bride and decided his choice was clear. Brushing deliberately past his knight's shoulders to ensure the man knew his foolishness had been witnessed, Otto too stalked from the hall.

He would deal with Andreas de Montain later.

The air was cooler as soon as he stepped from the great hall. Away from the piping music and raucous laughter, he could think more clearly. His frenzied jealousy abated, leaving him resolute.

Ariana had a lot of questions to answer.

But where had she gone? He looked from left to right, his ears pricked for running footsteps, but all was silent. If Ariana had returned to her bedchamber, he would have heard her ascend the stone stairs. The morning room then. But his instincts told him she was unlikely to take refuge in a closed off room so far from the bustle of the castle, especially after her recent ordeal.

Otto gnashed his teeth together, entirely unaccustomed to the melting pot of emotions he was now experiencing. One moment he was determined to interrogate his bride, the next he wanted nothing more than to carry her away and protect her from the terrors of the world.

The quiet of the castle mocked his plight. He was Earl of Darkmoor, yet his mastery of this very domestic situation was entirely lacking. Althalos was right. If Otto could not command discipline in his wife, what hope had he of leading loyal troops into battle?

A whisper of wind caught through his tousled hair and Otto's gaze swung towards the entrance hall. Mayhap the front doors have been left open. Which meant that Ariana could have gone outside.

She was a fool to leave the protection of the fortress. Otto strode forward, resolved to find her immediately and bring her back inside. The lands of Darkmoor were usually peaceful—Otto's own reputation saw to that—but on Beltane night, who knew what thieves and vagabonds may be lurking in dark corners? His pulse quickened at the thought that even now, Ariana may be in danger.

Or was she creeping outside to another secret assignation?

Dread wrapped cold fingers around his midriff as the suspicion settled inside him. If she sought a meeting with someone, it could be a lover, or even a spy from Kenmar. He didn't know which would be worse, but his lips pressed into a thin line and his pace increased. He would find Ariana and put an end to this wild speculation.

Before the night was over, she would give him the answers

he sought.

If anything, the air was warmer when he stepped outside. The spring night was balmy and thick with the scent of wildflowers. A series of flaming torches cast circles of light around the inner courtyard, but Otto stepped out of their comfort and blinked until his sharp eyes grew accustomed to the blanket of darkness. He would not give himself away by carrying a torch with him. If Ariana were really meeting someone out here, that person would not know of Otto's presence until his hands were around the intruder's neck.

He crept quietly over the gravel, cursing his heavy boots for the crunching sound they made. An owl hooted overhead, and another whisper of wind caressed his bare skin. It was a night made for romance. And if Ariana had come out here with that in mind, she would most certainly have made her way to the gardens. Those lovingly tended lawns she had gazed out upon from the morning room. Otto knew another clutch of anger in his chest.

Had he been taken for a fool?

He ducked under a stone archway, quieter now that he strode over grass. Nighttime insects buzzed around his face, but he ignored them with the implacability of a warrior about to attack. As he rounded the next bend, the moon slid out from behind a cloud and illuminated the scene before him.

Ariana stood in a circle of lawn, her arms crossed over her chest and her luxurious red gown spread out all around her. Her head was bowed. She was alone.

Otto's relief was palpable. He all but staggered into a gorse bush but righted himself at the first prick of the thorns.

No secret assignation then. Neither a lover nor a spy. Ariana simply wished to partake of the night air.

He stepped out of the shadows and said her name.

"Ariana."

It was a whisper. A caress.

Her head rose sharply upwards, green eyes shining in the

moonlight. A look of alarm settled into something calmer when she recognized him. "Have you followed me out here?"

"Aye." He nodded in admission. "I wanted to be sure you were safe."

She paused, still holding his gaze. "Well, now you know it."

Suspicion flared within him. He stepped closer, disliking her instinctive retreat.

"Are you keen to be rid of me, wife?"

She hugged her arms across her chest, but it was a gesture of defense rather than defiance. "You have made your own feelings clear these last days."

Otto's forbearance was at an end. He closed the distance between them and placed a firm hand around her shoulder, not allowing her to shake him off. "You are the one to order sleeping draughts from the physician," he stated, his words raining down like icicles. His eyes bore into hers, making sure his meaning landed. "And you are the one disinclined to dine with me on more than one occasion. What am I to make of it all?"

Something about the look in Ariana's fearful eyes tugged at him. There was anger of her own, misplaced for sure, but also doubt and a good deal of confusion. He was not looking into the face of a deceitful bride. More a brave soul who had been through an ordeal and did not know which way to turn. He loosened the grip of his fingers, noticing how the moonlight glinted on the jewels around her neck.

Ariana lifted her chin. "I was under the impression your lordship had finer company to keep."

He had never been spoken to so impertinently by a woman. Her words were delivered as a slap across the face. Otto recoiled, at first in shock and then with a cold anger. But the anger was not solely directed at Ariana.

"My uncle's words still trouble you." He spoke through gritted teeth. It was a statement, not a question.

She looked away. "It is not important."

"It is important to me." Gently now, he cupped a hand to her face and tilted it towards him. "Ariana, you have no reason to distrust me."

Her eyes flared. "We still scarcely know one another."

A shiver ran through her, visible despite the heavy folds of the gown, but the evening was not cold. Otto raised his eyebrows. What was it that made her tremble so?

"We shall not grow closer while ever you feast alone in your chamber." He paused, considering his next words. Once said, he could not take them back. But if he retreated from the matter, he would be forever beset by doubt. "Nor if you creep around my castle in disguise."

She flinched backwards, proving beyond all measure that his suspicions were correct. A knot of despair unfurled in his stomach. He had so hoped to be wrong.

Ariana swallowed and looked down, breaking their gaze. "You recognized me." It was a statement, not a question. "I knew it."

At least she had not attempted denial. Otto's scar throbbed and he clenched his hands together to keep himself from gripping her shoulders and demanding an explanation.

"Will you tell me why?" Despite his best efforts, it came out as a growl. Ariana moved away from him, and he couldn't help shooting out a hand to hold her in place. "Do not take me for a fool, Ariana."

"I would never do that," she breathed, a sob trembling beneath the surface of her words.

He believed her.

He dropped his hand. "You must explain your actions. I command it, not as the Earl of Darkmoor, but as your husband." His voice softened on the final words.

She was trembling now like a leaf caught up in a storm. Otto was torn between a desire to offer comfort and the urgent need to have her speak the truth.

"I have reason to believe that enemies of Darkmoor may even now be inside the castle walls," he said suddenly, driven by an impulse to explain. He fastened his gaze on the darkened blooms of his mother's roses and spoke from his heart. "I need to know that you are not one of them."

She lifted her face towards him, surprise and sincerity written clearly across it. "I am not your enemy," she whispered, the breeze fanning through her hair and bringing the pungent scent of rose petals towards them.

Her simple words were like sweet music to his ears, breaking through his barriers of fear and mistrust. He wanted to take her into his arms and kiss her, but too many questions remained.

"Then why?" He opened his arms wide to demonstrate the breadth of his confusion.

She stifled a sob and crossed her arms across her chest. "Will you trust that I am not your enemy?"

He had not anticipated such a challenge. While he pondered it, an orange fox slunk out of the undergrowth and fled silently across the lawns, the white tip of its tail glowing brightly in the darkness.

Did he trust Ariana?

Nay, it was not in his nature to trust. He had not been trained for it. On the battlefield he placed his trust in a handful of his closest knights, those he had fought side by side with on a multitude of muddy fields, splattered with the blood of their enemies. In times of peace, he was wary of all.

He gritted his teeth and answered truthfully. "I hope that in time, I may have that faith."

Her eyes widened as she considered his words. "At least you do not lie to me." Her lips quivered with the beginnings of a smile.

He inclined his head. "You have done me the same honor."

She put a hand to her breast, unconsciously clenching her fingers around an item of jewelry.

"My mother's broach?" His voice lifted in surprise. "You wear it still?"

"I do." She paused, her breath catching in her throat. "I treasure it."

Her words sealed his conviction that Ariana was not here simply as a spy for Sir Leon. Hers was not the mind behind the devious plots to threaten their recently secured peace. And right now, he had no wish to dwell further upon such things. Tomorrow would be time enough to gather his most loyal knights and share the grim news that Gaius had so unwillingly burdened him with.

Tonight, there was just one person on his mind.

Moving slowly so as not to startle her further, Otto closed his own hand on top of Ariana's. Her fingers were chilled to the touch, and he longed to offer her comfort.

"Do not fear me," he said, his voice tight with meaning. "You have no need to flinch away. No need to run and hide."

Her lips trembled. "I sensed from the first time we met, that you would not harm me."

"I would not." He slid his hands around her waist and pulled her closer, inhaling the sweet fragrance of her hair. "I would not harm any woman, but especially not you."

She stood as still as chiseled stone, unyielding to his touch, even when Otto dropped the lightest of kisses on the side of her face. Her eyelids fluttered and he knew she was struggling against her desire for him.

"But I have not told you the full truth," she blurted out, as he rained a soft line of kisses along her jaw.

In that moment, he didn't care. "You have not lied," he stated, bringing his hands up her sides and running them the length of her arms, enjoying the slight tilt of her body towards him. She was surrendering to the pleasure of his touch, just as his own mind was relinquishing reason over sensation.

"I will not lie," she breathed, closing her eyes as he encircled her with his arms.

He paused, pulling back to regard her quizzically. Her breathing had become ragged, much like his own. "You mean, if I do not ask awkward questions about why you were running around

Darkmoor in disguise, you will refrain from telling me an untruth?"

Her eyes flickered open, her gaze clashing with his own. A beat passed. All Otto could hear was the rustle of the wind through branches overhead. His heart beat heavily like the banging of the minstrel's drum.

Eventually, Ariana nodded. "That is what I mean."

Her audacity should have inflamed him, but somehow the corners of his mouth turned up in an indulgent smile. "That is what I thought." He lowered his head, whispering directly into her ear. "And will you ignore Sir Althalos the next time he attempts to discredit me in your eyes?"

She reached up a pale hand and rested it on his cheek. Such a simple touch, but it was his undoing. "I will."

He had waited long enough. His lips met hers and his arms wrapped hungrily around her waist. One part of his mind told him to slow down, but another urged him on, especially when Ariana pressed her body against his.

With great effort he pulled away, cupping her cheeks with both hands and gazing down into her beautiful green eyes. "Have a care, wife," he whispered. "I cannot promise you restraint if you press against me like that."

Ariana snaked her arms around his shoulders, seeming to delight in tracing her hands over the muscles of his upper arms. She stepped closer, so there was not so much as a breath of air between them.

"Who says I want restraint?" she whispered in reply.

Chapter Twelve

ARIANA HARDLY KNEW herself. Who was this daring young hussy, kissing handsome warriors in castle gardens and not allowing them to take a gentlemanly leave?

The embarrassment and insecurities that had dogged her footsteps through her life had vanished, leaving her free and unabashed. She wanted to kiss Otto. Wanted to feel his lips on hers. His arms around her waist. His warm breath on the side of her face. More, she wanted more than that. In a rush of courage, she shifted her weight closer to him, reveling in the solidity of his broad chest.

His usually fierce eyes were gazing down at her, but they weren't fierce anymore. Instead, they were hazy, almost unfocused. A smile played around his full lips. She reached up to feel the sharpness of his dark stubble.

"You do not wish for me to show restraint?" he echoed her words, his voice both throaty and playful. "My dear Ariana, do you know what you are saying?"

This was her chance to back away. To cast her eyes modestly down and apologize for her impropriety. But she had no intention of taking it. For the first time in her life, she felt feminine, desirable even. And it wasn't just because of the elegant gown Otto had gifted to her—though that was no doubt responsible for the stir her arrival had caused in the great hall earlier. It was because of the way Otto spoke to her, like she was an equal whose opinion was worth hearing. It was because of his smile, sometimes dangerous and sometimes kind, and mostly because of the fizzing sensation that his mere proximity sent skidding along her spine. Standing in Otto's arms, Ariana didn't feel awkward or overly tall. She wasn't worried about saying the wrong thing or stumbling over his feet; or generally making a fool of herself in front of the Earl of Darkmoor, a man who could take his choice of women.

Instead, she had the most wonderful feeling that she was standing exactly where she was meant to be.

She nodded firmly, allowing her hands to run down his spine all the way to his waist. "I do."

For a moment, he paused, and she wondered fleetingly if she had displeased him with her boldness. But then his lips crashed down upon hers and she wondered no more. All thoughts deserted her as she submitted to the wonderful sensation of kissing this mountain of strength. She gasped as his tongue met hers, moving closer into his arms and arching against him as he stroked a gentle line over her collarbone, settling his palm against the curve of her breast.

"Ariana," he whispered, nibbling her neck and sending waves of pleasure rippling down her body. "If we go further, I shall not be able to stop."

In answer she gripped his hand and pressed it more firmly against her breast. "I do not want you to stop," she enunciated clearly.

Her words unleashed something inside him. He immediately picked her up, as if she weighed no more than a child, and carried her a few steps closer to the rose bushes, where they were more shielded from accidental onlookers.

"I am glad of it," he grunted, laying her down gently in the soft grass. "I do not know how much longer I could have waited for you."

He expertly unfastened the front of her bodice, and she gasped again as his warm hands made direct contact with her sensitive skin.

"You said I could take all the time I needed," she reminded him breathlessly, winding her fingers into his tousled hair.

"Aye," he agreed, lowering his head to kiss the flesh he had so recently exposed to the night air. "I will be more careful with my promises in future."

Her whole body was tingling now with a mixture of excitement and longing. She wriggled in the long grass, not knowing how best to remedy the intense need growing inside her. "Otto," she gasped, as his hand pressed beneath her skirts.

"Do you want me to stop?" he asked, his voice muffled by her breast.

"No," she answered quickly. "No, never."

His fingers stroked her thighs, gently pushing them apart. Ariana felt as though someone had lit a fire inside her. A fire that deepened as Otto finally found her curls. He shifted onto an elbow and kissed her lips as one finger slipped slowly inside her.

"Oh," she gasped, rearing against him.

He quietened her by deepening their kiss, claiming her whole mouth as his hand caressed her. The pleasure he was inducing in her grew into a sharp point of need. She pulled helplessly at his tunic, wanting to feel the warmth of his skin and the beating of his heart.

He moved away and swiftly removed his clothing. Ariana had but seconds to admire how the pale moonlight illuminated the contours of his muscular body before his nimble fingers were gently divesting her of her gown. She bit down on her lip as the balmy evening air washed around her body, gasping out loud as Otto gripped the hem of her chemise and lifted it smoothly over her head.

He paused for a moment, his dark eyes raking over her body. But Ariana didn't feel shame over her nakedness. She held herself still and unabashed, enjoying the way Otto's attention feasted on her womanly figure. He reached out a hand and skimmed it over the curve of her breasts. The flame of desire pooled within her as Otto gathered himself.

"Are you ready?" he whispered.

In answer, she wrapped her fingers into his hair and pulled him down upon her, relishing the tingling she felt as his long, hard body made contact with her own softness. He kissed her again and she felt the first nudging of his desire between her thighs. He cupped her cheek as he gently pushed himself inside her, filling her up with his warmth. The brief stab of pain was quickly followed by wave upon wave of rhythmic pleasure as their bodies moved as one. She closed her eyes and surrendered to the wealth of sensations, her hips rocking beneath him, her hands roving over the hard ridges of his muscular back. Slowly her pleasure increased to a crescendo she couldn't help crying out over. Her teeth fastened onto his shoulder as new sensations rippled through her, leaving her limp but replete. Through her haze, she was dimly aware of Otto thrusting more urgently inside her, then giving a low moan of release.

Gradually, she recovered her senses becoming aware once more of Otto's weight upon her, the hard beating of his heart, an owl hooting far above their heads. His stubble rasped against her cheek, his breath was warm against her ear. She linked her fingers around his neck as her breathing slowed.

Otto propped himself onto an elbow and dropped a kiss onto her lips, before moving away from her onto his side. Immediately, she was cold and bereft, longing for the comfort of his warm skin, but then he reached for her and pulled her closer. She nestled her head onto his broad chest, enjoying the sensation of his hands smoothing her back.

"You are beautiful," he said gruffly into the silence.

She could only respond honestly. "I am not."

He brought a finger to her lips, pressing it gently against them. "What is this now? You tell me I am wrong?"

She shuffled closer, entwining her legs in his. "I have long known my assets and shortcomings," she said. "I am content with my lot."

Otto grunted. "I should hope so." She laughed lightly, her

mouth against his shoulder, but he lifted her chin and forced her to look up. "You are beautiful," he repeated, more firmly this time. "I want you to know it."

For the first time she felt a flush of self-consciousness stain her cheeks. Her anxious mind presented her with a series of images— golden ringlets, slender shoulders, a lady with the singing voice of an angel—but with a tremendous effort she shoved them away. Otto wanted her for who she was; exactly *how* she was.

What an extraordinary gift.

"Mayhap, in your eyes," she said hesitantly.

"Are not my eyes the only ones that matter?" he demanded.

"Why yes," she began, stuttering, but then saw that he was jesting with her, and she allowed a smile to break through. "Thank you, Otto," she said with meaning.

"For what?"

"For your kindness," she replied readily, settling her palm against his side. *For not demanding to know why I dressed in disguise just yesterday*, her mind supplied, but she swallowed it down.

He took her fingers and interlinked them with his own. Through the darkness, she could see only the gleam of his eyes and the outline of his jaw.

"I had small hope of happiness in this marriage," he said. "But I begin to believe that we may make a strong success of it, you and I."

Ariana felt as if she were standing at the edge of some preci-pice. She could fall into the treacherous depths or else she could soar above them. She held Otto's hand more tightly and squeezed her eyes shut for a brief moment. "I would like that," she said, her voice small. "I confess, such hopes were beyond my wildest imaginings when I first came to Darkmoor."

"You thought me a brute."

His abruptness took her by surprise, but it was a statement, not a question. She swallowed hard. "I knew you only by reputation."

He leaned closer, his breath fanning against her cheeks. "And now, Ariana, do you think there is more to me than a merciless killer?"

She felt the strong rhythm of his heart beating against her chest. His voice was tight. Could it be that Otto cared about her answer?

Such a prospect made Ariana momentarily dizzy. She took a breath. "It is true, of course, you are a mighty warrior." Never had she been more aware of his height and strength. "But there is more to you, yes." She reached out to place her palm against his angular cheek and he clasped her hand inside his.

"Thank you," he whispered.

Ariana's own deception seemed to hover over them, a gauzy sheet of duplicity capable of smothering this new-found ease, this path towards happiness. She opened her mouth in a sudden urge to confess, but closed it again for what could she say? How could she shatter this fragile state of trust that had so recently sprung up between them?

And what good would it do now? The deed was done. Ysmay was free. Ariana had no further cause to go behind Otto's back for anything, ever again.

She exhaled, releasing all her doubts and anxieties into the night. She would be a good wife from now on. She would give Otto no reason to doubt her. Their marriage could, as Otto said, become a success.

She settled her head against him, relaxing to the feel of his hands stroking her back. As the tension left her shoulders, she grew aware of something new. A faint flutter of hope, deep down inside her belly. She and Otto could grow to be happy, together.

She'd never wanted anything so fiercely.

THEY WALKED BACK through the darkness to Ariana's bedchamber and spent a restful night together sleeping deeply under her blankets, but Ariana woke with the first cock crow. The quiet of the castle told her it was too early to worry about the maids coming in, and she was far too awake to contemplate further rest.

Strips of morning sunlight slanted through the heavy shutters, illuminating the man who slumbered just inches away. As she gazed at him, the fizzing sensations that had rippled through her out in the rose garden seemed to make a new home in her heart. Her whole being sang with life and hope. For the first time in her life, happiness was within her grasp.

Who would have guessed that *Feared One* held the key?

That long-feared moniker had now lost its power to terrorize her, for she had discovered the man beneath the warrior's mask. Hardly breathing, she gazed at this close-up version of Otto Sarragnac, longing to reach out a skim her hand over his stubbled jaw. In repose, the usual lines of tension had faded from Otto's brow. He looked younger and softer, she thought, until her gaze reached his muscled forearms, then he was every inch a warrior. Her lips parted as she drank in her sleeping husband. She had grown accustomed to a constant energy radiating from the Earl of Darkmoor, accustomed to the piercing gleam of his dark eyes and the instinctive suspicion that he was somehow conscious of her every waking thought. To see him now, was to look upon a much calmer, more contented man. One without the burden of responsibility which Otto had long carried on his broad shoulders.

It was but a fleeting state, which would vanish the moment his waking mind took hold. Ariana was seized with an urge to capture it forever.

Moving slowly so as not to disturb him, she shuffled out from under the blankets, wincing a little as her bare feet came into contact with the cold floor. Clad in only her chemise, she stretched her arms above her head and rotated her neck slowly, half smiling when she caught sight of the clothing they had so carelessly discarded just hours earlier. Her body ached with the memory of the pleasure they had shared, and a certain soreness made her walk more gingerly over to the wooden chest which had travelled with her from Kenmar. She swung open the lid with deliberate slowness, squinting in the half-light to make out the objects she sought.

Her tin box of charcoals and a roll of parchment. Her hands fell upon them eagerly and she brought them out with all the reverence of a fine lady handling cherished jewels. Since childhood, these had been the tools of her escape from the bleak drudgery of Kenmar, from a life lived in the shadow of Sir Leon's disapproval. With the charcoal in her fingers, Ariana could switch off from the world around her and lose herself in sketching. Not that she showed her art to anyone. It was something she did purely for her own pleasure. Over time, she had captured the sparkling wonder of a winter landscape, the chubby arms of an infant reaching out for his mother, and the surprising grace of a hunting party.

Now she would capture the image of Otto at rest.

First, she unrolled the parchment and secured it to her writing desk, swiveling around to get a better view of the bed. Otto's brawny arms were flung sideways, free of the blankets. His tanned face inclined towards her, a look of almost boyish innocence about his brow. But that blameless purity was cast into doubt by the jutting edges of his scar and the defined curve of his biceps. He was a man of fierce contradictions, and Ariana's charcoal danced over the parchment, impatient to capture every detail of him in this moment before it was gone.

She became so engrossed in her work that the gradual stirrings of the castle did not reach her. She didn't hear the clattering of horses' hooves out in the courtyard, nor the rushed footsteps beyond her chamber door as servants started their daily toil. The sun grew stronger, casting Otto's stubbled jaw in a halo of light and Ariana drew with increasing ease and confidence, jolted from her studies only when Allys bade her a surprised good morning.

Ariana put her hand to her chest. "Allys, you startled me."

But Allys was not looking at Ariana. Her stricken gaze was fixed on the bed, where a bleary-eyed Otto was awake, yawning and scratching his head.

"Forgive me, milord, milady." Allys bobbed into a timid curtsy. "I did not know. That is, I was not expecting…"

Otto sat up in bed and the covers fell away from his sculpted chest as he smiled lazily at the servant. "Never apologize for bringing food to a hungry man." He gestured to her heavily loaded tray. "What do we have here?"

Allys stepped forward nervously, darting a gaze at Ariana. "My lady likes to break her fast with fruit and freshly baked bread."

Otto sniffed and nodded in satisfaction. "A sensible choice. You may leave the tray with us."

"Yes, milord." Allys maneuvered it onto the sturdy bedside stand and folded her hands behind her back, averting her eyes from the half-naked figure of the earl.

"Thank you, Allys. You may go," Ariana spoke up, offering rescue.

"Milady." Allys bobbed into another bow and scuttled from the room.

"Have a care, Otto," Ariana said, hiding her smile as Otto stretched widely, gloriously unaware of his rippling muscles.

"Mayhap you should have a care yourself, smuggling men into your chamber and giving your maid a fright." Otto tore off a hunk of bread and chewed it ruminatively, his eyes resting on Ariana and making her newly aware of how the dappled sunlight showed the pink of her skin through her chemise.

She should have pulled on a robe, but it was too late now. Awkwardly she put down her charcoal and folded her arms across her chest.

Otto tutted, striding from the bed and closing the gap between them in mere moments. "'Tis a little late for modesty, wife," he stated, closing a warm hand around her shoulder and dropping a kiss onto the side of her face. Ariana felt the heat of her blushes subside as she stepped into the comfort of his embrace. "Are you well rested?" he enquired.

"I am." She nodded. She had slept like a babe with Otto by her side.

"I am pleased to hear it." He settled his hands around her waist and drew her closer towards him before his attention was snagged by her drawing. "What is this?"

She blushed anew. "It is a mere hobby of mine."

He nodded appraisingly, his eyes raking over the parchment. Ariana saw her sketch with new eyes, conscious of the clumsy lines and disproportionately large hands, but Otto smiled in approval.

"I can say nothing of the subject, of course, but you have a gift for drawing."

"Thank you. It is not yet finished."

He inclined his head. "Another time." He stroked his hands down over her shoulders and sighed. "Alas, duty calls. As much as I would like to stay up here with you, I am afraid there are less pleasant tasks I must attend to."

Her regret was mingled with relief. As much as she warmed to Otto's words and touch, Ariana was used to spending time alone with her thoughts. More pressingly, she was not convinced she wanted to display her flesh to her handsome husband during daylight hours. What he had seen and touched under cover of darkness was one thing, but the stark light of morning was quite another.

"Of course," she demurred, noticing how his brow had already grown strained as he considered the day ahead. "Is all well?" she asked on impulse.

Otto stalked to the window and inched open the shutters so that more light poured into the room. He observed the busy goings on in the courtyard with another sigh and then turned to face her.

"Ariana, I must confess, there is trouble brewing."

Anxiety gripped her. "Of what kind?"

He ran a hand through his already tousled hair. "That I cannot tell you, not for sure. I live in hope that the peace we so recently obtained will prevail, for a while at least." He turned back to the window, scratching his bare arms. "A prisoner escaped yesterday."

She felt as if she couldn't breathe. All the air had been sucked from the room. Otto's stance was casual and relaxed. He couldn't know of her involvement with Ysmay. *Could he?*

She forced out the question. "What prisoner?"

He waved his hand, still gazing outside. "No one important. A woman. Honestly, her escape was a blessing in many ways. It saved me making an impossible decision." He broke off, seemingly lost in thought, but when he looked back at her, his dark eyes were impenetrably sharp. "My knights suspect spies from your father's lands have broken through our outer defenses."

His words brought a chill to the shadowed chamber, and she clasped her arms further about her. "Spies?" she repeated, frowning as her mind raced with confusion. "To what end?"

He shrugged expansively. "You are from Kenmar…" He left the sentence unfinished.

She shook her head, bewildered by this revelation. "Otto, honestly, I have no idea…"

He interrupted her stuttering protests with a chuckle. "Have no fear, Ariana. I do not suspect you of killing one of my guards."

All the strength in her legs deserted her and she sat down heavily upon the desk chair. "Which guard?" she asked, her voice no more than a whisper. She ran the tip of her tongue over lips that had suddenly become dry.

His eyes flickered over her. "I'm afraid to say I did not know him personally, though he died in the service of Darkmoor." He picked up his discarded tunic from a heap on the floor and shook it out. "He was killed at Traitor's Gate, most probably when our prisoner escaped."

"But I didn't kill the guard," she said unthinkingly. Her limbs growing cold in horror at the thought of the smiling young man she had dared to flirt with, now cold and lifeless.

"Of course you didn't." He pulled the tunic over his head, frowning in her direction. "That was never my inference."

Ariana put her head in her hands, all thoughts of deception far from her mind. *How had this happened?* She had never meant for anyone to get hurt. And now Otto suspected her father of sending spies into Darkmoor. But surely Sir Leon would never seek to stand against the might of Otto's army. Especially not so soon after the battle of Branfeld when his men were so vastly depleted.

This must be somehow her fault.

"What is it, Ariana?" Otto crossed the room to stand by her side, concern giving a new edge to his voice. "Forgive me, I didn't mean to upset you."

His hand grasped her shoulder and she put her palm over his, taking no comfort from his height and strength. All she could think of was the sequence of events she had so unwittingly set into motion.

Had the sleeping draught been stronger than she realized?

"It is nothing," she murmured, trying her best to recover her composure. "Only that I am sorry to hear of your troubles."

She spoke reflexively, giving little thought to her words, but Otto grimaced in agreement.

"I should be spending the early days of my marriage in bed with my wife," he declared with feeling. "Not preparing for some needless squabble. But have no fear, Ariana, whoever did this will soon be caught. And I promise, they will feel the full wrath of Darkmoor." He smiled down at her. "I am not known as the *Feared One* for nothing."

He turned away, rummaging amongst their hastily discarded clothing for his sword belt and cloak, blissfully unaware of the turmoil his bold statement had caused his young bride.

Ariana was numb with shock. *How had she thought she could double cross the Earl of Darkmoor without facing consequences?*

"I bid you a good morning," he quipped, dropping a chaste kiss onto her forehead. "Will I see you at dinner tonight?"

It was a question for which there was only one answer. Ariana nodded, desperately trying to find her voice. But Otto's mind was already on other things. With a faint wave of his hand, he strode from her bedchamber, the door swinging noisily shut behind him.

Ariana took a deep, heaving breath and crossed her hands over her heart.

What had she done?

She glanced down at her drawing. Already it seemed to be from another time. Would she ever spend another night wrapped in Otto's arms, ever wake again to the sight of him sleeping peacefully in her bed? It would only be a matter of time before he discovered her treachery and perhaps consigned her to her own imprisonment at Traitor's Gate.

Ariana felt a wave of nausea. She had come so close to happiness. Happiness which she'd dared to think she deserved. And now it would come to naught. All because of her father. What business did he have sending spies into Darkmoor? She had believed he wanted peace with his powerful neighbor. Her marriage to Otto had been conceived to deliver that peace.

She shook her head, knowing that Allys could return at any moment. She must dress and go about her day as if nothing was wrong.

A knock at her chamber door proved her correct.

"Come in," she called, not worrying about covering herself with a robe, for it would only be Allys. But it was not her maid who entered the room, eyes cast bashfully down, but a young errand boy.

"I have a message for you, milady," he addressed the rushes on the floor.

Ariana folded her arms across her chest, protecting her modesty as best she could in the thin chemise. "You may leave it there." She raised her eyebrows to indicate the nightstand.

The boy placed the sealed scroll on the polished wooden surface and took his leave, closing the door quietly behind him.

Ariana recognized the seal of Kenmar from where she sat.

The coat of arms seemed to mock her plight. Would she never escape her father's avarice?

Angry now, she strode over and deftly unfurled it, skimming Sir Leon's familiar hand. The missive contained no surprises. He enquired only after Ariana's progress in securing the ruby necklace, offering no hopes or well wishes for his daughter's welfare. Nor any hints of plotting against her husband, she noted.

Could Otto be mistaken?

She crumpled the parchment in her hand, staring pensively at the dappled sunlight on the white-washed wall. She should throw open the shutters, allow the morning light to fully penetrate her gloomy chamber.

She should not spend any further time ruminating on the actions of a selfish, small-minded man.

Decisively, she flung the message into her unlit fireplace. As soon as Allys came in to tend the room, Sir Leon's words would go up in smoke, which was no less than the fate it deserved.

Ariana was the Countess of Darkmoor now. She would concentrate on the future and leave the past where it was.

Chapter Thirteen

OTTO SAT ASTRIDE his black horse and gazed with satisfaction at four long lines of mounted men before him. He held up his hand for silence and immediately his request was granted, as if the entire training ground had fallen under some magical spell. Not a horse snorted, not a man so much as breathed. All he could see was a gleaming mass of horse flesh and a formidable array of muscle, topped with polished plate armor and the fluttering red and gold colors of Darkmoor.

High above them, heavy clouds shifted to block the mid-morning sunshine and the field fell into shadow. A strong wind whipped through the surrounding trees, forcing the flags to stream and snap. Otto saw the ears of his horse flicker back and forth with unease and he held her steady with his long legs, demanding obedience.

Then he spoke. "At ease," he commanded, his voice echoing through the ranks. And like a rippling wave, the soldiers of Darkmoor relaxed their stance. "Thank you, men." He smiled, feeling rather than seeing their murmured relief. "That was a good training session. Each of you do Darkmoor proud. Pray, remain alert in the coming days. We look for peace, but we prepare, as ever, for battle."

His words were met with a valiant chorus of 'ayes.' Otto pressed his spurs into his charger's sides and turned away, trotting along the wide path which led back through the woods to the bailey. The air was cooler today, threatening rain, but his spirits were nonetheless high.

He had awoken by Ariana's side. He had found all he hoped for and more in his intriguing bride. And now, after this morning's display, he was confident that the army of Darkmoor was as formidable as ever. Stronger even, he countered, for the young squires were growing every day into brave and highly skilled warriors. Soon they would be ready to fight by his side, though he prayed that such a battle would not come for many a year.

Could Darkmoor be a land of peace? He had heard of estates where the men grew fat and jovial, with fires flickering in the hearth and children at their knees. Where the women embroidered and arranged grand balls, where food was plentiful, and laughter filled the echoing halls. The home of his distant kinsman, Angus de Neville, was a beautiful castle which had never known the threat of an advancing army. Over to the east, his cousin Guy, Earl of Rossfarne, had hung up his sword amidst the domestic tumble of a young family.

He reined in his horse as they came in view of the crenelated bailey wall. Could Darkmoor Castle ever become a home first and a fortress second?

His hopes sputtered like a candle in a draught. It was like wishing for a horse that could fly, or a tankard that was never empty. Darkmoor had always been a land of warriors. Otto knew no other way of living, neither did most of his men. But that didn't mean he shouldn't *try*.

Mayhap Ariana could show him the way? Though she had been raised surrounded by as much bloodshed and avarice as anyone here.

Together though, could they build a different kind of future? If they stood side by side, might they create something beautiful, much like they had last night in the rose gardens? He smiled at the memory of her soft flesh and gracious curves. He had buried his face in her sweet-smelling hair and forgotten, for a long, glorious moment, what it was to be the Earl of Darkmoor with the weight of duty on his back.

The first droplets of rain splashed against his shoulder plate, and he urged his horse on. As they clattered over the drawbridge, the rain began to fall steadily. Soon the reins were slick and wet. Otto shifted in the saddle as water ran down his neck and beneath his chainmail. The earthy scent of dampened grass followed him inside the castle gates, where two familiar figures stood waiting for him.

Otto's heart sank as he recognized the cold eyes of Sir Althalos beside the anxious face of Gaius. Two men who were not natural allies.

"A welcoming committee," he quipped, throwing one long leg over his horse's back and springing down onto the squelching mud. "To what do I owe this pleasure?" He looked around for the stable boy and handed over the sodden reins.

Gaius clasped his hands behind him and waited for Sir Althalos to speak. His silence struck another wrong note. Otto cursed the drip of rainwater down his neck, suspecting that Althalos, clad in his warm cloak, was enjoying his discomfort. The clatter of hoofbeats had long disappeared before his uncle spoke.

"I bring grievous news, nephew."

Otto's impatience surged. "And will you make me wait all day to hear it? Speak, uncle, please, before we are all drowned."

"Shall we go under cover?" Gaius suggested, motioning towards the nearby stables, but Althalos shook his head.

"You would not wish us to be overheard," he stated.

Rain was now falling in heavy sheets, splashing noisily into fast-forming puddles all around them. Gaius pulled his hood over his head, half covering his eyes. The loyal knight had not been present at training, though Otto was willing to allow such liberties in one so skilled and experienced. Still, his absence was unusual. No doubt Althalos had had a hand in it.

Otto had been hoping to escape into the morning room, where he fancied Ariana may be found, complete with a crackling fire and mayhap even a tray of pastries. He shifted with impatience.

"I believe every man but us has taken shelter," he observed. "We can be sure of privacy out here in this deluge."

Althalos cleared his throat self-importantly. "My news concerns Lady Ariana, the Countess of Darkmoor."

That caught Otto's attention. Suddenly he cared little for the rain or the discomfort it caused him. "What about her?" he asked sharply.

Gaius looked down, but the cold eyes of Sir Althalos remained fixed on Otto's face. "We have reason to believe she is working in league with our enemies."

"Never," Otto retorted, quelling a flare of protective anger. "What reason have you for making such an allegation?"

Gaius leaned towards him. "It is not conclusive, my lord."

"You can read her words for yourself." Althalos flung out a piece of parchment. "Here."

Within seconds the parchment would be drenched, rendering any words of Ariana's illegible, for better or worse. Otto snatched the parchment from Althalos, clumsy in his gauntlets. He sheltered the message as best he could with one hand, while straining to read it through the rivulets of falling rain. The message was short and made little sense to him.

He fixed Althalos with a stare. "What is this she refers to? The Rose of Kenmar?"

"'Tis a jewel of high value," Gaius spoke up. "A ruby, I believe."

"Taken from Kenmar?" Otto clenched his jaw, frustrated with the narrative.

"From the druids, after the battle of Branfeld," Althalos told him smoothly.

"And where is this jewel now?" Otto didn't know whether to rip the parchment to shreds or shield it from the rain. Part of him railed in anguish at the possibility that his bride had betrayed him, while another cautioned that a missive to her father was hardly a crime.

"It is safe in our vaults," Gaius said. "I had the guards make certain this morning." He ducked his head. "That is why I was absent from training."

Otto acknowledged his explanation with a brief nod. "If the jewel is safe, what case do you make against Lady Ariana?" He brandished the increasingly sodden parchment at Althalos.

His reedy uncle did not so much as flinch under Otto's steely gaze. "I intercepted this letter some days ago. At the time, like yourself, I thought little of it. But now, with the druid witch escaped and one of our own men killed, it is time to act."

Otto's scar began to ache. He fought against an urge to stride away across the courtyard, forcing his legs to remain still. "And what action do you suggest?" he asked through clenched teeth.

Althalos smiled slightly. "That is for you to say, my lord."

Otto would have liked nothing better than to strike the impertinent smirk from his face.

"It is no crime to write to her father," he voiced his thoughts out loud. "I have not forbidden it." He shrugged, eager to bring the conversation to a close.

"It is a crime to express intent to steal from our vaults," Althalos corrected him, his voice as smooth as honey.

"But she has not stolen anything," Gaius interjected, saving Otto the trouble.

Otto cast a quick glance at the older knight. He looked thoroughly uncomfortable, though whether that was due to the inclement weather or the difficult subject, or both, Otto could not tell.

"Not yet," Althalos said.

Otto could not contain a grimace of impatience. "I shall question her." He turned to leave, his chainmail suddenly grown heavy against him.

"She deserves more than mere questioning," Althalos spoke up, his voice dangerously loud. "It is not wise to leave a would-be traitor unpunished."

Otto restrained himself from grasping the man by his scrawny neck. "I shall be the one to decide if my wife deserves to be punished."

"It is widely known that one of our guards was killed when the druid witch was set free," Althalos pointed out with infuriating calmness. "Rumor is already rife among the knights. We must expect word to spread about the jewel soon enough. After all, Gaius here does not usually enquire as to the security of the vaults." He treated them to a thin-lipped smile which Otto was in no mood to return. "Mark my words." He dared to point a thin finger in his nephew's direction. "Your people will turn against you if they have the slightest reason to suspect you favor the girl from Kenmar over the safety of their own families."

Otto took a deep breath, damping down the tiny flame of self-doubt that Althalos had so cunningly ignited. "You are being ridiculous, uncle. The people of Darkmoor surely expect me to protect the interests of my own bride."

He saw immediately that he had played into Althalos's hands. His uncle's dark eyes glinted with triumph. "The people of Darkmoor expect you to uphold the knights' code, as instilled by your father. *Show no weakness. Show no mercy.* You know this better than anyone, Otto. Has some frenzied desire for this dark-haired wench overcome your sense and learning?"

Gaius reached out a restraining hand and Otto forced himself to stay rooted to the spot, though every inch of him burned with the wish to pummel his uncle to the ground.

"What would you suggest I do?" he asked for the second time.

Althalos took a moment to pretend to consider. "Traitor's Gate would be a step too far," he mused. "Mayhap the woman should be flogged?"

Otto shook off Gaius's hand. "The *Countess* will most certainly not be flogged," he said icily. "Anyone who lays a hand on her will have me to answer to. Is that clear?"

Gaius nodded quickly, but Althalos did not move. "What is your solution then, nephew? And I pray, do not let your youth and naivete blind you to what must be done. Peace in Darkmoor must be protected, at all costs." His eyes narrowed. "At the very least, the *Countess* should be locked up."

"Do not lecture me, Althalos," Otto replied, knowing that every word his uncle spoke was chipping away at his hard-won self-control. "I am the Earl of Darkmoor, and I will act in the best interests of my people." He gnashed his teeth together, the heat of his anger dispelling the chill of the rain. "Including my wife."

"The guards are already gathering," Gaius flung out, preventing Otto's departure.

Otto clenched his fist, frustration churning in his belly. He was seconds away from losing his composure. "Who gave the order?"

He didn't need to see the quick flicker of Gaius's eyes towards Althalos to know the answer.

"I thought it was wise." Althalos straightened his cloak. "My actions are only ever intended to assist you, Otto."

Otto bit down on his lower lip until he tasted the metallic tang of blood. "From now on, please assume that I have no further need of your assistance."

He delivered his words slowly and emphatically, before swiveling on his heel and finally taking his leave, his leather boots splashing through the puddled courtyard as he strode towards the keep. He needed to put as much distance between himself and Althalos as possible, else there was a real risk he might strike the man down. He allowed himself to imagine the moment, picturing the impact of his fist against his uncle's weak chin, seeing him fall to the ground. But then he shook his head to dispel the fancy. Otto was the one to favor peace over violence; it would be an ill start to his time as earl if he felled his father's only brother.

Gaius had been right to warn him. The castle guards were already gathering inside the hall, their heavy boots echoing on the stone floor. Several of them carried spears, with sharpened tips pointing up at the vaulted ceiling.

Spears, against a woman?

Otto broke into a jog which took him halfway up the staircase and clapped his hands together.

"Silence," he roared.

The assembled guard amounted to at least twenty men, all clad in the red tabard of Darkmoor bearing the rearing lion of the Sarragnacs. They stood sharply to attention at the sound of his voice.

"Well done for gathering with such speed," he called out, improvising quickly. "Your services are not required this day, but we all sleep more easily in our beds knowing we have the best guards in the North here in Darkmoor. You are dismissed."

A murmur of confusion rippled through the hall and Otto thought for a chilling moment that his words might be disobeyed, but then a tall man near the front held his spear aloft and dipped down onto one knee.

"Thank you, my lord."

He raised himself up and the guards filtered out of the hall behind him, moving as one. Otto exhaled with relief as the last of them marched out into the courtyard. But the trials of the morning were not yet over. He had bought but temporary reprieve for Ariana, and for himself. He did not pretend that Althalos was not capable of fanning the flames of rumor and discontent amongst his men. For some reason, his uncle had taken against his bride. And Ariana would not be safe inside the fortified walls of Darkmoor Castle until Otto had unpicked that reason.

In the quiet of the empty hall, Otto took a deep, calming breath and gazed up at the Sarragnac coat of arms, blazoned above the vast stone fireplace. A golden lion standing out on a background of rippling red. The lion represented strength, courage, and resilience.

Show no weakness; show no mercy.

Otto's scar began to itch as his mind raced from one conclusion to the next. His new bride was an honest young woman who deserved his protection.

His new bride had plotted against him and could yet undermine the tentative peace he'd won for Darkmoor.

He was the earl; he had no choice but to act against a potential thief and traitor. Althalos was right about that. Mayhap he was right about the rest. The people would turn against Otto if they saw him taking the coward's way out.

Otto knew a surge of anger at the thought. He could never countenance being seen as a coward. On a broiling tide of conviction, he stalked through the shadowed halls to the back of the keep, barely hesitating on the threshold of the morning room.

He flung open the door and strode inside, immediately conscious of his chainmail and muddy boots amongst the delicate furnishings.

Ariana was sitting in an upholstered chair by the window. She was dressed in a simple pale gown with her hair loose around her shoulders and as soon as he saw her, the fight drained away from him.

"Otto," she exclaimed, rising to her feet and smoothing her gown. "What a surprise."

A muscle twitched in his jaw. How he longed to walk over and take his bride in his arms. But could he trust her?

He folded his arms across his chest, coming to a halt in the center of the room. For a short while, all he could hear was the lashing of rain against the castle walls.

"It has been a morning full of surprises," he said, eventually.

He watched her expression change from pleasure to concern, spying another emotion at work behind her wide green eyes.

Guilt.

He knew it clear as day. And the knowledge sickened him, like a dog.

She broke her gaze, looking away from him out of the windows. He saw a new tension in her shoulders and his resolve hardened into ice.

"I am sorry to hear it," she faltered.

Her words were almost the undoing of his certitude, for he believed she spoke the truth. She was sorry. Her sorrow was evident in the downward cast of her eyes and the tremble in her voice.

"Aye," he said, briefly.

Was that a tear he saw shimmering in her eye?

In that moment, he could have stridden forward and taken her in his arms, kissing away her tears and asking for an explanation, husband to wife.

He could have asked her for the truth, and she might have told him.

But Otto didn't know how to show weakness. There was only one way to handle betrayal in Darkmoor, and that way didn't involve kisses and kind words. He was the earl. She had done him wrong. And he had already saved her from guards. He had no intention of compromising his position further.

"You must come with me," he stated firmly, lifting his chin and avoiding her anxious gaze.

"Where?" she asked tremulously.

He pointed to the door, insistent that she walk out ahead of him. "You shall see."

Chapter Fourteen

ARIANA WOULD NOT give Otto the satisfaction of hearing her rain her fists upon the fastened door, but as soon as his footfall faded from the stairwell, the tears she had been so valiantly holding back began to fall.

He had locked her in his tower. She was now a prisoner of the man she had begun to love. And his countenance had shown not the faintest glimmer of remorse for it. Had he uncovered details of how Ysmay had been rescued? Perchance one of the castle guards had kept watch on her progress all the while. If only she had told him the truth, when she had the chance.

"You have no reason to distrust me," he had said, out in the rose gardens. But she hadn't trusted him. Not enough.

What bitter irony that he had imprisoned her in the place they had first kissed.

Just days earlier, Ariana had stood over by the high window and experienced the dizzying sensation of stepping into Otto's arms for the first time. Now, those same arms were closed to her. Albeit, he hadn't struck her, nor even grasped her with any force, but she'd been all too aware of Otto's size and strength as they journeyed across the outer courtyard. Her puzzlement was quickly replaced by dread when she recognized their path and realized where he was taking her on this cold trek through the unending rain.

She was chilled to the bone, the hem of her gown sodden and slick with mud. Otto hadn't even allowed her a cloak, despite the ravages of the weather. Her hair was a tangle of knots from the howling wind, which had whipped around them as soon as they turned the corner from the keep. She had staggered to one side with the force of it, flinging out her hand in unconscious hope that he might steady her against him.

He had not.

He had not extended his hand once, neither in friendship nor chivalry. Certainly not with any love or respect for the woman he had embraced so tenderly after the Beltane Ball.

She had been a fool to believe that the Earl of Darkmoor was anything more than a cold-hearted warrior. The *Feared One*.

Should she fear him herself?

She spun around, taking in her new surroundings through the heavy blur of tears. The circular chamber was exactly as she remembered it, complete with a bare wooden table and two upholstered chairs pulled around an unlit fireplace. Dull light filtered through the clouds into the regularly spaced windows, but when night fell, she would be encased in darkness.

A prisoner.

A possession, not a person.

Her father had treated her as a commodity to be traded with. Now Otto was doing the same.

Shock and anger coursed through her limbs, chasing away the cold and dulling the edges of her despair, for now. She paced from the door to the opposite window, scanning the castle grounds for signs of activity, but the usually bustling walkways were unnaturally quiet, save the drumbeat of heavy rain and the whistle of the wind. Was it the inclement weather that kept everyone inside, or was the cause more sinister?

Her heart grew heavy. Mayhap she should have pushed aside her pride and asked Otto why exactly she was being punished in this way. If she had appealed to him, put her hand on his, might that have broken through his newly aloof exterior?

A sob escaped her, breaking the dam, within seconds she was doubled over with grief. Happiness had seemed within her grasp but now all was lost. Otto was every inch the man she had feared to marry. Hard as granite. Unfeeling. Unflinching. What had happened to the smiles and intimacy they had shared? They were lost to the wind, like a puff of smoke from a failing fire.

And it was, at least in part, her own fault.

Ariana gripped the window ledge as this realization settled heavily in her stomach. If she had only put her faith in Otto. Told him the truth, as he had so softly requested just hours earlier. It had been a golden opportunity. And she had squandered it.

She sniffed in a most unladylike fashion before dashing her tears away. Self-pity would not free her from this predicament. She must do what she had not been able to bring herself to before now: appeal to Otto's clemency.

She stood on her tiptoes and craned to identify a flash of red down by the outer door of the tower. The pouring rain made it difficult to see anything in detail, but after a few seconds she was satisfied that her suspicions were correct. Otto had installed a guard by the tower.

Immediately her remorse hardened into resentment. Was her husband so intent on keeping her prisoner that one locked door was not enough?

She stamped her foot in frustration, the wooden patten banging hollowly against the bare floor. His treatment was unjust, causing her newly opening heart to harden against him.

Wilting now, with cold and worry, Ariana turned from the window and threw herself down in one of the upholstered chairs. It creaked beneath her, offering little in the way of comfort. Ariana drew her knees up to her chest and hugged them with her arms, trying to retain what little warmth she still had.

There was nothing for her to do but wait.

SOMETIME LATER SHE was jilted awake by the distant sound of a door banging shut, followed by the tread of heavy footsteps ascending the spiral staircase.

Stiff and cold, Ariana held herself rigidly still in the chair, hardly daring to breathe. She must have slept, for night had fallen and brought darkness to her tower-top chamber. However, her slumber had brought little in the way of reprieve. She had never felt so awkward and sore. Her gown clung damply to her body, and she had a cramp in her legs from curling them tightly against her.

What fresh torment was coming her way now? She dared not hope for warmth nor blankets, much less food or water. Her stomach rumbled as soon as the thought presented itself, but her thirst was a more demanding concern.

The footsteps came closer, and she strained to make out the shape of the doorway, but the night was cloudy, and the moonlight offered little illumination. Ariana closed her lips over a whimper as she realized she would be entirely at the mercy of whomever was making their way towards her.

Let it be Otto, she prayed. Better the *Feared One* than some unknown knight of Darkmoor. Too late, she realized she should have sought to hide behind the door or under the table, though she would have been hard pressed to make them out in the gloom. She heard the turning of the key in the lock and shrank back against the chair as the door swung open, bringing in a blaze of light so bright she had to turn her head away.

A torch swung in an arch, coming to rest on her face. She heard a small grunt of acknowledgement, then the creak of the door closing shut.

"Ariana," said a familiar voice, gruff but not unkind.

She held a hand over her face, not yet accustomed to the light. Her squinting eyes recognized Otto, holding the torch aloft in one hand and a large sack in the other. In her state of nervous apprehension, the sack brought her a stab of fear.

He strode towards her, and she covered her face with her hands. "Please, leave me alone," she gasped. She had intended a command, but it came out as a plea.

His stride didn't falter, but nor did he touch her. After a while, Ariana peeked through her fingers to see that Otto was holding the torch to a bunch of dry kindling he'd positioned inside the grate. Moments later, the fire took hold with dancing flames bringing the promise of warmth. Otto sat back on his haunches and regarded his handiwork.

Slowly she lowered her hands, unable to resist the temptation to hold them out towards the warmth.

"Thank you," she murmured.

Otto stood up abruptly and walked away, giving her permission to slip off the chair and kneel closer to the fire, holding her sodden gown out towards the flames.

"Be careful," he warned from the far side of the room where he was fixing the torch to a bracket in the wall. "You'll be singed or worse, if you get too close." She sniffed, biting back a curt query about why he should care. "I brought you this," he added, returning to rifle inside the sack and draw out a woolen blanket. He shook it out and draped it over her legs.

The sudden warmth and unanticipated kindness brought fresh tears to her eyes, but she bit down on her lip and blinked them away, determined not to be so easily won over. What did it matter if Otto brought her a blanket when he had assumed the role of her goaler?

"What else do you have in there?" she asked instead.

"Bread, berries, and a flagon of small ale." He paused awkwardly. "And your charcoals."

He laid his offerings out on the table, making Ariana's mouth water in anticipation of food and drink, but she wouldn't give him the satisfaction of seeing how grateful she was.

"You bring enough to keep your prisoner in basic health," she observed tartly.

Otto cleared his throat. From the corner of her eye, she saw him fold his arms over his chest.

"Who said you were a prisoner?" he asked. There was an

edge to his voice, but Ariana couldn't decide if it stemmed from anger or regret.

"The fact you have stationed a guard by the outer door tells me as much." She looked away from him, focusing her gaze on the flickering yellow and orange flames. Despite her resentment, Otto's presence unsteadied her. In truth, she was tired and upset and longed for the comfort of his strong embrace.

Ridiculous, she told herself.

Otto appeared silently beside her. After a moment's hesitation, he knelt down next to the hearth, his body disturbingly close to hers. She could feel a new source of warmth radiating from him. His proximity made her pulse quicken and she drew the blanket more closely around her shoulders, conscious of her damp, clinging gown.

"The guard is a knight," he said, following her gaze into the fire. "His name is Gaius, and he is one of my most trusted men." He placed his hands behind him and leaned back against them. Through the orange light of the fire, she could make out a rasp of dark stubble coating his jaw.

"Forgive my ignorance," she spoke up, unable to keep the sarcasm from her tone. "You have stationed a trusted knight outside my door. That makes me feel so much better."

"It should," he countered, shifting his gaze to her face. She could feel the force of his glittering eyes, even though she looked resolutely away. "Gaius is not tasked with keeping you inside, Ariana. He is tasked with keeping others out."

Lazily, he picked up a nearby poker and rearranged the logs in the grate. The fire spat and crackled as Ariana digested his words.

"Why?" she asked. "Who in Darkmoor wishes to find me, to do me harm? No one here cares in the slightest about me." She clamped her lips shut, disliking the self-pity evident in her words.

Otto paused before answering. She held herself taut with anticipation that he may declare some feelings of his own towards her wellbeing, but he disappointed her.

"There are those in Darkmoor who are displeased with your actions," he stated, his voice even and calm.

It was no more than she feared, though her heart pounded in her chest to hear it said aloud.

"And you are amongst them?" Her breath caught in her throat as she awaited his answer.

"Alas, yes."

She waited for more, but Otto fell into silence.

"I'm sorry for it," she said, truthfully, her voice breaking over the words.

He angled his head towards her and again, she felt the scorching heat of his gaze. She looked down, nudging her hair forward to hide her expression, unable to find the strength to meet his eyes. Guilt and fear washed over her in equal measure. This was the golden opportunity she had been waiting for. Now was the time to speak up, to explain why she had rescued Ysmay and plead for clemency.

Had Otto been a man of normal size and stature, with a reputation for passivity, Ariana fancied she may have found the words. But despite his gentleness towards her, she could not dampen down the knowledge that this man, her husband, was a mighty warrior accustomed to showing no mercy. He was not a man to be crossed.

And she had crossed him.

Mayhap he didn't know for sure that she was the one to rescue Ysmay. Mayhap he only suspected it. Would her confession see her transported directly to Traitor's Gate?

As she looked into the flames, she decided it came down to one simple question; did she trust Otto?

She swallowed hard, her mind a quagmire of uncertainty.

Otto spoke up first. "You have not asked me why you are here." A slight tremor in his voice betrayed his investment in the conversation, but in all other aspects he appeared cool and composed. "I ordered you from the morning room and stationed you here, with neither food nor light, nor the comfort surely expected by the Countess of Darkmoor." He pronounced her title with deliberate slowness and Ariana felt goosebumps break out on her arms. "And you ask nothing?" Hot tears formed in the corners of her eyes as he jumped to his feet in frustration. "Damnation, Ariana. Can't you see how this speaks of your guilt? Your complicity?"

A searing pain lodged itself in her heart. Ariana bent her head and allowed the tears to flow. "I am guilty," she said, the admission tearing from her in a rush.

He took a pace backwards, reeling in surprise. "I didn't want to believe it."

She clenched her hands together, willing to beg for clemency in that moment. "Otto, I never wanted to deceive you."

She forced herself to look up at him, to see the betrayal lodge in his dark eyes. He stood with one hand fastened in his unruly hair, his legs wide apart. "What am I to do with you?" he asked, seeming to pose the question more to himself.

"I'm sorry." She wanted to get up and stand beside him, but she didn't trust that her aching legs had the strength in them.

Otto took a deep breath and Ariana grasped comfort in the fact that he hadn't shouted, hadn't struck out in anger, hadn't even turned away from her. This was her moment to explain herself. All she had to be was honest. After all, she had every wish to be a proper wife to Otto, an honorable Countess of Darkmoor.

"I'm sorry, too," he said bitterly.

"Otto, please." She pushed herself up, trying to ignore the shooting pains in her cramped thighs.

"No." he held up a hand, warning her away. "Don't, Ariana. Not yet."

"I must." She abandoned all notions of pride and dignity. Suddenly it was clear that the only thing that mattered was Otto's belief in her integrity. "I should have told you before."

He shook his head, still flinching away from her. "How would that have helped? How could any man countenance his wife going in league with her father against him?"

She had opened her mouth to explain, but Otto's words left her bewildered. "I have never been in league with my father," she protested. "Not even as a child." She held her palms up towards him, pleasingly.

He grasped her arm and pushed it away. The first time he had ever touched her unkindly. "Do not lie to me, Ariana."

"I'm not lying." She bit down on her lip, knowing she must persevere despite his displeasure. But as she staggered to her feet, the resonant clanging of the warning bell sounded through the castle walls, its deep, penetrating tone obliterating all other concerns. She heard Otto inhale sharply, but he had moved into the shadowy recess of the chamber, and she could no longer see his face. "What's happening?"

"I don't know." He strode over to the window and looked out. Just then, she heard the lower door of the tower bang open and a torrent of running footsteps come up the stairs. "Gaius?" he called, questioningly.

The tall, gray-haired knight burst into the room, scarcely acknowledging Ariana. "My lord Otto," he spluttered. "The outer walls are breached. Soldiers bearing the colors of Kenmar are already within the castle grounds."

Otto dragged a hand through his hair. "Already inside? How is that possible?"

Gaius turned to the side, avoiding Ariana's desperate gaze. "Someone must have let them in."

Ariana felt winded. How could her father's men be so foolish as to penetrate Darkmoor Castle? It would be a suicide mission. Even taken by surprise, Otto's knights would easily overpower any so-called warriors from Kenmar.

Otto's gaze slid from Gaius to her. She felt rather than saw the force of passion in his eyes. "Ariana," he said slowly, "are you behind this?"

Her shock turned to anger. "I have been locked up here all day."

His expression did not change. "I must go to my men. But when I return, I shall expect an explanation."

Chapter Fifteen

"I HAVE YOUR horse ready for you, my lord." Robin, the young page, handed Otto his shining helm as soon as he and Gaius appeared in the outer courtyard.

They had run all the way from the tower, keenly aware that every second held vital importance. Otto caught his breath as he paused to consider his next move, holding his arms out to receive the heavy chainmail which Robin fastened around him. His mind was whirring with regret and betrayal. Surely this invasion proved that the one person in Darkmoor who he thought he could trust had turned out to be working against him. Realization cut through him like the sharpest blade, leaving wounds that would fester for many moons to come.

Otto stretched his hand inside his gauntlet reflexively. This was no time to be thinking of Ariana. He must concentrate all his wits and energy on the battle ahead. Sir Leon's men had the advantage of surprise, but the knights of Darkmoor were an elite group of highly trained warriors. The situation could still be turned around if he moved quickly and cleverly.

Otto nodded his thanks to his page. "Are the knights already assembled?" he asked Gaius.

"Aye, sir. They headed to the meeting point at the first sound of the warning bell." Gaius sheathed his sword and turned to his own waiting horse.

Otto sprung up onto his battle charger, the spirited animal half rearing beneath him. "Let's go," he said shortly. They both knew there was no time to lose. Together, they clattered over the cobbles and through an ivy-strewn archway to the knights' meeting point. Already the sounds of the battle were growing closer. Otto clenched his jaw at the familiar clash of steel on steel, the shouts of victory and the sickening groans of the injured.

Ten knights bearing the distinctive crimson colors of Darkmoor were waiting for him, their armor gleaming in the darkness, their horses snorting in anticipation. Otto held up his hand, commanding the attention of all.

"Your speedy arrival does you credit," he said, speaking quietly but forcefully. "Tonight, much will be asked of you in the service of Darkmoor. Enemies are within our very walls; threatening everything we hold dear." His horse pranced beneath him, splashing in puddles caused by the afternoon's downpour. Otto took a tighter hold of his reins and flipped up the visor of his helmet so he could better see his men. Drizzle fell like a gauzy blanket, muffling sound and making everything shine in the torchlight "We do not know how many we face. We do not know how many of our soldiers are already fallen. All we know is this, the enemy must be defeated. We fight, for the honor and glory of Darkmoor."

His knights cheered as one, Gaius amongst them. Otto spun around in the saddle to face the encroaching battle. Once they were out over the drawbridge, who knew what carnage they would discover? He looked back at his knights, their red cloaks fanning about them in the evening's breeze. "Gaius and Edmund, I want you to go quietly through the western gates to approach the enemy from the rear. With luck, they will be focused on our attack. You'll be able to pick them off, one by one."

"Very good, my lord." Gaius nodded to the tall, red-haired knight by his side and together, they split off from the group.

"The rest of you, on me." Otto pointed forward with his sword and dug his spears into his horse's side. The animal broke into a canter, moving quickly over the drawbridge and out into the unknown. Otto led his small band of knights as he had done on countless occasions. He sat tall in the saddle, knowing that all warriors, however strong and experienced, take courage from the one in the front.

Show no weakness; show no mercy.

The knights' code had been writ for occasions such as this. Darkmoor must prevail, especially against such dishonorable opponents who struck without just cause or fair warning.

Somewhere to their left, a dog howled in misery and a gust of wind brought a splatter of rain through Otto's visor. He blinked away the raindrops, pricking his ears for clues as to where the enemy were situated.

A clue came with the piercing whistle of overhead arrows. Otto had no sooner shouted a warning than he heard the sickening thud of one of them meeting its mark. From the corner of his eye, he saw the knight diagonally behind him clutch at his chest, then fall to the side, heavy as a rock. As he tipped over, his helm came off to reveal a shock of brown curls.

Otto's heart sank into his leather boots. *Not young Benedict.*

He yanked hard at the reins, but his horse had already carried him far from the fallen boy, and Otto knew that this could well be the first of many casualties amongst his men. Still, sorrow for the senseless death washed over him as his horse bolted forward. Just days earlier, he had spared young Benedict in the joust, only for the young squire to take a fatal arrow the first time he rode out to battle.

His burgeoning grief hardened into fierce resolve as the shouts of fighting grew nearer. He would wield his revenge on Sir Leon of Kenmar, whatever it took.

Soon he was amongst a sea of bodies, thrusting with his sword and battering would be attackers away with his shield. His horse snorted and reared as the deafening clang of steel on steel filled the night air. He clamped his thighs around the saddle, holding himself steady as he bent low over the horse's neck to deliver a fatal blow to an enemy knight. The metallic tang of blood mixed with the earthy scent of wet mud and hot horseflesh assaulted his nostrils as he pushed through the fray. Otto's mind was fixed solely on the task in hand, and he carved up the encroaching army with deft flashes of his sword. He had been raised to fight like this. Man on man. Sword on sword. A splintering whinny broke through the battle cries as a horse crashed onto its side. His own horse stumbled, and Otto knew a thrill of alarm as the muddy ground rose up to meet him, but he drove down into the saddle and shifted his weight backwards, allowing his charger to recover her footing with seconds to spare. Otto plunged his sword into the chest of a man on a magnificent towering beast beside him. In another moment, the man would have swung his sword and sliced straight into Otto.

High overhead, the clouds shifted, and a sudden burst of moonlight illuminated the battleground. Otto had forced his way through the melee to come out on the other side, where Gaius and Edmund, as instructed, were making short work of taking out the straggling Kenmar soldiers.

He twisted around in the saddle to survey the scene. Billowing red outnumbered the purple. Darkmoor had the advantage.

His sword arm throbbed, and his ribs ached, where someone had jammed the hilt of their sword into his side before Otto swiftly dispatched them. But it was not yet time to rest. He knew he must ride back into the heat of the battle and help his knights finish the job. Before he could turn his horse around, a glint of steel far off in the distance caught his eye. Focusing his gaze onto the rolling hills to the east, he spied a lone figure on horseback, a plume of purple helmet feathers giving his identity clear away.

Sir Leon of Kenmar.

His wife's father.

Otto gathered his reins, hatred boiling in his gut. The man was a no-good coward, attacking would-be allies under the cover of darkness and sending his men off to fight while he stayed safe atop a distant hill.

How Otto would love to gallop over to him, right now, and challenge Sir Leon to one-on-one combat. His pulse raced with temptation as the sour taste of malice filled his mouth. The idea of slicing into the man who had ordered his father's death was hard to deny. But he must. If he rode away and abandoned his knights to pursue his own ambitions, he'd be little better than a coward himself.

Channeling all his rage into a roar of determination, Otto pressed his horse back into the blood-soaked throng.

No more than an hour later, the skirmish was over. What remained of Sir Leon's army had fled into the hills. The Darkmoor castle guards rounded up a dozen torn and bloody prisoners and Otto ordered them to the dungeons; he would question them tomorrow.

As Robin led his tired horse back to the stables, Otto tossed his helm aside and sank down onto a low wall. He tilted back his head to look up at the magnificent fortress which had successfully withstood yet another assault. The familiar granite stone was illuminated with pools of light from numerous flaming torches affixed to the pillars. He had defended his home, his lands, and his title today, but had his instinctive trust of Ariana brought danger to his people?

His heart ached more than the bloody gash in his side, and he waved away the physician when he came bustling over to tend his wounds.

"It is nothing but a scratch, Merek," he stated calmly. "Others need your ministrations more than I." The memory of Benedict floated through his mind, and he put up a muddy hand to scratch at his scar. "Have the bodies of our dead been recovered?" He forced out the question.

"It is underway, my lord." Merek bowed his head.

"See they receive the proper rites." Otto sighed. There was still much to be done out here in the courtyard, but he could not properly dedicate himself to his duties before he had confronted the woman who had brought such treachery to their gates.

"Of course." Merek hesitated. "If I may say, my lord, you appear out of sorts. Shall I prepare you a restorative draught?"

Otto waved his hand. "Perchance later, Merek. I need my wits about me for now."

On tired legs, he walked through the darkness to the back of the castle. His mind played a spool of images from the short time he and Ariana had spent together. He saw her tremulous smile and her cascade of dark hair, he recalled how they had ridden down to the river, conversing easily as friends, then coming together instinctively as lovers. He had been impressed by her courage from the first; but her nerves of steel had been employed to the betterment of his enemies.

How could she have betrayed him so?

At the bottom of the tower, Otto paused, leaning an elbow against the rough stone. He closed his eyes and felt his body sway like the trunk of a young tree. He was bone weary and despairing. Most bitter of all was the realization that his cold-hearted uncle had been right all along.

Perchance Althalos was right about everything, not just Ariana. Mayhap the men questioned his leadership, thinking him soft. The events of the past day had certainly given credence to such allegations. His father's earlship had never been challenged from within, never so much as queried.

Show no weakness; show no mercy.

Was this the only way to rule after all?

Otto would have to embrace the code, else face Darkmoor turning to chaos, just as Sir Althalos had predicted.

Unable to swallow down his rage, he beat his fist upon the heavy wooden door, starting back in surprise when it swung noiselessly open. Immediately, he was on high alert. He'd left orders for this door to remain locked and bolted. Even with his best men fighting at the castle gates, his bride should not have been left undefended.

Cautiously he lifted a flaming torch from a nearby wall and shouldered the open door aside. All was quiet in the stairwell; the stone steps rose silently upwards just as they always had. Breathing softly, and cursing the ache in his ribs, he began to ascend.

He was less than halfway up when he realized something was wrong. Even with the light from his torch, the stairs were too bright. That could mean just one thing; the upper door was open.

Swallowing down instinctive panic, he broke into a jog, bursting into the tower room with a roar of rage intended to intimidate anyone still lurking inside.

But he didn't have to search the chamber to know that it was empty. The fire he had lit earlier still flickered in the grate; its embers glowing a deep orangey red which cast shadows up the walls. He swung his torch towards the table, noting the half-eaten meal of bread and fruit sitting beside an unfurled parchment. Had Ariana left in something of a hurry? The blanket he'd brought her was abandoned on the bare floor. He picked it up, wishing some narrative of the night's events could be gleaned from its folds.

"You're a fool," he said aloud, sitting heavily on the nearest chair. He didn't need anything or anyone to explain what had happened here. It was clear enough.

Ariana had stayed loyal to Kenmar; she'd been plotting tonight's escapade long before exchanging marriage vows with Otto. Although she must have been working with an accomplice, he mused. One who opened the gates to receive the soldiers and told them where to find her. The fact that Sir Leon's forces had been defeated did not in any way lessen the fact of her betrayal.

Otto's fist clenched around the blanket. To think that he had softened towards her. Just hours earlier, he had dreamed of a future for them, together.

He had dreamed of a new way to rule Darkmoor.

Up until this moment, he'd been but a boy, full of naïve fancies. Now he was a man, ready to put his innocent hopes aside, determined to defend his people and his lands against all who intended harm. He would embrace the lessons espoused by his father, a warrior earl who had given his life for his lands.

And if he ever saw Ariana again, she would regret crossing the Earl of Darkmoor. No matter how his heart still pined for her.

Chapter Sixteen

THE FIRST PINK rays of dawn had just begun to penetrate the heavy darkness of the forest as Ariana was forcibly carried across the gushing river which denoted the boundary of Darkmoor lands. She half-hoped the horse beneath her would slip and fall, but he was sure-footed and confident, splashing through the shallows with barely a moment's hesitation. Her heart sank as he scrambled up the opposite bank, taking her officially beyond the outer reaches of Otto's domain.

The last time Ariana had ridden on horseback, she'd been journeying to a much smaller, prettier river, with Otto by her side. Such excitement had darted through her belly on that occasion. She'd sat tall in the saddle; thrilled to find her husband's glittering dark eyes focused on her, daring to flick back her hair and hold his gaze. Back then, the future was painted bright with possibility. How could it be that mere days later, she was reduced to circumstances such as this?

Ariana was sitting astride a muddy cob, whose short stride jolted her at every step. Her hands were bound behind her, making balancing in the saddle almost impossible. Her thighs were chaffed and sore; the simple gown she'd been wearing in the tower proving thoroughly impractical as riding attire. At least her captors had provided her with a dark cloak; though Ariana suspected this was more for the purpose of concealment than comfort against the nighttime chill.

There were three of them ahead of her and at least twice as

many behind. While they had been within striking distance of Darkmoor Castle, she'd entertained plans of slipping down her horse's back and making a mad dash for it. But she'd known then that her chances of success were minimal, and now that they had left Otto's lands, those chances had diminished further. She'd be caught within moments. And the Kenmar guard had shown no reluctance to handle her roughly even when she'd put up no resistance. She shivered to think what they might do to her if she attempted to flee their control.

It felt as if she had been captive for days, but in reality, it was just a few hours since she'd been bundled out of her tower-top chamber. What a fool she'd been to walk straight into the hands of her enemies, assuming so naively that the footsteps coming up the tower steps belonged to Otto. She'd turned to face him with a smile, relief spreading through her that the skirmish at the outer gates was over so quickly. But the man who appeared at her chamber door was a head shorter than her husband, with greasy hair and cold eyes which shone with momentary triumph as soon as he spied her.

Sir Althalos. All along, he'd been her adversary. But she had never anticipated him betraying Otto, his own flesh and blood.

"She's here," he'd called over his shoulder.

With shock coursing through her, Ariana had stayed still and unmoving as three burly soldiers came marching up the stairs and through the door, making the chamber seem small with their muscles and height. She didn't need to look closely to know that these men did not answer to Otto. Their scuffed armor and ill-disciplined air gave them away as much as their shabby purple cloaks; they were her father's men, soldiers from Kenmar.

Sir Althalos was working with them.

Otto's own uncle was a traitor to Darkmoor. Ariana's mouth had opened to scream, but before any sound could come out, an evil-smelling rag was stuffed inside it, making her gag and retch.

"Don't give us any trouble, milady," the largest of them advised. "We're in short temper and who knows what dangers might befall a lady like you on the road?"

She wanted to spit out that she was her father's daughter; once the first lady of Kenmar. How dare these soldiers treat her with such disrespect? But fear had already lodged deep inside her stomach. Fear laced with a bitter acknowledgement that her father had never exhibited concern for her welfare, even when she'd been a small child. She had always been little more than a bargaining chip for Sir Leon, her marriage to Otto was proof of that. Now, as Countess of Darkmoor, she would have slid even further down the ranks of priorities for a man consumed by avarice.

Her horse bounded down a muddy path towards a silted-up stream and Ariana bounced uncomfortably in the saddle. If only her hands could be released, then she could balance herself with the reins or a fistful of the cob's coarse mane. But even if she could summon the courage to ask, it would be no good as her mouth was still bound up with the gag. Salty tears stung her eyes, making her vision blur. With every step they took, the prospects of rescue by Otto's knights became smaller. Though even as that distant hope presented itself to her, she dismissed it.

Otto must believe she had allied with her father against him. When he had asked her for the truth, he hadn't been referring to her rescue of Ysmay. He'd even told her directly that the druid's escape was of little consequence to him. But she hadn't listened.

With her back aching and her eyes blinded by tears, Ariana realized the full extent of her stupidity. All of those opportunities she'd had to speak up, confess her crime, and beg his forgiveness. Every one of them squandered. And now, she must face this ordeal alone, without her protector. Otto would not mount a rescue for a woman he considered a traitor.

One of the men upfront turned in his saddle and shouted to the rest.

"We'll halt a while here."

Ariana tried to blink away her tears as her cob was led from the path into a small copse of tall trees. Around her, the men dismounted heavily, talking in low voices and swigging from leather pouches of wine. She was ignored, but that was better than the alternative. Her horse lowered its head to crop at the fresh grass and she sat silently, a mere passenger, her senses growing dull from weariness and sorrow.

Minutes passed. The sun was rising in earnest now, casting a rosy glow over the forest of Kenmar. Ariana was not familiar with every acre of her father's lands; but this part she recognized as a favorite haunt of the druids. Fluttering, faded ribbons around an overhead branch confirmed her suspicions. She had played here as a child, picking berries and climbing trees, happy to be away from the disapproving glare of the Kenmar court. The recent rain cast a shimmering hue of moisture over the canopy of leaves overhead. Before her tired eyes, the greenery seemed to dance in the morning light.

She risked a glance back to her tormentors, who had now formed a tight little group and were talking avidly, taking regular swigs of rich wine and wiping away the residue with calloused hands. The air smelled fresh and clean, suddenly full of tantalizing possibilities.

She could urge her horse onwards. They would be gone in minutes. Mayhap these rough, untrained soldiers would fail to find her amongst the maze of trees and thick gorse. She could make her way to the druid camp and seek shelter there. The possibility of escape seized her by the throat, she must take her chance.

Cautiously, she nudged the cobb with her stockinged heels, her lips pressed together as she silently cursed her impractical attire. Her pattens had long since slipped off her feet and the animal's coarse hair made him less responsive to her cues, especially when he was grazing so determinedly. Greatly daring, she risked a sharp kick, gratified when the horse raised his head, pricked his ears, and launched forward into the undergrowth.

Her heart pounded so loudly she feared her captors would hear as they made lurching progress beneath the trees. She ducked forward over the horse's neck, wincing as water droplets fell down her neck, yet rejoicing at the realistic possibility of freedom. No shouts of warning came from the slovenly soldiers; they had not yet noticed their prisoner's absence. All she needed was a little more time.

A flock of crows took flight, squawking and flapping their wings. Her horse shied to the side, nearly throwing her from the saddle, but worst of all was the cry that went up from the copse.

"She's gone."

Frantically, she urged the horse forward with her legs, having no recourse to use her hands or her voice. The animal broke into a trot and she pressed herself against his hairy neck, fearful of the branches whipping past her head. Her cloak snagged on a bramble, and she heard a tear as the fabric ripped. But the cloak was thick and sturdy, it did not give easily enough, and the next moment Ariana found herself pulled backwards in the saddle. Had she been holding the reins, she could have righted herself easily enough, but with her hands tied behind her, the small pull of resistance was enough to unseat her. With a muffled shout of alarm, she tumbled from the horse's back into the sharp prickles of a gorse bush.

Pain ripped through her cheek and wrists, and the sting of blood mixed with the salt of her tears as she struggled to her feet. She could still escape. It might even be easier on foot. She could run and hide, fling herself into a ditch and cover her cloak with dried leaves as she'd known the druids to do. She darted forward, unsteady with her hands still bound, and wincing at the sharp press of twigs beneath her feet. She spun around the trunk of a mighty tree and barreled straight into the unyielding chest of one of her captors.

"Where do you think you're going?" He grabbed a fistful of hair and pulled back her head, leering down at her. She smelled the sourness of his breath as her mind raced for a way to escape his clutches. But it was no good; he held her in a vice-like grip, she'd be a fool to struggle against him.

Instead, she forced herself to be still, raising her head and meeting his eyes. She mumbled through the dirty rag, knowing he wouldn't understand her.

"I've got her," he shouted back towards the copse. "What will we do with her?" he enquired, as one-by-one his fellow soldiers trooped towards them.

"Put her back on the horse," said the man she'd identified as their ringleader.

"The horse has gone," replied her captor.

Ariana held onto hope that they may yet remove the filthy rag from her mouth, to hear her side of the story, but they had little interest in conversing with her. All they cared about was transporting her back to Kenmar like a haul of timber. She'd already decided to blame her horse. She would claim it had carried her off into the trees, with her unable to either change its path or sound an alert. But her excuse was unnecessary. She had no more autonomy than a dull, senseless animal.

The ringleader swore, then spit on the damp ground. "She'll have to come up with me then." He took a step closer, and she couldn't help flinching away from the strong, unwashed aroma wafting from him. "I'll keep a tight hold of you, milady."

Guffaws of laughter greeted his words. Ariana found herself with a strong man at either side of her, gripped by the arms and all but carried back through the forest to the waiting horses. They made short work of throwing her up onto the ringleader's saddle. Her skirts rose up around her thighs, scarcely covered by the torn cloak, but there was nothing she could do about it. The soldier hauled himself up behind her, clamping an iron arm around her waist and breathing hard onto her neck.

"Don't try anything else, Lady Ariana," he whispered menacingly. "I've never yet had a countess." His other hand danced a deliberate path upwards from her knee and Ariana knew a further clutch of fear as his dirty fingers wandered beneath the hem of her gown. "We've had orders to deliver you unharmed, as far as possible. But who's to say what's possible all the way out here?"

More tears seeped from the corner of her eyes, but thankfully the man removed his hand to snatch at the reins. "Let's go," he called to his men, and they set off at a canter towards the sloping path leading out of the forest towards the castle of Kenmar.

Ten days later…

"My lady, you must eat something."

Ariana forced open her eyes, dimly recognizing the small, stout figure of Chiara, the castle cook, at the foot of her bed.

"I'm not hungry," she croaked through dry lips. It was true, the very idea of food made her stomach churn and she'd had nothing to break her fast even though the sun was high in the sky, casting determined pools of light into her narrow, cheerless childhood bedchamber.

Chiara wrung her hands in her stained apron, tutting loudly. "But you've hardly eaten a thing since coming here. And you always had such a healthy appetite as a child."

Ariana forced herself onto her elbows, blinking in the dappled sunlight filtering through the shutters. The chamber was bare save her narrow bed, a singular wooden closet, a rickety nightstand and a footstool pulled up near the window. "You speak as if I am a guest," she grumbled, shielding her eyes as she accidentally moved into a burst of light. "Close the shutters more firmly, please Chiara." She couldn't bear to glimpse the outside world and know that life was carrying on beyond these cold walls.

"I will not." Chiara stood up tall, letting her apron fall to her sides. "It's not right, you up here all alone in the darkness, sending back every plate of food barely touched. You'll fall ill."

"It doesn't matter." Ariana sank back onto the thin mattress; the small effort of conversation having exhausted her strength. "It is probably what my father wishes, truth be told."

She closed her eyes, opening them again when a sudden dip in the mattress indicated Chiara had perched next to her. She smelled of sweet pastry and flour and warmth, and Ariana had to fight down a new surge of sorrow at such homely comforts.

"I'd say it's not clear to anyone what Sir Leon wishes right now," she said in a confidential tone. "Not even to Sir Leon himself. All his plans have come to naught."

Ariana shook her head, conscious of the wild tangle of her unbrushed hair on the hard pillows. How could she explain that she wasn't interested in her father's plans? When she first arrived back in Kenmar, she had brimmed with defiance, determined to find a way back to Otto. But after just one failed attempt to escape, her energies had dissipated. For three days now, she had not even risen from her bed; a prisoner of twisting nausea and bleak regret.

Chiara cleared her throat, obviously intent on saying her piece, despite Ariana's silence. "It was a bold move, storming Darkmoor Castle."

"Bold or stupid," Ariana interjected, unable to help herself.

"That's exactly it. Sir Leon was expecting more in the way of assistance, which could have made all the difference." Chiara shifted on the bed and Ariana wriggled in protest. "Will you let me brush your hair, my lady? Seeing as I'm here."

"You're a cook, not a lady's maid," Ariana stated. "Chiara, I'm grateful for your concern, but I'd like to be left alone."

Chiara continued as if she hadn't spoken, forcibly rearranging Ariana's pillows with surprisingly strong arms.

"That's better," she observed, helping her to a more comfortable position. "Well now, where was I?"

"I don't know." The sudden movement had made Ariana dizzy, and she lurched forward, fearful she might vomit. Thankfully she had nothing in her stomach, but she retched anyway, the dim walls of her bedchamber circling around as she gripped onto her thin blanket and waited for the pain to stop.

She heard rather than saw Chiara cross the floor and pour

some water from her pitcher. Moments later, a cold compress was applied to her forehead, bringing slight relief.

"Sit back," the cook urged, steadying Ariana's shoulders with her small, calloused hands.

"I feel terrible," Ariana murmured. Her body was hot one minute and cold the next. It had been that way since the marshal thwarted her attempts to steal out of the keep by hiding amongst the weekly wash. A fine plan, she had thought, until she found herself being bodily lifted from the stained linens to meet her father's unflinching gaze. Since then, Sir Leon had ordered her to be locked in her room.

Chiara pressed her lips together and made a noncommittal noise. "You don't look none too clever either, if I may say so."

Her honesty made Ariana smile. That failed bid for freedom had been the last time she had left her chamber, even though Sir Leon had grudgingly given word that she should be allowed outside once a day. Racked with nausea, she had taken little interest in anything. But part of her now railed against this inertia. She had learned long ago that there was nothing to be gained by moping.

"You may brush out my hair, as long as you take it slowly."

"Very good. It's about time someone saw to you." Chiara took up the hairbrush and carefully began to draw out the tangles. "Sir Leon's at a loss, you see?" She abruptly returned to her earlier conversation.

Ariana closed her eyes, half enjoying the soothing rhythm of the hairbrush. "Honestly, Chiara, my father kidnapped me and locked me up, for reasons I don't yet understand. It's hard for me to care if he's at a loss."

"I'm not saying you should care. I'm saying you shouldn't give up hope." She paused, gazing down at Ariana with meaning stamped across her blue eyes. "Especially now."

Ariana fumbled for the tankard of small ale kept on her nightstand and drank deeply, partially to avoid the question she sensed would come next.

"How long have you known?" Chiara asked.

Ariana straightened her blanket, desperate for distraction, but the two women were at the top of the keep and unlikely to be disturbed. "I don't know anything, not for sure. Not really." She closed her eyes against another swell of nausea. "It's too early."

"Well, I've seen this before." The cook smoothed a hand across her forehead. "I'd wager you're with child, my lady. That's why you can't bring yourself to eat even a morsel. The early days can be the worst for sickness. But you must keep your strength up. You'll need it in the months ahead."

"I don't want it to be true." She leaned back against the wooden headrest, uncaring of the hard ridges which dug into her scalp.

Chiara looked shocked. "Why ever not? A babe is a blessing."

"I know. I've always wanted children of my own. But not like this. Not far from my husband. A good man who thinks I betrayed him." At this, the tears came again, and Ariana hung her head. Her eyes were sore from constant crying.

Chiara knitted her brows. "Does anyone else know?"

"No." Ariana shook her head violently. "I've barely even admitted it to myself."

The cook folded her arms nervously, her foot tapping against the bare floor. "But time is passing. The maids will find out soon enough. And they'll report it to Sir Leon. You must keep it from them for as long as possible."

Ariana sniffed and dried her eyes with the back of her hand. She hadn't had such a long conversation in weeks and the constant flow of information was tiring her out. "Why?" she asked, shrugging expansively. "Why should my father care if I am pregnant with Otto's child?" But even as she said the words, the answer loomed large in her mind. "God's Bones." She reached out to grasp Chiara's hand. "If my father plans to take over Darkmoor and I, his prisoner, am carrying the rightful heir to Darkmoor…"

"That's a mighty prize for Sir Leon," Chiara finished for her.

"It will strengthen his position and make matters worse, won't it?"

The cook nodded reluctantly. "That's what I fear."

Ariana's apathy and exhaustion disappeared in a heartbeat. She fought an urge to leap out of bed and stride up and down the narrow room, so great was her agitation. But she couldn't face another bout of nausea, so she stayed still on the uncomfortable bed she'd known since childhood. "Tell me what you know," she urged.

Chiara settled herself once more on the side of the mattress. "In truth I know little," she admitted, "only what rumors go round the servant's quarters. But I know that Sir Leon had an ally on the inside of Darkmoor Castle."

"An ally which my husband believes to be me," Ariana interrupted hotly.

Chiara grimaced. "This ally was meant to have troops ready and waiting to join Sir Leon's assault. Only when he stormed the castle, there were no extra troops. Only those men that Sir Leon had taken with him. And they weren't strong enough to withstand the knights of Darkmoor."

Ariana knew a rush of pride in Otto and his highly trained knights, but her mind was already racing ahead of her. "It was Sir Althalos. The brother of the old earl," she added, seeing Chiara's blank face. "He must have double-crossed Father at the last minute."

Chiara picked up the hairbrush and resumed her ministrations to Ariana's hair. "Be that as it may, it's left Sir Leon in a quandary. For what can he do? He were expecting to be overlord of both Kenmar and Darkmoor by now, but instead he's holed up here, on high alert for retaliation."

"Otto may not retaliate for some time," Ariana ruminated. She knew him to be clever in all aspects of warfare. He'd attack when his enemy least expected it.

Although why had he not sought revenge already, she pondered?

Mayhap because revenge, on this occasion, would be closely

entwined with rescue.

And mayhap he did not wish to stage a rescue.

Ariana told herself the tears pricking at her eyes were a result of Chiara's comb encountering a particularly stubborn tangle. "I fancy your father was wanting to use you as bait, to lure the earl here, if he didn't manage to finish him off in the battle." Chiara spoke conversationally, as if what they were discussing had no more importance than the pie she was cooking for luncheon. "What gives me hope is that he's keeping you here, in your own chamber. Not the dungeons. He's a hard man, Sir Leon, but deep down, he's still your father."

"You mean he may let me go free?" Ariana raised her eyebrows.

"Who knows what that man may do, besides drink himself into a stupor? I'm praying for him to do right by you. But there's no denying that the babe complicates things. Mayhap your best chance is for the Earl of Darkmoor to come here and retrieve his bride."

"Otto will never come to rescue me, not while he believes me a traitor." She swallowed down her pain.

Chiara's face creased with compassion. "I'll not say as I was pleased to hear of your marriage to the *Feared One*. But I can see you've grown attached to him. I'd hope you've also grown accustomed to better than this." She looked pointedly around the sparsely furnished room.

"I have. I had. He was never anything but kind to me. But what good will it do?" Ariana felt flattened by her lack of hope.

"It never does any harm to have a fierce warrior on your side. An earl no less." Chiara nudged her shoulder. "We know not what the future holds, milady." Her face fell. "Only that, once your father learns you're carrying the heir to Darkmoor, there's no chance he'll let you go free." She placed the hairbrush down on the nightstand with trembling fingers and pressed her hands together as if in prayer. "You must hope and pray Otto Sarragnac finds it in his heart to forgive you for whatever he thinks you've done, and soon as well. Else you may never escape Sir Leon."

Chapter Seventeen

A FINE RAIN fell over Darkmoor, despite the approach of midsummer. It seemed it was always raining, ever since Ariana's betrayal and the painful loss of three good men, including young Benedict. Otto strode through the outer courtyard, accustomed to his hard leather boots splashing through puddles and the fine layer of drizzle which clung to his hair. Chickens clucked in his path, and he spun on his heel to avoid them. Nothing must slow him down. If he didn't make it over the drawbridge before the cock crow, the demands of the day would claim him. Today the castle court was sitting, and Otto, as earl, must preside over proceedings. He would be detained in the great hall for many hours, dispensing justice in a matter of a stolen foal, some purloined coin, and a cheating wife. The latter case, he could well do without.

But he would fulfil his role to the best of his ability. He only needed an hour or two first, to walk and to breathe and to forget. This regular morning exercise was a recent habit, discovered through a combination of insomnia and bottled-up grief. A brisk walk up a steep path helped lend an air of calmness and grace to the rest of his day.

On this gray, unprepossessing morning, he was headed to the Caldon Hills which lay behind the castle. It would be faster on horseback, but then he would have to trouble the stableboys and wait for his horse to be made ready. On foot, Otto only had to rely on himself.

As he walked, he looked from left to right, assessing the condition of his lands and property. All looked well in Darkmoor. Walls stood strong and upright and plenty of lush grass grew in the pastures to feed the livestock. If this godawful rain didn't stop soon, this year's harvest would be threatened, but there was still time for nature to smile upon them.

His pulse quickened as he began to climb up the rough earthen path, his boots slipping occasionally on the loose ground. Otto let his arms swing by his sides and increased his pace, his long strides swallowing up the ground beneath him and his focus narrowing to the path ahead. As his muscles flexed and his body grew warm, he allowed himself, briefly, to acknowledge the sense of loss and regret which hadn't diminished any since Ariana fled his castle. Each morning, alone and unobserved, he would screw his eyes tightly shut and let out a roar of pure anguish, projecting all the pain and sorrow in his heart out into the heavy morning air.

When he opened his eyes again, the top of the hill was in sight. Otto slackened his pace and tugged off his cloak, allowing the brisk breeze to ripple through his tunic and cool his limbs. He felt momentarily better and lighter, freed of the constant weight of his bride's betrayal. It wouldn't last, he knew that, but it would enable him to battle through the day.

Otto stood until his heartrate returned to normal, his hands on his narrow hips, surveying his kingdom. From here he could see the towering walls of Darkmoor Castle, the Sarragnac coat of arms fluttering from the highest tower. He could see the swaying trees of the forest and the neatly laid out pastures, dotted with grazing cattle. If he lifted his chin, he could even make out the swirling sea beyond the cliffs. All of this he was sworn to protect.

That was the nugget of certainty he clung to, despite the incessant grieving of his heart for an untrue wife. He was the Earl of Darkmoor. Duty first. *Show no weakness.*

He would take his revenge on Sir Leon of Kenmar. His men were ready for the order. But first, he must decide what he would do with Ariana when he found her.

THE COURT PROCEEDINGS were long and boring. Otto sat on his carved wooden chair atop the dais, listening to the proclamations of the accusers and the lengthy arguments of the defendants. Their concerns seemed trivial to him; but he knew that for his people, a single horse could mean feeding their family versus watching them go hungry.

The great hall was emptier than usual, with just a single row of trestle tables positioned opposite the dais. A member of the castle guard stood at the door and two others escorted in the petitioners and defendants, ensuring no one left until justice had been served. Otto did his best to focus on proceedings, not allowing his mind to wander back to days past, when Ariana had worn a beautiful gown of ruby red and danced on the polished floor directly below him.

At last, they reached the final case of the day. Otto was in no mood to hear from a cheating wife and despite his determination to be fair-minded, had already decided in favor of her husband long before the couple were brought before him. But the modesty of the short-haired, slender woman, who stood by the table with her head bowed and her hands meekly folded, brought him up short.

This was not the bold hussy he'd been anticipating.

His gaze flickered to the husband; a great brawny brute of a man with a florid complexion and vivid blue tattoos snaking down his muscular forearms. He sat with his legs apart and his arms crossed over a stained tunic, the unmistakable scent of ale wafting from his unwashed body.

Otto cleared his throat. "Who brings this case?"

The man turned beady black eyes in his direction. "I do."

Otto drummed his fingers against the arms of his ornate

chair. "On your feet when you address me," he said, with misleading calmness. Immediately the complainant scraped back his chair and pushed himself upright, breathing hard with the exertion of this simple movement. Otto saw his wife take a subtle step to the side, putting a greater distance between them. "What is your name?" he demanded.

"Jeremiah. This is my wife." He flung his arm out to the side, without looking in her direction. "And she's been on her back with Benjamin the blacksmith."

One of the guards broke the silence with a poorly muffled bark of laughter. Otto glanced upwards, noting who it was and determining he would be rightly disciplined as soon as the court was out of session.

The wife seemed to cower further into herself at the allegation. Her head was still bowed, which displeased Otto who was intent upon seeing her face.

"May I ask your name?" he addressed her.

Jeremiah stiffened. It seemed he had not anticipated the Earl of Darkmoor seeking his wife's view on anything; it was not customary for a woman to speak up on such occasions.

The woman raised bewildered brown eyes to Otto's. "My name is Sarah," she said, so quietly that Otto had to lean forward to hear her.

"Sarah," he repeated. "And what say you to this charge?"

Jeremiah's face was slowly turning the color of an over-ripe plum. Otto ignored him.

Sarah's gaze shifted to her husband and then back to Otto. Her whole body was trembling. "I deny it, milord," she eventually whispered.

Jeremiah banged his first on the table. "You laid down on your back and he ploughed you, not once but many times." His angry voice carried through the near-empty hall.

Otto fixed him with a glare. "Sit down," he ordered. "No one speaks in this court without my permission." He returned his attention to the wife. "Is that true?"

Her eyes widened as her cheeks drained of color. "I would never do such a thing. Never."

"What cause have you given your husband to think it?"

Her voice shook. "I took Benjamin a cup of ale when he came to fix our horse's harness." She looked down. "We got to talking, that's all. I was never in his house. Not once. Nor he in ours." For the first time, her words were firm.

Otto looked back at the puce-colored husband. "What say you to that?"

Jeremiah pointed an angry finger at his wife. "She's a nag and a scold with me, always complaining about how much time I spend at the alehouse." For the first time, he noticed the large stain on the front of his tunic and his hand brushed at it ineffectually. "But with him, she's all smiles."

Otto had heard enough. "A wife should never be a nag or a scold," he observed. "But a husband should provide for his family, not spend all his time at the ale house. Treat your wife with more kindness, Jeremiah. And Sarah, save your smiles for your husband."

He waved a hand to confirm the case was dismissed and rubbed his temples, doing his best to ignore the dull itch of his scar. The guards ushered away the couple and closed the double doors behind them. Otto was alone, at last.

His gaze travelled around the great hall, seeing not a bare and empty room but one full of ghosts. His father's figure lingered here, striding through the doors and demanding attention. So too did Ariana, as she'd been for the Beltane Ball; smiling brightly, glittering with jewels. If Otto closed his eyes, he could still hear the minstrels' band and the heavy stamp of booted feet on the dance floor. Such thoughts led him somewhere darker. To the melancholy banging of a single drum and the unstoppable wailing of a grief-stricken mother. Young Benedict's funeral procession had started from here just days earlier.

He was so deep inside his memories, he hardly heard the double doors squeaking open and the patter of footsteps towards him. He jolted to his senses when a deep voice spoke up.

"I'm sorry to trouble you, my lord."

"The court is no longer in session," Otto replied automatically, rubbing at his tired eyes. He opened them and started in surprise. "Gaius, my friend. What can I do for you?"

The old knight hesitated before shuffling to the side. Behind him, Otto beheld a young boy of about fourteen years, white-faced and trembling. Otto raised an eyebrow and turned his questioning gaze back to Gaius, who was clad in a rich tunic of pale gold.

"This is Matthew, my lord, one of the stableboys."

Otto's mind was racing. Something about the boy looked very familiar. He snapped his fingers. "You look after my horse, don't you?"

Matthew's face grew red. "That's right, milord." He gave a clumsy half bow.

"Come closer," Otto ordered. "And stand easy. I don't bite."

"Go on," Gaius prompted.

The stableboy shuffled slightly closer to the dais. His cheeks had recently been scrubbed clean, but there was still a tidemark of dirt around his neck. He flung a terrified look back at Gaius. "I can't do it," he whispered.

Gaius held up a reassuring hand. "Allow me to tell the story for you, Matthew. You can step in whenever you want."

The boy nodded, evidently relieved.

Otto waited expectantly, but it was the turn of Gaius to grow uncomfortable. The loyal knight dragged his hand through his tufted gray hair and sighed deeply. "May I speak freely, my lord?"

"I would be grateful for it," Otto replied drily. "It seems many hours since I took my seat up here. Speak freely and speak quickly, pray, for my sake."

Gaius shifted his weight from one foot to the other. "This was not a matter fit to be heard in the court," he said eventually, weighing his words. "It is for your ears only."

Otto gestured around the empty hall, then folded his arms

and assumed an expression of strained patience. In truth, he knew Gaius would not trouble him with trivial matters; the stableboy must have committed, or witnessed, some very grave crime indeed.

"It concerns Sir Althalos," Gaius added.

That got Otto's attention. He sat up straighter in his chair and beckoned them closer still. "I'm listening," he said.

Gaius cast a glance down at Matthew, but the stableboy's gaze was firmly fixed on his shabby boots. "Our young friend here overheard something some weeks since. He thought nothing of it at the time. But today, matters escalated."

Otto saw a variety of emotions cross over Matthew's face, the last one being puzzlement. "He means things became worse," he explained, and with an inward sigh of resignation he rose from his chair, feeling his cramped muscles first complain, then stretch with relief. "I shall come down to you. Let us all speak eye to eye." He jogged down the stairs and joined them by the trestle tables, pleased to be upright once again. "Tell me what you overheard," he said to Matthew.

The stableboy swallowed and Otto thought for a moment he might refuse. But then he spoke up in a high, clear voice. "'Twas Sir Althalos's men. None of us like them. I'm sorry to say it, but it's true." His eyes flickered nervously between the two great warriors on either side of him. Otto waved a hand for him to continue. "Anyway, they were saying how the earl can't command an army, not properly, not like the old earl." Matthew stammered out the last few words and Otto clamped down on his instinctive anger for fear it would throw the boy entirely off course. "And that our knights would do better fighting for Sir Althalos."

Otto looked at Gaius, but he wouldn't meet his eye, silently confirming the boy's story. Otto cleared his throat. "And what of our men? What did they make of this?"

Matthew shook his head. "I never heard anything disrespectful against you, milord, not once."

"Your knights are unswervingly loyal," Gaius said levelly.

Otto knew a swell of impatience. "Does this tale continue?"

"Aye, milord." Matthew lifted his chin. "Last night, when I went to check on the horses after dark, Sir Althalos was in the barn talking to three of his men. They were huddled up beneath the hayloft, but I listened hard, and I heard what they said." The boy swallowed. "One of them was well into his cups. He was laughing. He said that killing the guard was a masterstroke."

Otto's mind raced. "The guard outside Traitor's Gate?"

"I dunno, milord. But he said that Sir Althalos was pulling your strings like a puppet." Matthew's cheeks flamed with embarrassment. "I dunno what that means either, milord."

Otto smiled reassuringly, even as bile rose in his throat. "What happened next?"

"They said how you locking Lady Ariana in the tower played right into their hands for when the Kenmar army arrived. But then Althalos spoke up and said how that were true, but none of it mattered now. That Sir Leon was weak, and he didn't need him no more. He would go it alone and get twice the prize."

"Go it alone?" Otto flicked his eyes towards Gaius. "What is he about?"

"Tell him, Matthew," Gaius nodded encouragingly.

Matthew fixed his gaze on the floor. "Sir Althalos said that soon all of this would belong to him."

"Holy Hell," Otto exploded, a pulse pounding at his temples. "Arrest him, now."

"It is too late for that." Gaius stepped forward. "Sir Althalos has gone."

Several beats passed. "Gone?" Otto repeated.

Matthew nodded. "He's taken his horses and all his men. They've cleared out. Gone."

Otto spun around to face Gaius. "Did he say anything to you of these intentions?"

"Not a word," Gaius declared, folding his arms over his heavily embroidered tunic. "I saw him this morn and did not think anything amiss. That was before Matthew came to find me."

Otto scratched at his scar, thinking hard. "He told me he would be gone by midsummer, but that is still several weeks away. It's strange that he has fled without word to anyone."

"Most odd." Gaius nodded emphatically. "It looks as if he is planning something."

Otto met his eye and nodded once, sharply. "You're right, Gaius. I want extra guards stationed at all look out points, day and night. Can you carry that order back to the gatehouse?"

"Straight away."

Otto clapped him on the arm and nodded his thanks to Matthew. "If Sir Althalos means to attack, then we shall be ready for him, have no fear. And that's thanks to you. I won't forget this, Matthew."

The stableboy reddened, but with pleasure not embarrassment.

"What will you do now?" Gaius asked.

Otto came to a quick decision. "Later tonight, I will join the look out," he promised. "But first, there's someone I need to speak to."

Someone he mayhap should have spoken to days earlier, if only his pride hadn't gotten in the way.

He left them both in the great hall, determined to fulfil his goal before anything further happened. Servants were preparing for the evening meal, carrying platters of food on heavy trays which they lifted swiftly out of the way when Otto appeared before them. His cloak billowed out behind him as he strode through the keep. He had never had cause to enter Merek's chamber before, but he knew where it was situated. A gust of balmy air caressed his cheeks as he entered the inner courtyard and he noted with faint relief that the rain had finally stopped.

He raised a fist and hammered on a bolted door, uncaring of the curious eyes upon him. Now that he had realized the extent of his uncle's treachery, his thoughts turned to questioning Ariana's role in recent events. He had presumed her guilty, but had she been a victim of Althalos's game-playing?

It was a dizzying possibility.

The physician shot back the bolts and opened his door quickly, bowing down low when he identified his visitor.

"Good evening, my lord. Are you taken ill?" He was clad in a stained apron and his untidy gray hair reached his shoulders.

Otto strode past him into the cramped room, unable to help a curious glance around. Dozens of bottles glistened on narrow shelves covering every wall, and earthenware bowls of colorful herbs were scattered here and there. Merek appeared to be midway through mixing up a potion using a pestle and mortar on his scrubbed wooden table.

"I need to speak to you," he said, by way of greeting. "And I need you to tell me the truth, Merek." Otto put a hand to the hilt of his sword and then thought better of it. He fixed the ageing physician with a meaningful glare instead. "On pain of being branded a traitor to Darkmoor."

Merek's pale eyes had followed the path of Otto's hand. He met his gaze without a tremor. "What is it you wish to know?"

Otto knew a flicker of guilt for showing such aggression towards the man who had once saved his life. "It concerns the Lady Ariana."

Merek blanched at that. He tugged at his beard thoughtfully and sighed with resignation. "May I sit?"

"Of course. 'Tis your own chamber, Merek." *For now,* Otto added silently.

The physician sank into a hard wooden chair by the table. "I knew Lady Ariana's mother, many years ago."

His words piqued Otto's interest and he too sat down in the opposite chair. Immediately the sweet smell of lavender assaulted his senses from a nearby bowl.

"Before you came to serve us in Darkmoor?"

"That is correct."

"What about Lady Ariana?"

Merek nodded slowly. "I knew her as a child, yes." His tone

was guarded.

Otto folded his hands on the table and decided to be frank. "For many days now, I have believed Lady Ariana guilty of conspiring against me." Otto paused to gauge Merek's reaction, but the old man didn't move. "With her father, Sir Leon," he added.

Merek pursed his lips. "There was no love lost between Lady Ariana and her father. It was always said Sir Leon regretted his match with her mother." Merek looked down at his herb-stained hands. "She was a druid, you know?"

"Ariana's mother?" Otto's tone revealed his surprise.

Merek nodded slowly. "She taught me much." He indicated the tools of his trade. "I owe her a debt of gratitude."

"So Ariana had sympathy with the druids?" Otto's mind was racing. He drummed his fingers on the table, coming dangerously close to unsettling the bowl of dried lavender.

"That's true." Merek paused, indecision flickering across anxious eyes which eventually landed on Otto. He took a breath. "Ariana did conspire against you, my lord, but only to rescue the druid prisoner."

Otto's heart pounded against his ribs, but he didn't know if his primary emotion was rage or relief at hearing Merek's confession. "Why would she do that?" he asked, finally, his hands clenching into fists.

"The prisoner was her aunt," Merek stated calmly. "Ysmay was sister to Ariana's mother. She was also a healer of some renown." He paused. "The druids know her as the Rose of Kenmar."

The Rose of Kenmar.

Otto sat still for a moment, piecing it all together. Ariana had written to her father of her intention to free her aunt, not steal a jewel from their vaults. Any duplicity had been rooted in love. "Why did no one tell me?" His fist slammed down on the table. "Why did *you* not tell me?"

Merek reached out for the earthenware bowl of dried herbs

and nudged it to safety, his eyes cast down. "If I may say, we feared your anger, my lord."

His words pierced the fog of emotion swirling in Otto's mind. He gripped the edge of the table and breathed deeply to calm himself down. The scent of lavender was a balm, even in the midst of his confusion. "I can't blame you for that," he said eventually. "I had more than a hand in creating my own reputation. The irony is, after much deliberation, I had decided to release the druid prisoner. She was an old woman and once my senses cleared, I could see that she bore no blame for my father's death." He raised his hands. "If only Ariana had come to me with this." His sorrow was imbued with bitter regret.

Merek nodded slowly. "It would have been a wise choice." He risked a glance towards Otto. "That was my advice to her, my lord. To bide her time. But Ariana has always been a spirited young woman."

"Aye," Otto sighed. It was Ariana's spirit that had first attracted him to her; he could hardly berate her for it now. "To be clear, Ariana had no part in the battle Sir Leon brought to our gates?"

"None that I know of, my lord."

Otto pursed his lips. "I came here only to see if Ariana had mentioned something to you during a consultation. But you have given me much more than I hoped for."

Merek bowed his head, his long gray hair falling forward and obscuring his face. "I am glad to have been of service."

He took his leave of the physician and walked through the gathering dusk to his private tower at the back of the castle. The events of the day; the cases at court, his morning walk, even his conversation with Gaius, all seemed to have taken place in the distant past. His mind was full of this latest revelation; Ariana had not been in league with her father after all. She was no traitor to Darkmoor. She had told him no lies.

He stopped short, felled by this mighty realization. Ariana had kept her word and not told him anything that wasn't true. Was it her fault that Otto had failed to ask the right questions?

With leaden feet, he climbed the spiral staircase to the tower top chamber where they had had their final conversation. For all these weeks, he had imagined Ariana leaving here gladly. The thought had pained him but the alternative, he realized, was much worse. She must have been taken against her will. And he had done nothing about it.

"Damnation." He slammed his fist into the solid wall then shook his grazed knuckles to rid himself of the pain.

He had done nothing.

He had been too quick to let the poison of Sir Althalos seep under his skin. His uncle was the only traitor to have been given hospitality in Darkmoor. Ariana was guilty of loving her aunt, no more, no less.

The connection he'd felt to his bride had been real.

The natural ease of their conversations, the instinctive trust that had sprung up between them, the sense of a shared past and a future where they would be stronger together, all of that was real. Beneath his burden of worry and regret, Otto began to feel the first glimmers of hope and joy. He hadn't imagined the sincerity shining in Ariana's eyes. Hadn't been intoxicated by fine wine or base lust when he felt that she was the only person he could be his true self with. Their relationship had been burgeoning into something beautiful, before Sir Althalos had laid his cunning plan.

He walked quickly to the tapestried chair and picked up the blanket he'd draped over Ariana's legs, wanting to warm her chilled limbs even while he doubted her intentions. He pressed it to his nose and inhaled deeply, but no scent of her remained and he flung it away in frustration.

Still, she had been here. She had been *his*. And she could be again. It was not too late, he felt it in his bones. He had vowed just this morning to defend Darkmoor with his last breath. Now he berated himself for not retaliating sooner against Sir Leon of Kenmar. Ariana deserved his protection. He need not fret about how to punish an untrue wife; he needed only to rescue her and bring her home.

It seemed so long ago that he'd come here with his sack of modest offerings, hoping to help her pass the night more easily. Even then he had instinctively doubted Althalos's words. He should have listened to his gut.

Otto wandered over to the table, which had yet to be cleared. No servants came in here; it was his own private domain. He wrinkled his nose at the stale bread and wizened, moldy berries. Clearly Ariana had been stolen away before she could satisfy her hunger. He hoped she was well-fed, wherever Sir Leon had hidden her.

A roll of parchment was at his feet. He bent to pick it up, starting in recognition at the vivid image etched onto it with charcoal. It was smudged, the lines drawn hurriedly, but its meaning was clear. Otto's hands trembled as he gazed down at Ariana's depiction of him: a man, not a warrior.

A man at peace.

A man drawn with love.

Any remaining doubts as to whether Ariana wanted a future here in Darkmoor evaporated like morning mist.

Otto placed the drawing reverently on the table and stood back, drinking it in.

His resolution was clear-cut and shining, like the brightest jewel in the vaults. He would rescue Ariana and bring her back to Darkmoor. And he would rule his estate in his own way, no longer suffering misplaced doubts about his own moral code.

Otto fished in his pocket for the token Ariana had given him at the long-ago joust. He clenched it inside his fist, drawing strength from the memory.

A man could be both a warrior and a husband. Could live a peaceable life but stand up against his enemies.

He pressed his lips to the token, then returned it to his pocket and drew his palm over the familiar hilt of his sword. He had done enough thinking on this matter. It was time to act.

Chapter Eighteen

ARIANA GAZED OUT of her narrow window to confirm that nothing had changed, that no armored warriors were descending across the moors, then she resumed her frantic pacing of the chamber.

She had grown weary of sitting around and waiting to be rescued.

Somewhere between waking up and breaking her fast with the usual meager offering of small ale and stale bread, the unrelenting tedium of her incarceration had become too much to bear. She needed something to happen. *Anything.* If it meant putting herself in fresh danger…

So be it.

She dressed quickly in a plain tunic, belted at the waist and ornamented with Otto's broach. Her hair, she plaited into a long braid over her shoulder, securing it with a faded ribbon plucked from a pile at the bottom of her closet. Rummaging further, she was pleased to find an old pair of goatskin shoes which she dimly remembered wearing several summers past. They were cracked at the soles, but far better than nothing.

She felt better for being up and properly attired. More herself. As if she'd shaken off her sluggish despair along with her bed linens.

When her father had given the order for Ariana to be locked in her chamber, he'd made provision for her temporary release each morning to take the air in the inner courtyard. Up until now,

Ariana had ignored the guard when he came to escort her, turning her face to the bare wall and waiting for him to go away. But today, as soon as she heard the key turn in the lock, she rushed towards the door with the brightest smile she could muster.

"Good morn," she greeted the dour-faced guard.

He pursed his lips. "I am come to take you for your walk, milady."

She nodded graciously. "And I am pleased to accept."

The guard stood aside to allow her to pass out into the narrow stone stairwell. "You can walk afore me, milady. But know that there are men stationed all over the keep. It would not be wise for you to try to run."

"No indeed." Ariana cast another smile over her shoulder. "I shall not run."

Their progress was slow down the steep turns of the tower, and Ariana was glad of her shoes on the cold, worn steps. When they reached the antechamber at the bottom, she paused. "Where are we to walk?" She already knew the answer, but she was playing for time until she could formulate a plan.

"The inner courtyard."

"How pleasant." She offered the man her arm, and he was too surprised to do anything but accept it.

They progressed together out of the main doors and out into a brisk breeze which whipped up Ariana's plait and made her eyes water. The inner courtyard was a grand term for a patch of rough grass, across which smoke from the bakehouse billowed. But Ariana's gaze had shifted to another section of the castle. At last, she settled on her goal.

"Is my father in his solar?" she asked nonchalantly.

"I cannot say, milady."

"I should like to go and see." Bright with determination, she altered their path to the low-slung stone building which housed Sir Leon's private quarters.

"Sir Leon should not be disturbed." The guard's voice was

stern.

Ariana turned wide eyes towards him and bit down on her lip. "I must make an apology."

The guard raised his eyebrows.

"I should not have tried to escape." A plume of smoke caught in her throat and made her cough. "It was wrong of me." The guard looked unsure. Ariana knew that he could easily refuse her request. Worse, the marshal could appear at any moment, and he was not a man to be easily fooled. "Allow me to at least knock upon his door?"

Without waiting for a response, she tripped across the patchy grass and rapped her knuckles upon the solidly built door.

A growl came from within. "Go away."

She winced, recognizing both her father's voice and the temper within it. She had long lived in fear of Sir Leon's rages. But she would not give up now.

"It's me, father." She tried the handle and found, to her surprise, the door was unlocked. "I have come to apologize."

At first, she could make out little in the gloomy chamber. A grimy sort of light filtered through one window, which was partially obscured by an oil cloth. The fug of the room was most unpleasant: stale rushes, woodsmoke and ale. Her father sat slumped at a desk, surrounded by scattered parchments and spilled ink. He did not even raise his head at her entry.

"Go away," he repeated, loudly.

"What are you doing?" Ariana swallowed down her fears and inched further inside, pleased at least that the guard had not followed her beyond the door.

"Why are you out of your chamber?" He finally acknowledged her presence, dark eyebrows arching over his unshaven face.

Ariana couldn't help blanching at her father's unkempt appearance. Sir Leon had always been a vain man, but it looked as if he had not shaved for several days. His tunic was rumpled, and his sword belt lay abandoned on the floor.

"Have no fear, Father, I am being carefully guarded," she trilled, with a smile towards the man waiting outside.

He grunted in response. "I'm busy, Ariana. Leave me in peace."

She regarded him for a moment, her mind whirring. She had thought she might plead for her freedom, but he showed less interest in his daughter's presence than in the tankard of ale he was now draining. Her gaze jumped to the parchments on his desk. They were letters, all written in the same elegant hand.

"Who has been writing to you?" She moved closer, but he covered the parchments with his large hands before she could see anything of note.

"That is no concern of yours." He made to rise from his chair as if to swat her away, but then he sank back into it with a low groan.

Ariana observed his red-rimmed, unfocused eyes and shaking fingers. The now empty tankard of ale, together with the fumes emanating from his half-open mouth, all confirmed her suspicions. Her father was drunk.

Her surprise quickly morphed into resolve to turn this to her advantage. Sir Leon may not be moved to sympathy for her plight, but mayhap he could be convinced to tell her of his intentions? Intentions which she could then somehow reveal to Otto.

Somehow.

It wasn't much of a plan, but it was the best she had.

"It was a clever idea, to wed me to the Earl of Darkmoor," she improvised.

Her father picked up the beer tankard and looked inside. "You think so?"

"It's true, I didn't think so at first." She picked her way over the littered floor to a hard wooden chair pulled near an empty fireplace. She lowered herself down and folded her hands on her knees. "But that was because I didn't understand."

Sir Leon regarded her with glazed eyes. "And now you do?"

"Yes." She put her head to one side and pretended to think. "Perchance not all of it."

Her father's response was a deep guffaw of laughter, which scared her more than his earlier shouting.

"You and me both, Ariana."

She took a deep breath, intent on persevering. "You mean, you don't understand either?"

He banged the tankard down onto his desk, unsettling more of the parchments. "I understand well enough when a man breaks his word."

"Sir Althalos," she guessed.

"That double-crossing snake," he hissed, looking suddenly like the fearful baron he was.

Ariana leaned forward. "You were in league with him against Otto? When you stormed the fortress at Darkmoor, he was meant to come to your aid?"

"Fifty men, he promised me." Sir Leon pointed a wavering finger in her direction. "Fifty men and fifty swords. Half my men were killed at the battle of Branfeld. I didn't tell him that, why would I?" He shook his head in answer to his own question. "But his fifty men could have made all the difference at Darkmoor."

Ariana felt a wave of nausea, unsure whether it was from her growing babe or the disgust she felt at her father's tale. But there was nothing to be gained by asking him why. The only information that could be of any use to Otto was what Sir Leon planned to do next.

"Instead, Sir Althalos watched your men be cut down, while his remained safe and well," she said softly, her eyes fixed upon his face. Despite her calm demeanor, inside she was braced to flee if her father lost his temper. In less than ten strides she could be out of the door. "Surely you must want to take your revenge, Father?"

"Revenge, aye, if only." His gaze became unfocused. "I have not the army for revenge."

"Then what?"

He sat back in his chair. "Then what?" he repeated. "'Tis a question I have asked myself over and over."

Ariana's fears gave way to impatience. "You had your men kidnap me…" she began.

"Aye. That was a mistake," he interjected. "I was watching the fighting at the castle walls. Althalos was meant to open the gates for me. Once the earl's men had submitted, I would ride through in victory." His full lips creased into an unpleasant smile. "You were taken to ensure the young earl didn't try anything once we'd taken him prisoner."

Ariana's head was pounding, though this confession was no less than she had expected. "My imprisonment here is a mistake?" she articulated slowly.

"Aye. It's become so, certainly."

Belatedly, Ariana realized that her father's cheeks had grown mottled with anger—a look she was all too familiar with from childhood. She rose quickly from her chair. "I will leave you, Father."

But Sir Leon was already shouting over his shoulder for the guard. "Take her back to her chamber," he ordered, as soon as the man barreled through the door. "And don't allow her to bother me again."

Ariana scuttled forward, not wanting to give the guard the satisfaction of dragging her from the solar. But once outside, he clamped iron fingers around her arm.

"Don't try anything else, Lady Ariana," he said with satisfaction. "Next time, I'll shout for the marshal."

But all the fight had gone out of Ariana, and she submitted to the walk back to her chamber without prevarication. What could she do now but wait?

SOME HOURS LATER, Ariana pulled a stool over to the window and knelt upon it, fixing her gaze on the dirt path through the distant trees. A strong wind whipped around the keep, howling between the stunted towers and causing the horses grazing in the paddocks to toss their manes and prance. Ariana bit her lip and leaned closer to the window, her hands joined together beneath her chin as if in supplication. Ever since Maria, the kitchen maid, had brought her a heel of bread in lieu of luncheon, Ariana's pulse had been racing. There was something about the frenzied wind, so unusual for the season, and the frantic pacing of the guards in the outer courtyard, that hinted change was coming.

And not a moment too soon.

Something certainly was afoot. She'd even spied her father talking to the guards, gesticulating vehemently towards the forest as the wind played havoc with his long cloak. He must have sobered up since this morn.

Could it be that the lookouts had brought word back to the castle of an advancing army?

She didn't allow herself to hope, but her insides crawled with nervous anticipation that even now, Otto was on his way to rescue her.

Her father's soldiers were assembling beneath the keep, fueling her suspicions further. The soldiers of Kenmar had never been a formidable force, but they had dwindled even further since the battle of Branfeld and the ill-fated skirmish at the gates of Darkmoor. Just a handful remained.

Ariana recalled her father's slurred words earlier in the day. *"I have not the army for revenge."*

He had not the army to mount a successful defense of the castle either.

The horses were led out by a gaggle of dirty stableboys and, one by one, the remaining soldiers mounted. Sir Leon watched them silently from the steps. He offered no words of praise or encouragement, no example either of fortitude or resilience. Ariana closed her fingers around Otto's broach, feeling her stomach clench and roll. Since leaving Darkmoor, nausea had been her constant companion.

Then she heard it; the thunder of approaching hoofbeats. It was unmistakable. The soldiers below heard it at the same time; their heads turning simultaneously towards the forest. The ears of their horses flickered forward and backwards, anxiety shining in their wide eyes. Several of them started in fright as the resonant clanging of the warning bell rang through the courtyard. Ariana's breathing became jagged as she gazed at the distant path and hoped with every fiber of her being that the standard of Dark-moor would soon appear.

The thunderous beat grew louder, sending vibrations through the ground and making the castle dogs howl. It was like the beating of a drum; a rhythmic sound which must surely herald the knights of Darkmoor. No other army could be so tightly disciplined, moving at such speed through the forest.

Her father's men cantered out to meet them. From Ariana's room at the top of the keep, she had a full view of the open plain to the front of the castle, where she had no doubt the fighting would shortly commence. She gripped Otto's broach so tightly her tunic snagged beneath it. All this could only mean one thing. *Otto was coming.*

Whether he was coming to rescue her, or punish her further, in that moment she hardly cared. At last, she would see him again.

Just as she was growing faint with wanting, the first riders came into view. Ariana's heart leaped for joy when she glimpsed the fluttering red standard, and her eyes strained further to make out the heroic figure of Otto, the *Feared One*, riding at the head of his army. Never had she placed so much value on his reputation. As they poured out of the trees, the approaching knights fanned out behind their leader into two equal lines.

That was her first clue that something was wrong.

She placed her forehead against the window, so anxious she'd have almost clambered through it if it were possible. Had Otto brought but half his men to mount his rescue?

Had something further happened in Darkmoor to diminish the forces it had to offer?

Her gaze focused on the leader and her pulse thrummed in her ears as she noted his slight stance. This man was small and wiry. Even as she watched, he reined in his horse and allowed his men to filter past him to start the fighting without him. Otto would never do such a thing. Her eyes jumped to the colorful emblem of the men's shields. Red for Darkmoor, just as she'd hoped. But instead of a rampant lion, these shields bore a blazing yellow cross.

Not Otto.

Not the knights of Darkmoor.

Disappointment made her limbs turn to cold stone and she sank against the window, exhaling all her hopes and dreams in a trembling breath which fogged the glass.

But who else would launch an attack against Kenmar?

Below her, swords clashed and horses whinnied in distress. She clasped a hand to her mouth, hardly knowing what outcome she sought. Were these unknown knights fighting in Otto's stead? Immediately she straightened up, scrutinizing the men for some clue as to their identity. Their tunics glowed red beneath polished armor. Their horses were gleaming and well-conditioned. Who else in these parts kept such a fine force of fighting men?

Her gaze alighted on their leader, sitting lightly astride a fine dapple-gray horse which she couldn't help but recognize. The horse had distinctive coloring; she had seen him in the stables of Darkmoor. A burst of fresh excitement was quickly followed by dreadful recognition.

This army was led by Sir Althalos.

Her heart beat hollowly inside her chest as she withdrew from the window and sank down on the corner of her mattress. Sir Althalos was her enemy. She could not look to these men for assistance, though they must know she was here. Her scrambled mind raced back to Chiara's observation that Sir Leon didn't know which way to turn. Perchance that was because he'd suspected he was to be double-crossed by his former ally.

Either way, it mattered not. Ariana was locked inside her room. She had no hope of escape. Whether it was Sir Leon's guards or Sir Althalos's knights who came for her; neither wished her well. A sob escaped her. She'd been so close to believing her troubles were over.

The distant sounds of the battle were growing louder: the animalistic roar of war cries, the harrowing groans of the injured and the relentless clash of sword on sword. But in amongst that constant hum, she became aware of closer activity. Doors banging shut, children crying, and frantic shouting.

Unable to help herself, Ariana resumed her post at the window, craning her head to the side to see a flood of servants and villagers pour from the western gates of the castle towards the river and possible freedom. They must believe that defeat was imminent; otherwise, they would be too much in fear of Sir Leon's punishments to think of saving their own skins. Ariana's shoulders sagged. Better than anyone, she knew of all the secret ways in and out of Kenmar Castle. There was an underground tunnel accessed through the vaults which led right to the other side of the river. She'd used it often to meet up with the druids against Sir Leon's wishes. But she was locked up and forgotten at the top of the keep, where her knowledge could benefit no one.

She looked back at the battle, wincing at the bodies of the fallen and the streams of red blood running through the grassy plain. Heavy casualties had befallen both sides and it was impossible to see who had the advantage. A loose horse, reins flapping, made a bid for freedom by bolting towards the forest. Ariana felt nausea swirling in her gut. It was all such a senseless waste. So much death and bloodshed and fear, children taken from their homes, husbands from their wives. And for what?

It was a rhetorical question; she knew the answer well enough. The pursuit of land, riches and power was behind such thirst for blood. She'd been raised upon it but had naively hoped that her forced marriage to Otto would signify unity between

Kenmar and Darkmoor. She'd believed Sir Leon when he said that was all he wished for. Peace with his neighbors. Plus, the priceless ruby: the Rose of Kenmar.

Now she knew better. All this time, her father and Sir Althalos had been working together in a bid to overthrow Otto.

As she watched the scene of the battle, Sir Althalos himself came back into view, his finely bred horse picking his path through the carnage towards the castle gates. His way into the heart of Kenmar had been cleared of all obstacles; no guard, knight, or villager brandishing a pitchfork came out to stand in his way. He had won, here in Kenmar at least.

Ariana pulled away from the window, she didn't want to see any more. It was only a matter of time before Althalos's men came to find her. She trembled to think what they might do to her, one hand going unthinkingly to her flat belly. At least they did not yet know that she was carrying Otto's child.

Althalos could well recognize Otto's broach though, and the sight of it could inflame him further. Fingers shaking, Ariana unpinned it from her tunic. She'd wanted to wear it always but couldn't bear the thought of it being thrown away or deliberately trampled underfoot by Otto's vindictive uncle. On a sudden whim, she crossed to her closet and picked through the crumpled ribbons until she found one of a dark purple hue. Purple; the color of Kenmar. Quickly, she pinned the broach to the ribbon in a defiant symbol of unity between the first lady of Kenmar and the rightful Earl of Darkmoor and placed the scrap of material atop her pillow. It would be found, someday, by someone.

Breathing hard, adrenaline coursing through her veins, she pondered her next move. There was nothing to be gained by hiding. She'd seen enough ransacking soldiers in her time to know that squeezing herself under the bed or inside the closet would yield little in her favor. They would drag her out with ill-concealed glee; any reprimand grown far greater for her attempts to outwit them.

But she couldn't sit here and wait, like some sort of sacrificial lamb.

Ariana bit down on her lip as an idea formed in her mind. Not an idea; a memory. Before her marriage to Otto, one of her ladies had whispered to her that dark plans were afoot. The lady had pressed a small, bejeweled dagger into her hands and urged her to keep it always to hand. Ariana had secreted it under her mattress. Could it be there still?

Grunting with the effort, she hauled the straw mattress onto its side, thrilled to see the familiar leather pouch laying innocently beneath it. She snatched it up and placed it inside her belt, feeling oddly comforted by the weight of it. She was ready now. Resigned to the worst; but determined to go down fighting, if only for the sake of her unborn child.

A hammering at her door made her jump with fright. Had they found her so soon? Despite her brave intentions, terror wrapped cold tentacles around her limbs. Ariana opened her mouth, but nothing came out. Then came the unmistakable sound of the iron key turning in the lock. The door swung open with a familiar creaking, and she forced herself to stand tall and steady, to meet whoever had come for her with at least the appearance of decorum. But it was Chiara's anxious face which peered into the narrow room.

"Lady Ariana," she whispered, "you're still here."

"You came for me." Relief and gratitude made her weak. "I thought everyone had left."

"Come quickly," Chiara urged. "The enemy are on their way to the keep. We have but seconds to spare."

Ariana rushed forward and grasped the cook's reddened hand. Together they ran wordlessly down the stone stairs; a seemingly endless journey which by necessity took them closer to the advancing army. The tight turns of the staircase made Ariana's head spin and twice she nearly stumbled. At last, they emerged onto the stone-flagged ground floor. The great hall was to their left, the main doors to their right. No one else was around.

"We must follow the others to the western gates," Chiara

huffed, her dark eyes flitting nervously around.

"I know a better way," Ariana urged, her heart pounding from the speed of their descent. "Through the vaults."

"The vaults." Chiara reared back in alarm. "I've no wish to go down there, milady."

Ariana was about to point out that this was no time to be afraid of the dark when the sound of marching footsteps up the front steps drowned out all thought and reason. She grasped Chiara's hand as three knights came into view; swords in hand, faces set and determined. A knot of dread unfurled in her belly as she recognized the middle knight.

"Lady Ariana," Sir Althalos purred, a callous smile playing around his thin lips. "We meet again."

Ariana staggered backwards, barreling into the stout figure of Chiara whose kind face was screwed up in fear. These men were armed warriors, already smeared with the blood of their victims; what hope did two women have against them?

"Let us go," Ariana tried. "We mean you no harm."

He laughed at that, and the two knights at either side of him joined in. Their laughter echoed around the empty hallway.

"I would like to see you try," one of them said, wiping a hand over his mouth. His sleeve was speckled with gray matter. Ariana didn't like to think what it might be.

Her mind went instinctively to the dagger at her belt; but she didn't need a lesson in warcraft to know that one dagger would not better three swords.

"My husband is the Earl of Darkmoor," she tried again, her voice trembling despite her best efforts. "If you touch me, the repercussions will be severe."

The knights regarded her with faint disinterest. Too late, Ariana remembered that these men had most likely been stationed at Darkmoor since the old earl's funeral. They would already have known who she was.

"Your belief in my nephew is touching," Sir Althalos said coolly. "But where is he now, when you need him?"

Ariana could feel Chiara shaking with fear beside her. How she longed to offer comfort with a declaration of faith that Otto's army would arrive at any moment. But for all she knew, he had no intention of coming to Kenmar.

Althalos must have sensed her doubt, for the corners of his mouth twitched in triumph.

"Seize her," he ordered his men, nodding at Chiara. "Leave the Countess of Darkmoor to me."

"No," Ariana cried, grasping ineffectually at Chiara's apron as the cook was forcibly led away. The last Ariana saw of her one remaining ally was her plump arms flailing against her attackers, then they turned the corner and were gone from her sight. She heard their boots clumping down the front steps and the crunch of gravel as they stepped onto the courtyard, then all was quiet.

"What will they do to her?" she demanded of Althalos.

He smiled humorlessly. "What do you think?"

"She's only a cook."

Althalos shrugged. "Don't pretend you don't understand how this works. It doesn't matter if you're a princess or a scullery maid. The enemy is the enemy." His dark eyes flickered with hatred. "Even if your husband is the Earl of Darkmoor." He raised his sword, his voice a mocking parody of Ariana's just moments earlier.

"And what of my husband?" Ariana demanded. If she could keep Althalos talking for long enough, mayhap she could figure out a plan. "Has he become your enemy now? You double-crossed him; just as you have double-crossed my father."

He inclined his head. "Events have moved swiftly, it's true. But that was always my intention. Sir Leon and I reached an understanding some years since about how best to take down Darkmoor once my dear brother passed."

"And then what?" She inched sideways…but to no avail as the tip of his sword followed her progress. "Your understanding came to naught once my father showed his hand."

Althalos smiled slightly. "Leon promised me the might of the

Kenmar army. But he launched an attack on one of England's greatest fortresses with too few men and not even the courage to lead them himself." He raised the sword so that it was level with her nose. "Such a weak ally might better be described as a hindrance."

"And such a devious ally might best be described as an enemy," Ariana declared. Inside, she quailed at the wisdom of angering the man further. But she couldn't escape to the vaults without somehow getting past him. Distraction was the only way.

His mocking gaze never left her. "Why should I share the spoils of victory when I can take both Darkmoor and Kenmar for myself?"

Ariana forced herself to stand tall. "What part do I play in the spoils of victory? Do you intend to take me prisoner, Sir Althalos? Or do you intend to kill me?"

She was gratified to see a look of faint surprise cross his face. "I'd say that all depends on you, Lady Ariana." He smirked, lowering his sword to the ground and resting both hands upon the hilt. "My men would prefer we take you prisoner. They'd certainly enjoy spending time with Otto Sarragnac's young bride."

Her stomach rolled with nausea. "I would prefer to die."

"That can be arranged." He stepped towards her, and the metallic stink of fresh blood, not his own, filled her nostrils.

Ariana leaned backwards, conscious of the stone wall looming behind her. She had no intention of being taken prisoner to be raped by the villainous warriors reporting to Althalos. But she had no one to rely on but herself. "You threaten me, Sir Althalos," she said calmly. "You should know, I'm a desperate woman. And desperate women should not be toyed with."

"Oh?" He raised a mocking eyebrow and came closer, so close she could see where his chainmail gapped over his blood-smeared tunic. "Do you threaten me now, Lady Ariana? That's good. I like to see some defiance in my women, before I thrash it out of them."

Her moment had come, and Ariana didn't waste it. She kept her eyes focused on Sir Althalos's mean black ones while her hand reached for the dagger, unsheathed it, and plunged into the gap beneath his chest plate, wincing with horror as her blade sliced upwards through flesh and scraped against his ribs.

For a second, it seemed as if her aim had missed. Sir Althalos blanched, but stayed standing, his glazed eyes fixed on hers. He opened his mouth and a reddish foam bubbled from the corners. Ariana scuttled sideways, numb with shock, knowing she must get herself out of reach of his sword. But she needn't have worried. In another moment, Althalos's legs buckled beneath him, and he sank to the ground, a deep-red pool of sticky blood gathering beneath his fallen body.

Ariana clamped her hands to her mouth, silencing her scream. She couldn't waste any more time. Enemy soldiers could be preparing to storm the keep, even now.

Without another look at her adversary, Ariana ran towards the vaults and the possibility of freedom.

Chapter Nineteen

OTTO WAS UNACCUSTOMED to feeling nervous when he faced his men, but on this warm mid-summer's morn, he had to chase down his apprehension before standing up to speak.

The knights of Darkmoor were gathered in the stone-flagged armory; yawning still because of the early hour, scratching their bushy beards and jostling one another good naturedly. A flagon of cider was making its way around them. The men drank deeply, smacking their lips in appreciation. Otto took a deep breath and strode to the center of the vaulted chamber.

"Good men of Darkmoor," he began, his voice rebounding around the whitewashed walls. "I have summoned you from your beds and gathered you here to ask a very important question."

"'Twas not his own bed you summoned Sir Tristan from," interjected Andreas de Montain, to a chorus of approving jeers.

Tristan, a young knight of just twenty summers, found the grace to laugh at their jesting. "Aye, well, the lady has promised me I'm welcome back any time," he said, his brilliant blue eyes alight with youthful zest.

"Glad to hear it, Tristan," Otto put in quickly. He looked around at the assembled men; every last face was tilted up towards him. They trusted him as their leader. But would they follow him so unthinkingly into battle when they heard what he had to say?

He cleared his throat. "You have served Darkmoor and done

us proud, some of you for more years than I have been alive." He nodded towards Gaius, who raised the flagon of cider towards him in a silent toast. "The knights of Darkmoor are known throughout the North for their fearlessness." A small cheer erupted at that. "Their unfaltering courage." Another cheer, accompanied by some table-banging. "And their strength, speed, and skills in battle." This time his words were met with roars of approval, feet-stamping, and back-slapping. Otto waited until the chorus had died down. "I would have it no other way." He raised his fist into the air, getting into his stride now. "But there is one change I would like to make." Immediately the mood in the room shifted as the men waited for his explanation. Otto rubbed at his scar and summoned the conviction from deep within him. "My forefathers created the Knights' Code for Darkmoor. We all of us know it. *Show no weakness; show no mercy.* It is a code that has served us well in battle." Otto lowered his voice, knowing he had the attention of every man here. "Darkmoor has never once fallen." Cheers erupted through the room and Otto held up his hand for silence. "Thanks to the fortitude of our ancestors, we find ourselves on the cusp of more peaceful times." He ploughed ahead, seeing doubt flicker behind the eyes of the closest young knights. "And I for one, would like to ride out under a different code. One that values fortitude and valor over all else." He paused for effect. "As knights, we show no weakness. But there are times, men, when it is a strength to show mercy. Or that, at least, is what I believe." He plunged ahead, taking courage from the nods he saw greet his words. "From this day forward, we defend our borders. We protect what is ours. We fight for *peace*, for our families and for the people of Darkmoor."

Gaius was the first to his feet. "Aye," he cried, bringing his mighty hand down onto the table.

The knights around him rose as one, brandishing their fists in the air and banging their swords. "Aye," they shouted.

Otto knew a moment of relief before he was swept up into the throng of back-slapping and good-natured thumping. The flagon of cider was pressed into his hands, and he drank deeply.

"And now to business," he roared, jumping onto a low wooden table to be seen above the fracas. "We have reason to believe that Lady Ariana is being held in Kenmar Castle. This war with Sir Leon has already taken too many lives, but we must protect what is ours. As the Countess of Darkmoor, Lady Ariana belongs here, with me. We must bring her home."

"Aye," cheered the men.

"Are you with me?" he bellowed, brandishing his sword above his head.

"Until the last," proclaimed Gaius, to a rousing chorus of approval.

"Then let us make ready," Otto ordered. "We have a long journey ahead of us."

The sun was still rising over the Caldon Hills when the knights mounted their horses in the outer courtyard and trotted over the drawbridge in a tidy formation behind Otto. They were followed by an army of a hundred men, with another fifty staying behind to guard the castle. Otto kept the pace steady, knowing they had some distance to travel and mayhap many challenges to overcome even when they reached their destination. But despite his trepidation over what lay ahead that day, he knew great peace of mind that he had at last spoken openly to his men.

As they progressed towards the river, a great heron flew overhead, flapping lazy wings and making stately progress through the clear blue sky. After so many days of rain, the change in weather was a good omen, boding well for their quest. The Sarragnac standard cracked in the brisk breeze and the horses stepped out smartly along the ploughed tracks. To their left, down in the valley, Otto could spy the rippling treetops of the ancient forests bordering Kenmar and Darkmoor. It was through those mighty oaks, he reasoned, that Ariana's captors had smuggled their prisoner. Keeping her hidden, for the most part, until reaching Sir Leon's cheerless fortress. He steered his men well clear of the woodland; they had no reason to hide and the winding paths within would only slow their journey.

At midday, they halted, dismounting from their horses and sating their hunger with bread and cheese. Otto saw that the horses were watered and allowed to crop at the lush green grass. The mood amongst the knights had grown more somber now they were so close to Sir Leon's stronghold. A strong wind whistled around them, making conversation difficult. The men ate steadily, with quiet purpose, filling their bellies so they could reap the strength in the upcoming battle. Otto had posted lookouts ahead, but he still felt a sharp sense of unease and was unable to keep his gaze from the distant trees, fearful of archers' arrows reaching them unawares. As soon as the horses were rested, he ordered his men back into the saddle and they resumed their march east.

Marching towards Ariana.

He remembered her cloud of hair; the way her lips would curl into an understanding smile. The softness of her curves and that instant spark of a connection between them. *Why*, he demanded of himself, *had he left her at the mercy of their enemies for so long?*

And not just at the mercy of Sir Leon, but mayhap Althalos, too.

It took all his inner steel not to urge his horse into a gallop.

After an hour of steady riding in strong sunlight, he beckoned Gaius forward and their two horses fell into step across the unprepossessing moors. The wind had died down, and flies buzzed around them from a stagnant, stinking pond somewhere nearby.

"What is your plan, my lord?" enquired the old knight.

"In truth, Gaius, my sole plan is to rescue the Lady Ariana and be gone from this grim place. I have oft wondered what beset Sir Leon's ancestors to situate their stronghold in such inhospitable surroundings." He nodded towards the bleak expanse of sparse moorland all around them. "Much as the desire for revenge boils in my veins, I have no great wish to spill more blood in battle with Kenmar. We have already lost too many men to this senseless fight." Otto held his reins in one hand so he could swat away an insect, closing his mind to thoughts of young Benedict. "But nor can Sir Leon's actions go unpunished. And I know not what will greet us over the next hill. We must be prepared."

"Sir Leon's ranks must be depleted after the battle at the gates," Gaius observed, spurring on his horse who was spooking at an oddly shaped gorse bush.

"Aye," Otto agreed. "And what caliber of man serves a master who kidnaps his own daughter?" He frowned as a hot rush of anger passed through him.

Gaius pursed his lips together, but wisely allowed a few beats to pass. "We await your orders, my lord. Mayhap one contingent should keep Sir Leon's men busy while you search the keep for the countess?"

"'Tis not a bad idea," admitted Otto, his mind racing. He opened his mouth to add more detail to the plan, but his attention was caught by the unmistakable thunder of approaching hooves. Glancing quickly over his shoulder to see that his men were attentive, he held up a hand to halt their progress. As one, the knights of Darkmoor reached for their swords, bodies tensed, eyes fixed on the track ahead. A growing cloud of dust announced approaching horses, but how many? "Stand ready," commanded Otto, hearing rather than seeing his men shift into formation behind him.

Before them, the barren moors rose to a brief incline which impaired their vision. Otto could do nothing but wait with growing impatience to see what manner of threat was about to descend upon them. His horse snorted and shied to one side when over the hill came a powerful warhorse in full charge. The horse's head was low, its eyes wide and distressed, its stirrups flapping freely. Behind it, galloped another two such riderless horses.

"Stand aside," shouted Otto, hauling at his horse's reins. With seconds to spare, the knights of Darkmoor cleared the path, and the three out-of-control battle chargers careered through their midst.

"Whoa," breathed Gaius, reaching down to soothe his horse's neck as she half-reared in protest.

"What are we to make of this?" Andreas de Montain twisted in his saddle to look after the departed horses.

Otto took a deep breath. The horses bore no colors or standards, but they were streaked with sweat as if they had been ridden hard all day. "I do not believe they are horses from Kenmar," he said, putting voice to his fears.

"Some other army has arrived ahead of us then?" Gaius cocked an eyebrow at Otto, leaving his unvoiced question hanging in the air between them.

The army of Sir Althalos.

"Then there is no time to lose," Otto declared, concern for Ariana twisting like a dagger in his gut. He swiveled in his saddle to rouse his men. "We ride into battle, as we have so many times before. You know your positions, gentlemen. On me." Plunging his heels into his horse's sides, Otto urged him into a gallop, crouching low over his neck as behind him, the Darkmoor battle horn sounded.

In a tight V-shape, with Otto at the head, the knights crested the hill and poured down upon the open plain leading to the craggy gray fortress of Kenmar.

The massive outer gates stood open. But Otto had no sooner acknowledged this, than his senses were assaulted by the sights and sounds of a battle recently ended. The stench of blood and death and the sounds of groaning men. He made out the purple colors of the house of Kenmar as his eyes swooped over the broken bodies scattered over the muddy ground. But among them he spied a couple of scarlet red outer tunics. His heart pounded hollowly in his chest as he recognized the yellow cross as the standard of his uncle.

"These men are sworn to Sir Althalos," he warned in a harsh

voice, pulling back on the reins to slow his horse as they passed, unchallenged, through the barbican and into the inner bailey. "Be on your guard."

Castle Kenmar was apparently deserted, bar the injured and dying, but Otto held his sword aloft, ready for any surprises. Their horses picked their way through the detritus of battle and into the cobbled courtyard, where the granite keep rose from the weeds. He cast his eye up and down the squat tower, making out a series of shuttered windows in the bare stone. Could Ariana be within? A dreadful fear that he was already too late had clamped around him like a vice, but he would search every inch of this cursed place for the woman he loved.

Althalos had come here. Otto's fist tightened on his sword. He would never forgive himself for allowing Althalos's poison to infect his thoughts and actions against Ariana. But worse, he would never forgive his uncle for his treachery. Resolve tightened in his belly. The man would pay for what he had done.

A sudden movement to his left had him reining in his horse further. Young Tristan had dismounted at speed and now held the tip of his sword to the chest of a torn and bloodied figure who he had pulled from behind an abandoned barrel.

Otto shifted his position in the saddle as Tristan marched the trembling man out towards them. He staggered slightly and held tightly to his left arm, which was bleeding profusely. The man had a gray beard and wore the ragged clothes of a villager.

"Who are you?" Otto demanded, straightening up to his full height.

The man's watery eyes flickered over the assembled knights, taking in their shining plate armor and powerful horses. "My name is Arthur," he said weakly, his voice thick with pain and exhaustion. "I am but a farm worker, milord."

"What has happened here?"

The man swallowed. "Soldiers came from the woods." He gestured behind him. "Sir Leon said we all must fight. All who were able, save the women and children."

"And where are the women and children now?" Otto demanded. Surely Ariana would be with them?

"Gone into hiding, down by the river." The man staggered to one side and Tristan quickly removed his blade.

"Stand easy," the young knight said, steadying the farm worker against him. "We will not harm an unarmed man."

"Is everyone gone?" Otto asked. He spun around his horse so he could take in a full view of the bailey, where not so much as a chicken scratched among the weeds. The fortress was deserted.

Arthur nodded, slumped now against Tristan. His face had turned an unhealthy gray color.

Despair clutched icy tendrils around Otto's heart. He was too late. Ariana would have already fled. Or worse. But he wouldn't allow himself to go there.

"Secure the fortress," he commanded Gaius. "I will take twenty men into the keep. We must search every room for the countess. But first, someone bind up this man's arm."

A knight hurried forward with a pot of salve and a roll of bandage pulled from a saddlebag well equipped with medical supplies. Otto sprung from his horse and unsheathed his sword, motioning to a group of nearby knights to follow him and putting one hand to his lips to show they must be quiet. Their enemies appeared to have already fled, but who knew what they would find within the fortified walls?

As one, they crept up the cracked front steps and through the wide oak doors which stood open as if waiting for them.

Was this a trap?

Otto paused to allow his eyes to adjust to the gloomy interior of the entrance hall, which was less than half the size of Darkmoor's. Narrow stairs ran up to his left, beside an unlit fireplace and a wooden door shut fast. Otto motioned for one of his knights to try the door, braced all the time for attack. But the man returned within moments to whisper that the chamber was empty, and not a sound came from elsewhere. Still the hairs on the back of Otto's neck raised high. A sour, cheerless air pervaded the keep, which stemmed not from the ravages of battle, more from years of quiet despair. He had always thought of Darkmoor being more a fortress than a home, but compared to this, he had grown up amidst cheer and light abounding.

How had Ariana's courage and resolve sprung from such a bleak place?

Andreas de Montain lit one of the bracketed wall torches over their heads and crackling orange light flooded the stone-flagged hallway. Otto nodded his thanks and led his men further into the keep. But no sooner had he turned the next corner than he came to an abrupt halt, young Tristan walking straight into his back.

Otto held up a warning hand for silence as he struggled to process the scene before him. Here, the narrow corridor widened into a windowless antechamber, into which what looked like the main staircase led. But the design of the fortress held little interest for him; what had seized his attention was the fallen, bloodied figure sprawled across the smooth stones. The face was turned away, but the man was instantly recognizable thanks to the color of his hair and the richness of his clothing. Otto took a deep breath.

"Althalos is dead," he announced to the men behind him, his voice reverberating off the rough walls.

He waited for a pall of grief, for despite everything, this man was his uncle, the last of his kin, but none came. He felt nothing. Not even relief. A small voice at the back of his mind bemoaned that he would never now take revenge on the man who had betrayed his trust and put his bride's very life at risk, but Otto quietened it down. His was not the hand that had plunged the jeweled dagger into Althalos's ribs, but someone had. That was enough.

Silently, his men fanned out around him, all quietly considering the dead man.

"He was a traitor to his family," hissed young Tristan, earning himself a warning look from his brothers in arms. But Otto nodded his agreement.

"That he was."

"Shall we move the body?" asked another.

Otto thought for a moment. "Aye. Do that. Take him out into the light where any of his remaining army may see him and know their battle is well and truly over." Immediately his men shifted to do his bidding, one gripping Althalos by the ankles and another hauling up his shoulders.

"Shall we search down here?" Andreas nodded towards the darkening corridor.

"Aye," Otto agreed again. "I shall go on up." His eye followed the line of the staircase. "Listen for my shout."

Before anyone could express their doubt in his solo quest, Otto strode forward, his heavy boots pounding against the stone beneath them. He made short work of the shadowy staircase, checking every chamber he came to with his sword held aloft, but finding no one within. Eventually, with a roar of frustration, he concluded he had searched to the very top of the keep. Ariana was not here. Nor was there anything to tell him where she might have spent the last weeks, or whether she even still lived.

No. He put a hand to his heart, silencing the thought. His wife still lived. He knew it deep inside.

Weary now, he allowed himself to sink down onto the low bed inside the final chamber. The bed creaked beneath his weight, but Otto hardly noticed. His eyes scanned the room, taking in a solitary wooden closet and a narrow window looking out onto the recent battleground. A footstool had been pulled beneath the window, as if someone had been on the look-out for approaching riders.

Otto's mind leaped. Could Ariana have perched there? Mayhap looking out for his approach? Immediately he cursed himself for the idea, which only brought him pain. Why had he not ridden out to rescue her days earlier?

It was too late now. Perchance the approaching riders Ariana had seen were the knights of Sir Althalos, coming to attack her father's depleted army. If so, she might have had time to escape.

Let it be so, he prayed, his hands fanning out over the rough woolen blankets. His fingers snagged on something sharp, and he looked closer, his eyes widening in surprise as he saw the familiar curves of his mother's broach. The token he had presented to Ariana on that long-ago day in the morning room.

He picked it up, his thumb smoothing over the crisscrossed lines and the shining stone at the center. There was no doubting this was the same piece of jewelry. Had Ariana despaired of waiting for him and abandoned his token? His heart constricted at the thought, even as part of him understood the impulse. He had believed his uncle's lies and forsaken her, after all.

"Ariana," he whispered. The broach had been warm to his touch, as if she had just recently positioned it on the bed. Mayhap he had missed her by no more than minutes. If so, there was still time to find her. *If she wanted to be found.*

His fingers pulled at a piece of ribbon pinned to the broach, and he idly wondered what it was. Holding it up to the dim light of the window, he saw that it was purple, the color of Kenmar. The satin glowed in the faint sunlight and Otto's lips twitched upwards. Had his clever wife left this as a sign for him? The houses of Kenmar and Darkmoor, forever entwined?

Was this but foolish fancy on his part? He pulled the ribbon out straight, noting how the broach had been deliberately pinned to the very center.

Nay, this was Ariana's way of telling him she still believed in their union. There was still hope.

Otto leaped to his feet, conviction burning within him.

He would find his wife.

Chapter Twenty

THE VAULTS WERE longer and darker than she remembered, although last time she had descended the narrow steps and picked her way through sloping tunnels dripping with damp, she'd been a spirited young woman, dodging the dictates of her father to spend time with the people she loved. Now she was fleeing for her life.

She should have thought to bring a torch. Blackness closed over her like a blanket as she turned a corner and lost the last speck of light from the kitchens of Kenmar castle. She shrieked aloud as something small and furry rushed over her feet, then clamped a hand over her mouth, summoning the resolve to stay silent from now on. If more of Sir Althalos's men were looking for her, she couldn't afford to give away any clues as to her whereabouts.

Shaking with a mixture of adrenaline and cold, Ariana inched her way forward, breathing in the dank musty smell of the twisting corridors carved from ancient rock beneath the fortress, glad she had thought to pull on the goatskin shoes that morning. If only she hadn't left her dagger inside the ribs of Sir Althalos. She would very much value its protection now, not knowing what horrors awaited her around the next bend. But the idea of leaning closer to her old adversary's lifeless body to recover her weapon had been more than she could bear.

She had killed a man.

The knowledge twisted in her gut and made her wretch. She

put a hand out to the rough wall to steady herself and breathed deeply, wincing at the sour, unhealthy tang in the icy cold air.

Enough. She must press on and spare no further thought for the wretch who had turned Otto against her and threatened her very life. He had deserved to die. Though her throat constricted at the thought of what his men might be subjecting Chiara to. Part of her longed to turn back and mount a rescue, but what hope did she have against so many highly trained knights? She knew that Althalos had only succumbed to her tricks as she'd harnessed the element of surprise.

She must protect her unborn child.

Her hand hovered over her belly. There was no decision to make. She must escape.

Swallowing her cries of anguish, Ariana forced her feet to take her on, deeper into the dark and further into the unknown. One hand reluctantly trailed along the rough wall, flinching occasionally at the rivers of damp. The cold crept into her very bones, making her shiver compulsively despite her constant movement. What she wouldn't give for a flicker of light and a warm cloak!

At long last, a distant pinprick of light ahead indicated the end of the secret passageway. Renewed with hope, Ariana began to run, her long legs striding over the rocky ground. As the light grew stronger, her lungs burst with effort, and she sucked in the chilled, stale air. Salty tears blinded her vision as she groped her way forward, climbing now. She remembered this slope from her childhood. It was here that Ysmay would be waiting for her, with a flickering candle, a warm smile, and a flask of restorative wine. They met no more than three or four times a year; anything more would have risked discovery. Even then, the notes they smuggled in and out of the keep could easily have been intercepted by her father's men. But the risk they took was well worth the reward of seeing one another.

Lost in her memories, her cracked shoes slipped on the damp ground and Ariana fell forward, her hands shooting out to break her fall at the last moment. Winded, she paused to catch her breath, steeling herself not to mind the sting of her grazed palms.

She was nearly there.

Pushing her braided hair behind her shoulders, Ariana straightened up. She would walk out of this passageway like the first Lady of Kenmar. Like the Countess of Darkmoor; the brave bride of a fearless warrior. She would not run and sob. She would stride.

Head held high, she headed for the light. The distant chirp of birdsong was the sweetest sound she'd known for many days. With it came a rush of fresh air. Ariana breathed in the scent of damp grass, her keen ears discerning the rushing of the river. It was all a far cry from the darkness of the passage, further still from the horror and bloodshed of battle. With one hand over her pounding heart, Ariana walked out into the light.

The warmth of the sun was like a caress. She tilted her face upwards and closed her eyes, allowing herself this moment of deep relief. Then she heard the scrape of a sword being un-sheathed. A familiar voice said her name.

"Ariana."

Dread pooled her insides, but she forced herself to stay still and open her eyes slowly.

"Father."

Sir Leon of Kenmar stood a few feet away, facing her, his sword half drawn. His purple cloak was torn and dirty, his unshaven face smeared with mud. Ariana's gaze flickered behind him, half expecting to glimpse an advancing army of Kenmar knights, but a rabbit scurrying into the undergrowth was the only sign of life, save the pulse of a vein flickering in her father's still beefy neck. He had always been a tall, strong man. She breathed deeply, quelling her instinctive emotional reaction to this man: her parent in name only.

"You escaped," he said.

Was that relief in his voice, or something else? And why did his hand still grip the hilt of his sword? Ariana eyed her father uneasily. She knew him to be volatile, greedy, and unpredictable. His mood swings were hard to judge, his temper even more so. *But he was still her father.*

"As did you," she commented evenly.

Sir Leon sheathed his sword but did not take his eyes from his daughter. "Did you meet Sir Althalos?"

Her mind raced, but she could think of no reason to hide the truth. "I killed him," she answered simply.

Surprise finally showed on Sir Leon's face, closely followed by an unmistakable look of respect. It was something she had never seen on her father's face before. At least, not aimed toward her. A gust of wind lifted his thinning hair from his lined face. "You did what I should have done."

Ariana swallowed down a new swell of emotion. Was her father verging on an apology? "No doubt," she said.

Sir Leon inclined his head towards the river. "Shall we walk?"

Ariana was in no mood to place her trust in one who had so recently betrayed her, but she reasoned that lingering so close to the mouth of the passageway was not in her best interests either. Even now, her enemies could be inching their way through the darkness towards her.

Folding her arms, she preceded Sir Leon down a winding path to the shore of the river, where birds darted for insects and white water foamed around rearing stones. Sir Leon leaned back against a rocky outcrop, but Ariana simply stood, braced to flee at any moment. She had played here as a child; this part of the forest was as familiar to her as her own hand. If Sir Leon showed the slightest sign of animosity, she would race away from him through the pair of willow trees standing across a grassy clearing.

"You owe me an apology, Father," she said eventually, resolved to say what was in her heart.

Sir Leon shook his craggy head. "I have always acted in your best interests, Ariana."

Her cheeks flushed with anger. "How was it in my best interests to plot behind my back with my husband's enemy? To have men kidnap me away and then lock me up? I trusted you when you told me you sought peace with Darkmoor, but it was all a lie."

"Aye, it was a lie." Sir Leon leaned towards her, his eyes belligerent. "Darkmoor has long been a thorn in our sides. They have the best land and a better yield come every harvest. Plus, a fortress that even the Scots have failed to penetrate." He spat with disgust into the long grass. "I saw an opportunity to take it for myself. For us," he amended, seeing the fury in his daughter's face.

"You wanted it for yourself. And you didn't care whether I lived or died." Ariana's voice cracked on the final words.

"That is not true." Sir Leon shook his head with vigor. "You are Countess of Darkmoor. You were essential to my plan."

"Your plan to furnish your coffers with Darkmoor gold." Ariana could feel the dampness of the grass seeping into her goatskin shoes and making her shiver. "With me as the sacrificial victim."

Her words had pierced whatever remained of Sir Leon's heart. She watched as an array of emotions played out across his face. "It's true, I put my trust in the wrong person." He stretched out an open palm towards her, but she deliberately looked away. "I was a fool to believe in Sir Althalos. And now I have paid the price."

"You have lost what little power you had," she stated. "And that is what upsets you now. Not the harm you caused your only daughter."

"What harm?" Sir Leon pushed himself away from the rocks and took a step towards her, making Ariana newly aware of her vulnerability. Her father was aging, but he had once been a trained warrior, and his sword was kept as sharp as any knight's. "You are alive and well, are you not?"

"No thanks to you." Ariana kept her tone icy, even as she inched backwards towards the trees.

"You are alive and well," Sir Leon repeated, his pale eyes

flickering over her. "And no doubt, when your husband finds out about his uncle's treachery, he will ride out to rescue you."

Ariana's heart beat wildly inside her ribs. Too late she saw that her plan to outrun her father was ill-conceived. Sir Leon bore no trace of weakness or injury. If she sought freedom, her only hope was to appeal to his reason, and that faint glimmer of humanity he had so recently shown.

"So you will compound your crimes against me by taking me hostage for a second time, is that it?" she demanded. "Have you no care at all for me, father? Do you doubt that your own blood runs in my veins?"

Sir Leon stopped in his tracks, gazing at her as if seeing her for the first time. "You are your mother's daughter," he all but whispered. "You resemble her in so many ways."

"You mean my druid ancestry?"

"I mean her strength and determination." Sir Leon put his hands on his hips and looked up towards the sun. "She was taken too soon, from both of us."

"On that, at least, we can agree," she said, her breath jagged and uneven. Was this her moment to flee, while Sir Leon was so distracted? Could she place any amount of trust in a man who had drawn his sword against his own kin?

"Don't move," hissed Sir Leon. His face screwed up in con-centration, and even as Ariana reeled in surprise at this sudden turn of mood, he strode towards his daughter and grasped her firmly by the arm.

"What are you doing?" She struggled against him, but his grip was firm and unyielding. A faint smell of stale ale wafted from his body.

"Listen," he hissed again.

Ariana forced herself to stay still. If she strained her ears, she could make out a distant sound of rapid hoofbeats, coming closer. She swallowed hard. Had they been found by Althalos's men?

"Get back," Sir Leon ordered, ushering her towards the rocky outcrop he had leaned against just moments ago. His fingers bruised the tender flesh of her arm, but she dared not cry out. Would her father hand her over to the knights? Or would he finally act as her protector? As she mulled over this choice, he clamped a firm hand over her mouth.

The hoofbeats stopped, to be replaced by the trampling sound of human footsteps. One man, Ariana thought, calculating their odds of success while trying not to breathe too deeply and gag. If Sir Leon worked with her, surely they could overcome one man? But she had no faith in her father's loyalty to anyone but himself.

The footsteps paused at the other side of the trees. Ariana was sure that whoever it was must be able to hear her heart pounding against her ribs. Sir Leon stood as still as the rocks behind them; his strong arms forbidding her the slightest movement. She heard the rustle of parting branches and a looming figure appeared between two slender birch trees. It was a figure she would know anywhere and immediately her body sagged with relief. She hadn't realized how much tension she was holding in her shoulders until she relaxed them.

Sir Leon stiffened, in recognition or in fear, and in that moment, Otto sighted them both. His dark eyes flashed with the realization that she was being held against her will, and before Ariana could signal anything further, the sword of Otto Sarragnac was pointed at the neck of Sir Leon of Kenmar.

"Release her," he commanded, in that rich throaty voice that Ariana had missed so much.

But Sir Leon would not be moved. "She is my daughter. Why should I release her to a brute like you?"

Otto laughed mirthlessly, his eyes trained on Ariana's face. She drank in the planes of his face and the familiar chiseled jawline. She had never thought she would be so happy to see the golden lion of Darkmoor.

"That was not a question you concerned yourself with when you willingly gave your daughter's hand in marriage." Otto pressed his sword against Sir Leon's skin until a tiny trickle of red blood ran down his flushed skin, but still, he did not budge.

Ariana had rarely seen her father display such bravery. Her gaze swung from one man to another, her mouth agape.

"Things have changed since then," her father croaked.

"Really?" Otto stepped closer, until his masculine aroma of horses and leather mingled with the beery smell of the Kenmar chief. "Have you finally found your heart, Sir Leon? Or have you discovered a more profitable way to use your daughter to your advantage?"

"Enough," shouted Ariana, wriggling free from her father's clutches in a sudden burst of courage. "I am here before you both. I will not be spoken of as mere chattel."

Otto inclined his head. "Forgive me, Ariana," he spoke through gritted teeth. "But the principle remains." He took another threatening step towards Sir Leon. "You conspired against me with my own uncle. Then kidnapped my wife and held her against her will. Is that not so?" His gaze switched to Ariana until she nodded her assent, relief rippling through her that Otto finally knew the truth. "Then give me one good reason why I should not run you through with my blade this instant?"

Ariana put her hand to her heart. Otto was saying neither more nor less than she had thought for herself, but she still couldn't bear to see her father slaughtered in cold blood by her own husband.

Her husband, who had come to her rescue just as she'd dreamed. Who stood before her now, every inch a mighty warrior. But as much as she longed to run into his strong embrace, there was still too much at stake.

"Because he is my father," she spoke out bravely.

Both men looked at her in surprise. "You wish me to stand down?" Otto asked, showing no inclination to do so.

"I don't know." Ariana wrung her hands in distress. "Father, you have put us in an impossible situation. How can we trust you?"

"You cannot," Sir Leon finally spoke up, his voice gruff. "And

I cannot ask it."

"Then what would you have me do?" Otto demanded.

Sir Leon held up one hand in a show of peace and with the other he withdrew his own sword and slung it to one side, where it clattered noisily against the rocks and sent a bird flying upwards in alarm. He held Otto's gaze until the younger man slowly lowered his own sword. "First, I ask for the chance to apologize." His eyes flicked from left to right and came to settle on his daughter. "Ariana, I did you a grave injustice. I allowed myself to be swayed by thoughts of wealth and power, and I am sorry for it." He gave a small bow in her direction, then transferred his attention back to Otto.

Ariana's hand went to her heart. This was the apology she had long sought, but in the current circumstances it carried little consequence. Deep down, she knew her father was finding the words to save his own skin.

He would always think of himself first.

Sir Leon cleared his throat. "Are you here alone?"

"I am." Otto's stance was still that of a warrior braced for attack. Ariana felt her knees begin to tremble anew.

Sir Leon glanced at Otto as if asking permission, then sank downwards onto a large, flat rock. He sighed wearily and stretched out his legs. "I am surprised that the Earl of Darkmoor has come alone into the forest of Kenmar," he remarked, almost conversationally.

Otto took in the relaxed stance of his adversary and sheathed his sword, standing back and folding his arms across his powerful chest. "I have a hundred men stationed back at your castle," he stated, with deliberate casualness.

Ariana's pulse leaped at this declaration of strength. A declaration which, despite his brusque apology, Sir Leon could not help but heed. She stepped forward to put herself between them, taking a deep breath to interject. But before she could speak up, Otto continued.

"But it matters not. I do not come here as the Earl of Darkmoor. I come as one man, to speak to another."

Ariana saw her father's bushy eyebrows shoot up. "And what is it you wish to say?"

Otto reached up to scratch at his scar, something he only did in moments of stress. "We have been enemies for too long. It has cost us both dearly. Especially me." Otto clenched his jaw with palpable tension. "You are here now at my mercy, Sir Leon. Surely you know that I could take you down in an instant?" His gaze flickered to the sword laying in a cloud of dirt at the foot of the rocks.

"But your wife has forbidden it." Sir Leon's eyes twinkled and Ariana, who was starting to know hope, was plunged again into despair.

But Otto did not retaliate, he merely shrugged his armor-clad shoulders, as unmoving as the granite stones all around. "My wife is a wise woman." He flashed her a smile, which made her insides melt despite the gravity of their situation. "But she only gave voice to my own thoughts."

Her father didn't miss a beat. "So you have come in search of peace?" His words resonated around the small clearing, making Otto's reasonable pronouncement sound foolish.

"The peace which was promised upon our marriage." Otto reached out his hand and clasped Ariana's. She grasped his fingers, taking strength and courage from the warmth of his flesh against her own. She'd always known him as a warrior, a fighter. But now she saw that her husband was every inch a thinker, a diplomat. Not only feared, but also wise. "Without Sir Althalos here to meddle, I live in hope that our two families may yet live side by side. Nay, I even dare to hope that we may yet be allies."

Tears sprang into her eyes at this. It was all she could have hoped for.

"Allies, is it?" Sir Leon's pale eyes raked over them both, his expression betraying nothing. "And what do I get out of this?"

Ariana's heart was beating painfully hard. Why was it her fate to have so stubborn and grasping a father?

"The chance to live quietly in your own home, under Darkmoor guard." When Sir Leon looked to protest, Otto laughed quietly. "You do not take me for a fool, do you, sir? After all these years of animosity, I will not leave you unchecked. I seek peace, not total destruction."

After a fraught moment, Sir Leon guffawed. "And the alternative?"

Otto's eyes sought Ariana's and she gazed back, knowing that his answer would be the right one. "I will not strike you down," he said quietly. "But you will come with us and spend the rest of your days under lock and key in Darkmoor Castle."

"And what say you to this?" Sir Leon's gaze swung to his daughter.

Ariana moved to stand closer to Otto, drinking in the living, breathing presence of her warrior husband. "I say you are to count your blessings, Father, that the Earl of Darkmoor gives you such a choice."

A flock of birds flew overhead, calling to one another in the deep blue sky. Below them, the river gushed downwards, and a faint breeze carried the scent of new grass and hope. Ariana clenched her fist, digging her fingernails into her palms and praying that her stubborn father would accept the generous terms on offer. Otto would not negotiate, nor was he likely to stand here and deliberate for much longer.

"Peace it is then," Sir Leon sighed. "Peace it is." He extended his hand to Otto and after a slight hesitation, Otto leaned forward and accepted it.

Ariana knew a dizzying moment of relief before Otto's strong arms wrapped around her waist and pulled her against him. "Now all we have to do is get you home," he murmured against her ear.

She placed her hands on his shoulders, barely able to believe that the hardship and worry of the past weeks were behind her. "I can't wait," she breathed, tilting her face upwards and closing her eyes as his lips pressed down on hers. "In fact, I long for it."

The next minutes passed in a blur. Otto signaled to his wait-ing men, who plunged through the trees to surround Sir Leon and march him into guarded quarters in the castle. Next, he ordered that their horses be made ready.

"Unless you would prefer to rest here for the night?" he asked her, concern etched across his rugged face.

Ariana shook her head with conviction, even as her body shook with weariness. "I do not wish to spend another hour in this terrible place." She looped her arms around his waist, knowing there were many words still unsaid between them. "Otto…" she began.

"I know 'twas not you who betrayed Darkmoor," he said steadily. "I have gathered the facts and I believe I know it all. I only wish you had felt able to trust me with the truth about your aunt."

Ariana felt heat rise in her cheeks, but she met his gaze un-flinchingly. "As do I."

"And I wish I had trusted you more," he said in a rush, taking her by surprise. "All of this could have been avoided." He inclined his head to one side. "I have much to learn about marriage."

A smile pulled at the corner of her lips. "Perchance we will learn, together."

"I would like nothing more," he sighed. "And I'm grateful for the chance of it."

Such a surge of emotion took hold within Ariana that her knees buckled and she swayed against him. Instantly, Otto swept her up into his arms, holding her close and safe.

"Speaking as a selfish man who has missed his wife, right now I should prefer to keep you here by my side," he said into her hair. "But I know of someone else who wishes to speak with you."

She groaned against his broad chest. "I have said all I intend to say to my father."

"Nay, not him." Gently he turned her around by the shoul-ders until she was facing the willow trees. "Go and see."

Ariana opened her mouth to protest again. She was weary to the bone and had no wish to take so much as a step away from her husband. But Otto was urging her forward, and his insistence piqued her curiosity. She forced her legs to carry her over the flattened grass and cautiously peered around the slender trunk of the trees. At first, she could see nothing save the dense greenery of the forest, but then a flash of white caught her eye.

"Who is there?" she called, her voice small amidst the ancient trees.

Silence. Not so much as a bird called from the branches in reply.

"There is no one here." She turned back to Otto, but he was sitting on a rock and gazing into the river, apparently lost in thought.

"It is I, Ariana," said a silvery voice near her ear.

Warmth and recognition flooded her. She spun around to face her aunt, her heart threatening to crack open with joy.

"Ysmay."

They embraced for a long time—long enough for Ariana to push past her worries about the frailty of her aunt's body and instead rejoice in the fact that they had found one another again.

"How long have you been watching us?" she asked when they finally broke apart.

"Long enough to know that the peace we have longed for is now agreed upon." Ysmay's beautiful face creased into a smile. "Thanks to you, dearest Ariana."

"You could have been hurt." Ariana frowned, thinking of how very differently the situation with Otto and her father could have gone.

"Nay." Ysmay's long white hair fell about her shoulders as she shook her head. "I was well protected." She motioned behind her, and two druid men stepped from the trees, each of them tall, strong, and carrying a well-strung bow. "My archers were also tasked with keeping you safe. Mercifully, their arrows were not needed today."

Ariana nodded her appreciation to the calm, silent men.

"It is Otto we should thank. He was the one to seek peace." Ariana bit down on her lip. "I should so like you to know him better," she whispered.

Ysmay put her head to one side, like a sparrow. "When last I saw Otto Sarragnac, he was splattered with the blood of his enemies."

"But much has changed since then."

Ariana thought her aunt would argue, but Ysmay smiled. "It does my heart good to hear you speak up for your husband."

"May I call him over?"

Ysmay nodded, and Ariana looked over her shoulder to find Otto already walking across the clearing. He came to a halt a few paces behind them and bowed to Ysmay.

"I am pleased to meet you properly," he said without preamble. "And I offer my sincerest apologies for the rough treatment you and your people once endured at the hands of my men."

Ysmay stood tall and proud. "Thank you for your apology, Otto Sarragnac. But let us look to the future now, not the past."

Otto placed his arm around Ariana's shoulders. "I promise to take good care of your niece."

"I have no doubt of it." Ysmay's kind eyes met Ariana's.

Otto cleared his throat. "And I believe we have something of yours in our possession. A ruby necklace. Is that right?"

Ariana gasped. "The Rose of Kenmar."

"Keep it for yourselves," Ysmay demurred, shaking her head. "I have no need of jewels."

"Nay." Otto's voice was firm. "The jewel is rightfully yours. I will have it returned as soon as we arrive back in Darkmoor."

Ysmay nodded her acceptance. "As you wish."

Ariana grasped her aunt's slender fingers. "We have no cause to stay apart from one another now. Everything has changed. Why not come back to Darkmoor with us?"

Ysmay squeezed her hands before reaching up to lay a palm against her cheek. "I do not belong in a fortress," she said softly.

"I could not breathe freely within granite walls. I belong here, in the forest where I was born."

"But Merek would be so pleased to see you."

Ysmay inclined her head. "Merek knows where he can find me." Ariana felt tears squeezing from the corners of her eyes, which her aunt gently wiped away. "Do not be sad, child. I shall see you again."

"Do you promise?"

"I promise," Ysmay repeated. "But now we must go. 'Tis a long walk back to our camp." She raised her eyes. "Fare ye well, Otto Sarragnac."

Otto bowed low, and Ariana bent to embrace her aunt once again. "Goodbye," she whispered, forcing down a lump in her throat.

"Goodbye, Ariana."

Without another word, the three druids melted soundlessly back into the forest. Ariana felt bereft, until Otto slipped his hand over hers and she looked up into his kind eyes.

"How did you know the druids were there?" she sniffed.

"I saw them when I came through here to confront Sir Leon. They were watching and waiting, but they stood aside to let me pass."

"They could have wounded you."

"Nay." He shook his head with a smile. "They would not waste their arrows on a man who meant you no harm." He glanced down at Ariana, and his eyes clouded with concern. "You do not look well."

"I just need a moment." But even as she spoke, a humming sound filled her ears, and her legs began to tremble. "I'm sorry," she whispered, breathing in his masculine scent as he carried her over to the rocks, setting her down on a flat stone overlooking the river.

"You have nothing to be sorry for. But you must take care. It has been quite an ordeal." Otto brushed back her hair tenderly. "You look tired. Beautiful, but tired," he amended quickly.

"I am not tired." The denial came instantly to her lips, before she sank back into his arms, leaning her head against his muscular chest. "Well, mayhap there is a reason I am tired."

Was it her imagination, or did his breath come a little faster?

"What is it?" he asked, lifting her chin so their eyes were just inches apart.

She swallowed, suddenly nervous. "Otto, I have reason to believe that I am with child."

Her words, though delivered quietly, seemed to carry all around the clearing. For a moment, he didn't react, his brown eyes calm but unreadable, but then the largest smile she had ever seen broke across his handsome face.

"With child," he breathed. "Truly?"

"Aye," she chuckled at his obvious delight. "'Tis still early. But I have been beside myself with worry that this child may grow up without knowing his father."

"Never." His rough palms cupped her face, and he kissed her softly on the lips. "I will be here for our child, the heir of Darkmoor. And our families will know peace. I promise you this."

"I believe you." She placed her hand over his. Above them, the sun burst through the clouds, bathing them in a dazzling shaft of warmth and light. Ariana held onto her husband's hand and smiled up at him. "I admit, I feel quite peculiar," she admitted.

"So do I." Otto's breath warmed the top of her head as a blackbird broke into song. "I think I know what it is," he whispered.

"What is it?" She moved closer, wanting to meld her body with his.

Otto ran a finger down her cheek. "I do believe that what we're feeling is happiness."

Chapter Twenty-One

Three Years Later…

THE CARRIAGE BUMPED along the dusty road, making Ariana's uncomfortable dress poke into her in all the wrong places. She shifted awkwardly on the plush seat, reaching for Otto's hand to steady her.

"How much longer until we are there?" she asked, aware that her voice held a note of complaint familiar from their two-year-old son and unable to keep from smiling at the comparison.

Otto made a show of looking behind him. "I thought we had left Alfred at home with the nurse," he said, his eyes wide with mock bewilderment.

Ariana dug her elbow into his side before letting a peal of laughter escape her lips. "I'm sorry, but we have been travelling for nigh on two days. And ever since this morning when you persuaded me to wear this ridiculous gown, I have longed for our arrival."

Otto put his arm around her shoulders and pulled her against him, shifting around so she could make herself more comfortable on the narrow seat. "It will be worth the pain, I assure you," he said, his lips pressed against her elaborately coiled hair. "And you will know when we reach the gates of Wolvesley. I promise you that."

"How so?" She reached up to twirl a strand of his thick, dark hair around her finger, enjoying the sight of her husband in his finery. Otto wore a rich blue tunic embroidered with gleaming gold thread. His glossy hair hung around his shoulders and his leather boots had been polished until they shone. This was a day to showcase the grace and elegance of Darkmoor.

Although Ariana felt as if she had been trussed up like a goose ready for the roasting spit in the heavy silken gown which Otto had ordered especially for this occasion. The dress was beautiful, no doubt, but these days she was happiest in the serviceable skirts which allowed her to play with their young son in the evergreen fields around Darkmoor. Her hand reached up to briefly touch the gleaming ruby pendant hanging around her neck. Ysmay's jewel, the Rose of Kenmar, was usually kept locked in her jewelry box, away from two-year-old Alfred's grasping fingers. She was pleased to bring it out into the light of day once more and feel a connection with her aunt, who by now had sadly passed on.

"I promise you will know," Otto repeated, a playful glint in his eye. "If you are growing bored with the journey, wife, I can think of other, more pleasing ways for us to pass the time…"

She pursed her lips together and shook her head, even as a flicker of desire shot through her. "You would rip my dress and ruffle my hair and have me presented at Wolvesley looking like a slattern," she said primly.

"I doubt Angus would mind," Otto countered, one hand already inching beneath her long skirts.

She slapped him away, laughing. "Behave yourself," she admonished, straightening up so she could see out of the window and swallowing her instinctive cry of frustration that the same view of rolling hills met her eye. Although, what was that in the distance? "Do I see something?" she asked eagerly, craning her neck for a better view.

"Perchance." Otto made a show of examining his cuffs, apparently disinterested.

"Look, please," she begged him.

"What can you see?"

"Great crenelated walls." She half stood, leaning against the lined carriage door. "They must be thirty feet high. And a wide path sweeping between some ancient trees." Her head was almost hanging out of the window now, a faint breeze threatening to spoil her coiled tresses.

"Come back inside." Otto tugged at her wrist. "You'll fall out, if you're not careful."

"But is this Wolvesley?" she persisted, widening her eyes in supplication to her husband.

"Is it the largest castle you have ever seen?"

Ariana's head snapped from Otto back to the window and she gasped as a rearing granite fortress came into view. The castle stood atop a steep hill and was surrounded by forest on two sides. Their carriage was making faster progress along the well-laid pathway and her eyes widened further as they passed over an arched bridge guarded by proud stone lions.

"I have only ever known two castles before," she pointed out. "But yes, forsooth, this is by far the largest."

"Then this is it." Otto treated her to a wide, boyish smile. "You will not have seen anything like it." He grabbed for her hand. "You must promise not to throw me over for my much wealthier, grander, and infinitely more good-looking cousin."

"I make no such promises," Ariana declared, as the carriage rounded a bend, and they came to a wide river upon which swam a group of impossibly large, impossibly white birds. "What are they?" she demanded.

Otto shrugged. "Why should I tell you anything more? I see you are already making plans to leave me."

She lunged forward and pressed her lips against his. "You know in your bones I would never do that. My heart belongs to you. And Alfred," she added with a giggle. "Besides, it isn't true that Angus is better-looking than you are. I remember him from my early days at Darkmoor. He was nothing by the side of you."

"That is good to hear." He linked his fingers with hers. "I wasn't sure if you would remember Angus. I seem to recall my uncle making that evening particularly unpleasant for you."

She squeezed his hand. "Let us not spoil our day with talk of Althalos," she declared. "In truth, I remember little about your friend, save his blond beard and blue eyes. "He is the younger brother, is he not?"

"Aye. His brother, Lord Lucan, is a number of years older. Alas, Lucan's wife died birthing their first child. The babe did not survive, either."

"How awful." Ariana bit down on her lip, her eyes instinctively filling with tears at the idea. It was not so long since she had faced that ordeal herself. "So there is no heir?"

"None save Angus himself." Otto paused to reflect somberly on the grave events before treating her to a flickering smile. "He is mayhap one of the jolliest men I have ever met. For the sake of his smile, I hope he is never obliged to take on the mantle of earlship."

Ariana glanced out of the window once more but could make out nothing save a blur of passing trees. "Is he married?"

"Oh no," Otto laughed. "He has been betrothed for many a year. I don't know what keeps them from marrying at long last. Mayhap we will find out during the course of the ball."

Ariana blanched at the thought of the ordeal ahead. Tonight, the Earl of Wolvesley was hosting a lavish midsummer ball which, as far as she could divine, most of the nobility of the country would attend. Lords and ladies, all of them far grander than she, would gather together to dance and feast while she hid in a corner and waited for it to be over.

In the jolting carriage, Otto saw her face and guessed where her musings had taken her. "It will be fun, you'll see." He nodded emphatically.

"That's all very well for you to say." She smoothed her skirts, hoping to hide the trembling of her fingers. "You're the Earl of Darkmoor and a warrior to boot. No one would dare so much as look askance at you."

"And you are the Countess of Darkmoor," he interjected. "The most beautiful woman to grace the great hall of Wolvesley

Castle on this or any other occasion." He looked at her consideringly. "Though if any man looks twice at you, I may resurrect my reputation as the *Feared One*."

They both laughed as the carriage finally drew to a halt within the inner courtyard of a bustling castle. Horses pawed at the ground and liveried servants ran back and forth, sparing hardly a glance at the Darkmoor carriage.

A page scurried forward to open their carriage door and Otto stepped down first, stretching his back and groaning a little before holding out his hand for Ariana. She emerged into brilliant sunlight, which fell on the fortress like a bright, glittering halo. Ariana looked around her, blinking dazedly at the display of great wealth. To their backs, a stone-carved fountain gushed jets of water upwards to the heavens before they splashed down into a wide circular bowl, at least as big as Ariana's old bedchamber in Kenmar. Ahead of them, wide stone steps rose gradually to an open doorway of gargantuan proportions.

"Has this castle ever been breached?" she whispered to Otto.

"Never," her husband replied, emphatically. "It has never even been attacked."

Ariana bit down on her lower lip, unable to stop gazing around and drinking it all in. A castle that had never known an act of warfare was an incongruous idea, like a horse who had never galloped, or a child who had never laughed. "So this is all for what?" she opened her palms. "For pleasure?"

Otto winked and grabbed her hand. "You will see."

"Otto Sarragnac." A great booming voice echoed around the vast courtyard. "As I live and breathe. You made it, my old friend."

Ariana skittered to the side as Angus de Neville strode down the wide stone steps to clasp Otto in both arms. He was a tall, strong man, equal to her husband in height and breadth, but with none of Otto's whip-sharp energy. Where Otto was a man bred for battle, Angus appeared to have been raised for the purposes of pure enjoyment. His youthful face was unlined, his blue eyes were bright, and his full head of hair was thick and golden.

"And your lovely wife. Ariana, I remember you well. Welcome to Wolvesley, my dear." Angus took hold of her hand and pressed his lips to it, making Ariana smile like a schoolgirl. He was so charismatic and handsome; she couldn't help her instinctive reaction to his charms despite being a happily married woman.

"Thank you for inviting us," she managed.

"Thank *you* for persuading this old rogue to set foot out of Darkmoor. I haven't managed it since he was yay high." Angus held his hand out at shoulder level and winked, leaving Ariana opening and closing her mouth, wondering whether she should admit that Otto had been the one to do the persuading.

"All that has changed, Angus," Otto quipped, snaking a possessive arm around his wife's shoulders and pulling her close. "I'm a family man now, you know? I've sheathed my sword and embraced a life of quiet pleasure."

"And you're quite the advertisement for matrimony." Angus looked his old friend up and down. "I've never seen you looking better. That frown that used to linger between your eyes is altogether gone."

Otto cuffed him on the shoulder good-naturedly. "At least we know our manners up in Darkmoor. It isn't the thing, you know, to leave ladies standing around in the midday sun. Are we to be invited in or not?"

Angus immediately dipped into a low, elaborate bow. "My good sir, my lady, please do follow me."

In a stately train, they followed their host up the wide stone steps and through the enormous arched door into a vast entrance hall, replete with circular pillars, a vaulted ceiling, and an exquisitely detailed mosaic floor. Ariana traced the colored tiles with the toe of her shoe, marveling at the craftsmanship, before her attention was taken by the vivid tapestries hanging on the white-washed walls. Her gaze rose upwards, following the polished wooden staircase to a gleaming gallery upon which two liveried maids were gossiping, their heads close together. Upon feeling her eyes upon them, they both bobbed into small bows and scurried away, leaving her wrestling with a pang of guilt.

"Go and freshen up, make yourselves at home." Angus waved airily towards a waiting servant who bowed smartly and indicated they should follow. "The gong will sound for dinner. Come straight down." He wagged a finger at Otto. "You won't want to miss any of what I have prepared for this evening."

Ariana reached for Otto's hand as they followed the servant down a high-ceilinged, bright corridor, lit with dozens of flaming torches as well as natural light from several well-spaced, tall windows looking out onto a small garden boasting yet another fountain. She had experienced much since becoming the Countess of Darkmoor, but wealth such as this was beyond her comprehension. The heavy scent of expensive perfume lingered all around, and she shivered to think of the well-dressed, well-connected women with whom she would no doubt have to converse at the ball.

They would think her a country bumpkin. And they would be right.

Otto squeezed her hand, as if he could hear her worries, and immediately they melted away. What did it matter if she came from humble stock? She had the kindest, bravest, and most handsome husband anyone could wish for. A man who still set her heart pounding with desire, even after two years of marriage and the labors of childbirth. Despite its origins, theirs was a union forged of love, and Ariana never ceased to be thankful for it.

"Here we are." Otto led her into a light, well-proportioned room boasting a vast canopied bed and a wide window overlooking green pastures behind a lake which sparkled in the afternoon sunlight.

"Oh." Ariana took a few paces further inside, looking around like a child at a feast. "It's lovely."

The servant bowed smartly and left, leaving them alone together.

"You like it?" Otto asked, smiling widely.

"I love it," she answered honestly. "Although all this grandeur can't help but make me uneasy. Shouldn't some of his coin be diverted to keeping an army?" She gestured helplessly out of the window. "I see barely any sign of fortification. It's more like a pleasure palace than a castle."

"That's exactly it." Otto looked pleased at her analogy. He brought her closer to the window and wrapped his arms around her waist, leaning his head upon her shoulder as they both gazed at the beautiful view. "Although, have no fear, Lucan de Neville leads one of the largest armies in the country. He just keeps them out of sight." He twisted to look down at her consideringly. "You don't wish we lived like this up in Darkmoor?"

"No indeed," Ariana declared. She had long grown used to dining amongst warriors. "Although it's interesting to experience." She craned forward to see the unusual birds swimming in the lake in more detail. "What *are* those creatures?"

Otto gave a short laugh. "They're called swans."

"Swans," she repeated, incredulous. "I have never heard of them."

"Nonetheless, there they are." His hands began to roam up from her waist, sending waves of anticipation shooting through her. But Ariana was still too perplexed by her surroundings to give herself over just yet.

"How long have you known Angus?" she asked, nudging his hand back towards the small of her back.

"Years," declared Otto. "His father and my father fostered together." He lowered his head and nibbled at her earlobe, clearly more interested in his young wife than his family history.

"I find it all so strange. I didn't know your father, of course, but I've always imagined him as an austere man. A warrior. Not someone given to excess."

"You have him exactly right." Otto's breath was warm on her face. She knew she had but seconds left before his touch and his kiss would drive all other thoughts from her mind.

"But all this." She pulled away from him, opening her arms to encapsulate their chamber, the lake, and the magnificent castle. "It's all so different, isn't it?"

"On the surface." Otto inclined his head, finally giving her words due thought. "But in a way, it's all just another form of warfare."

Ariana watched the stately progress of the swans, gliding across the gleaming surface of the lake. It didn't look anything like the warfare she was accustomed to. "How do you mean?"

Otto was not a man to countenance distractions. One hand inched up her back, slowly untying the laces of her gown even as he answered her question.

"This extravagance is not purely for show. Or rather, it *is* for show. But deliberately so. It's a display." He smiled as the shoulders of her gown gaped open. "A display of strength. Lucan is no fool. He trained at Lindon, although he left long before I arrived. I tell you, there is no better knight than the Earl of Wolvesley. He is one of the great warlords of England. But these days, he prefers to use his brain rather than his brawn." Ariana closed her eyes as Otto dropped butterfly kisses onto her collarbone. She no longer cared why an unknown man had swans swimming in his lake, but Otto had hit his stride. His warm hand slipped beneath her silken gown as he carried on explaining. "Lucan plays to his strengths. And his strengths are the size of his castle and the depths of his coin chests." He sighed as more of Ariana's gown came undone and he eased it over her shoulders. "Right now, he is facing unrest to the west. He has enemies in Powys, distant relatives who seek to lay a claim to his fortune. So instead of riding out to meet them with muscle and blade, he invites them to a ball, where they are successfully intimidated by his all too obvious might, rich resources, and powerful connections."

"He is a clever man." Ariana's eyes were glazing over with pleasure as Otto's hands ran over her naked flesh. But she snapped to attention and sharpened her gaze as he shrugged off his tunic, enjoying his whipcord strength and tanned body.

"A clever man," Otto agreed, scooping her up and carrying her over to the bed. "But not a man so lucky as I." He gently placed her down and then raised a quizzical eyebrow. "Do you have any further questions, or may I make love to my wife?"

Ariana reached out her arms. "I have no further questions."

THE GREAT HALL at Wolvesley Castle dazzled with light. Flickering candles were arranged atop long tables and around white-washed pillars while flaming torches blazed from high walls which were patterned with a rainbow spectrum of color. Open-mouthed, Ariana realized this was the reflected gleam from a multitude of jewels worn by the most notable families in the realm. Outside, the evening sun cast a burnt orange hue through the darkening sky, although shadows stretched across the courtyard and in the floral glades of the well-tended lawns. A trio of musicians played on a raised dais at one end of the hall, and the surrounding long tables had been pulled back to allow for dancing and entertainment. The air was heavy with the scent of perfume, heated bodies, and roasting meat.

Ariana held tightly to Otto's hand, conscious of both her heavy jewelry and her heavy skirts. But despite her physical discomfort, she found herself transported by the glittering spectacle. Elegantly dressed ladies fanned themselves against the summer heat while their menfolk drank deeply from silver goblets and clapped along to the music. The atmosphere was bright and festive, and she couldn't help her lips inching up into a smile.

"Happy?" Otto asked against her ear.

"Happy," she confirmed, as a smiling serving wench beckoned them forward to take their seats near the dais.

No sooner had they sat down than the musicians blasted out

a startling tune and the background chatter of conversation ceased as lords and ladies craned their necks to see what was causing the disturbance. After a moment's wait, a rippling sigh of appreciation passed through the hall, followed by a faint scattering of applause. From their position near the back of the large room, Ariana still couldn't see what was happening, but Otto, who was a head taller than she, looked mighty pleased with the view.

Finally, she saw it. It or rather them. The loveliest young woman she had ever beheld was proceeding through the great hall, carried aloft by two bare-chested strong men who had hoisted her onto their shoulders. The woman had long blonde hair hanging in waves down to her narrow waist. Her silken dress was sky blue, just like her eyes, and her voice was raised in a song of such unearthly beauty it brought goose-pimples out over Ariana's bare arms. Next to her, a petite lady got to her feet so she could more easily watch the display, and after short consideration, Ariana did the same. Now she could see that the three performers were not alone. Several more stood waiting near the heavy oak doors, all robed in sky-blue, with the men displaying their rippling muscles.

The first woman's voice soared up to the smoky rafters of the hall, capturing the attention of everyone within it. Otto's mouth was slightly agape, and his hunter's eyes were fixed on the singer, but no sooner had Ariana noticed this than he glanced up at her and treated her to a wide smile. Moving slowly, the two strong-men pirouetted on the spot, so everyone had the opportunity to admire the angelic face of their lady, before they slowly lowered her to the floor and all three of them dipped into a gracious bow. A roaring tide of applause burned through the room, but the performers were only just getting started. Now it was the turn of the tumblers, who advanced forward with a series of death-defying somersaults that had Ariana clasping a hand to her mouth. Next, the group formed a human pyramid, with the blonde-haired beauty balancing right at the very top, her arms outstretched to the heavens.

Ariana was overwhelmed with it all. She sank back down onto the cushioned bench next to Otto and took a restorative mouthful of good red wine. While she'd been watching the show, some diligent servant had delivered platters of delicious looking food to their table. Ariana's stomach rumbled and she followed Otto's example in helping herself, enjoying the opportunity to eat unobserved while those around her were transfixed by the entertainment.

But as Ariana's eye travelled across the hall, she saw one man who, like her, was not watching the show. Instead, his deep blue eyes gazed unseeingly towards the darkening window. He was tall and fair, with long tresses of golden hair falling forward over muscular shoulders. His robes were sumptuous, his face entirely devoid of expression.

This must be Lord Lucan, the powerful earl. He looked as lonely as his story suggested. Ariana quickly looked away, not wanting to pry on the man's grief.

Minutes later, the performers took their final bow and filtered out. Gradually conversation resumed and the hall thrummed with laughter.

"What did you think of my acrobats?" Angus demanded as he strode towards them. He was clad in a dark tunic trimmed with so much gold Ariana felt almost blinded by it. He banged his goblet down onto the table and beckoned for a chair to be brought for him. "I found them at Beltane and convinced Lucan to hire them for tonight. Rather good, aren't they?"

"The best I've ever seen," Otto declared, forking sweet pastry into his mouth.

"I've never seen anything like them," Ariana added, honestly.

"I rather liked her." Angus winked at Otto.

"I don't know what you mean." Otto raised his eyebrows and smiled broadly, his hand covering Ariana's and giving it a reassuring squeeze.

"She was very beautiful." Ariana was flushed with wine and

excitement. In that moment, she truly didn't mind if her husband's eye was turned by a beautiful performer. Only his eye, mind.

Angus raised his goblet in a toast. "I'll say."

Otto leaned across his wife to better address his friend. "Ariana asked me just this morning, how come Angus de Neville is not yet married?"

Angus treated her to a mock serious expression. "That is a very good question, my lady. It's one I have troubled myself with many times."

"And?" Otto pursed his lips in enquiry.

"And I am at a loss." Angus opened his arms wide, then turned back to Ariana. "Wolvesley is renowned for its hospitality, but still my betrothed finds distraction elsewhere. Can you think what I am doing wrong?" He affected a look of mournful misery.

"No indeed." She couldn't help a burst of laughter. "You keep a very grand home."

Angus nodded his thanks. "Lucan tells me his efforts tonight have not gone unnoticed by our special friends in the west," he said in an undertone to Otto. "I understand a missive has already been dispatched to Powys."

Otto looked impressed. "Lucan's strategy is to be admired. This grand ball has mayhap saved many lives." He took another swig of wine and smacked his lips. "Your brother will have to take me under his wing. With such help, perchance we can yet establish a reign of peace in Darkmoor."

"I am happy to send my troupe of acrobats up to your wild home, whenever you say the word," Angus laughed.

"You have everything here a man could wish for." Otto eyed their table, groaning under the weight of so much food. "You are blessed indeed."

"Blessed in all ways, except in love." Angus spoke into his goblet of wine. "In return for my acrobats, mayhap you will stay here, my friend, and teach me what you have so recently learned?"

Otto put down his goblet and reached for Ariana's hand, which she gave him willingly. He entwined his fingers with hers and spoke as if she were the only person in the room. "I do not believe that love is a lesson to be learned," he said softly. "More it is something that simply falls into place, when the right person is by your side."

Ariana's lips curled up in agreement as she leaned forward for the kiss she knew what was coming. "What a very wise man you are," she whispered.

The feasting and merriment around them faded into nothing as Otto's lips lowered towards hers and Ariana experienced a familiar swirling, bubbling feeling deep inside her stomach. It was a feeling she recognized readily now.

It was happiness.

THE END

About the Author

Elizabeth grew up in a rambling old farmhouse high on the Yorkshire moors, where a sense of history was never far away. She studied English at university, specialising in mythology and folklore and often bemoaning the lack of sword-wielding heroines. After graduating, she spent several years moving between northern France, southern Germany and London, where she worked in travel publishing and PR.

She now lives a stone's throw from her childhood home, with her husband, children and a feisty black cat who enjoys interrupting her writing. She plots most of her novels while walking in the rugged Yorkshire countryside, finding endless inspiration in the rolling hills.

www.ingramcontent.com/pod-product-compliance
Lightning Source LLC
Chambersburg PA
CBHW060439310726

48977CB00001B/259